If Wishes
Were Horses

Sallyann Sheridan

Sallyann Sheridan
x

IndePenPress

First published in Great Britain by Indepenpress

All paper used in the printing of this book has been made
from wood grown in managed, sustainable forests.

ISBN13: 978-1-906710-90-3

Printed and bound in the UK
Indepenpress is an imprint of Indepenpress Publishing Limited
25 Eastern Place, Brighton, BN2 1GJ

Cover design by Jacqueline Abromeit

For Precious Ramotswe and August Boatwright, with gratitude for the many enjoyable hours I've spent in your company.

"Out beyond wrong-doing and right-doing,
there is a field,
I'll meet you there."

Mevlana Jalaluddin Rumi
(1207 – 1273)

Chapter One

If the events of these two midsummer days were transposed, I have questioned whether the outcome would have been different. Would I still be sat here, drinking coffee and contemplating death or, more correctly, murder? The truth is, it does not matter. Because the events did unfold in the order in which they did and I am here. And I am contemplating death. And, more importantly, I am contemplating murder.

For almost 24 hours now, I have felt sick. Not the kind of sickness that would be accompanied by actual vomiting. More the sickly feeling I used to get when the boys were out late on their motorbikes. When they promised to be home before 11 o'clock and I would lie in bed and hear the green painted longcase clock in the hall strike midnight. The sort of sickness I experienced when I first learned about Peter's court case. A hungerless, empty feeling accompanied by a lightness of the body and an invisible tremor. Yet, over the years, I thought I had learned to dismiss mindless worry. Well, almost. I had learned that the things you need to worry about find you. You have no need to go chasing.

Seeing Marilyn's car draw onto the patchy, weed-strewn gravel to the side of the cottage, I slid the appointment letter into my tan leather handbag, switched on the answering machine and went to pull the heavy double oak doors shut behind me.

1

I noticed again the dusty dying fly on the windowsill. It was still there, giving the occasional weak, barely audible buzz. I removed my brown court shoe, raised it over my head and brought it down with hammer force on the insect. I only hoped my family would have the courage to do the same for me when the time came.

'You look extremely pale, Jetta. Are you alright?' Marilyn said as I slid into the passenger seat and pulled the seat belt around me.

'Not really. I was pleased when you offered to drive today.' Sensing she was about to ask more, I held up my hand. 'I'll tell you all about it later, promise. Over coffee.'

Marilyn, I decided, would be the first person I would tell. She was not prone to emotional outbursts and never made mountains out of molehills. Some considered her cold and detached. In truth she was level-headed and considerate. And in the few years I had known her, she'd become my most trusted friend.

The overgrown hedges and wild cow parsley made the single track lanes out of Hampton Stoke narrower than usual. The forecast was for yet another hot sunny day with isolated showers, and I lowered my window several inches, enough to let in a warm breeze. I was beginning to feel calmer. Less shaky. Less nauseous. Within 10 minutes we were on the A36 heading west towards Bath. Thank goodness my late morning appointment meant we avoided the rush hour. Driving, Marilyn and I had long since agreed, was no longer a pleasure.

Once in Bath, we lapsed into a comfortable silence; Marilyn followed the signs to The Royal National Hospital for Rheumatic Diseases, whilst I tried to concentrate on the everyday things that were my life. Jetta Fellowes' life. Eighty years young, I was a regular contributor to the Hampton Stoke parish magazine, organised charity coffee mornings, sent letters of protest and occasional praise to newspapers, politicians and potential reformers. I enjoyed social gatherings, the company of friends, meeting new people, my cats, books, reading and the Open Minds discussion group. Most of all I loved my family. But I didn't want to think of them right now.

Marilyn eased her navy Volvo into a tight space at the Theatre Royal end of Upper Borough Walls. Was this auspicious? Parking was not usually this easy.

'You go ahead,' Marilyn said, fumbling in her purse for pound coins to feed the ticket machine as I struggled to get out without scratching the paintwork of the car alongside. 'I'll meet you in Maddison's in an hour or so.'

With rain spots the size of half crowns starting to fall, I hugged the hospital side of the pavement as I made my way towards the entrance. It was ludicrous how many parking slots they fitted into such a small area. I'd write a letter to the council headed 'Revenue over Comfort'. Although I knew I wouldn't. Not now.

Once inside the spacious Georgian building, I handed the receptionist my appointment letter. 'Doctor Bhalla at 11.30.'

Hearing the doctor was running slightly late, I bought a coffee from the vending machine and gazed at the portraits around the walls. A pastel of Mrs Morris, wife of the first apothecary, dated 1742; an oil painting of her husband, John, together with an oil of Ralph Allen, born 1694, died 1764 who was both president and benefactor. Eventually I sat down near the consulting room on a high backed chair beneath a watercolour of the hospital under which a brass plaque explained it was presented by Doctor George D Kersley in 1993. From the pile of magazines on the table, I picked up an old *Country Life*, turning its pages at regular intervals as I sipped my hot, bitter coffee. I didn't want to make conversation. Not today.

'Mrs Fellowes.'

The consultant's voice cut through my thoughts. I glanced up to see the tall, lean doctor pick up a set of notes from a shelf outside his door. I had expected a longer wait. The nurse suggested it could be as long as half an hour. As I looked around for a space to set down my coffee and magazine, I noticed him glance down, raise his head and say, 'Mrs Fellowes. Mrs Bibby Fellowes.'

That's when the numbness started. Mrs Bibby Fellowes? It couldn't be. It couldn't be her. I set the vending cup down on the magazines, spilling most of the now tepid coffee. The numbness suffused my body. To my right, several seats nearer the consulting room, a tall, slender woman stood up, smoothed her blue cotton dress across her hips, flicked her shoulder-length blonde hair back from her face and followed the doctor into his consulting room.

It was her. I'd glimpsed only her profile, yet it was un-mistakably her. I twisted my hands, one within the other, anything to stop them trembling, and looked down to where a rivulet of coffee ran from the magazine table onto the floor.

'Don't worry,' someone was saying, using paper tissues to mop up the spilt coffee. 'Could happen to anyone.'

Please heart, please slow down. Please.

'Are you alright?' One of the clinic's nurses knelt beside my chair as several of the patients turned to see what was happening. I knew only one thing. I had to get out of here before she came out of the consulting room.

I stood and clutched my handbag. 'I need to get some air.'

The nurse put her hand beneath my elbow, steadying me as I headed towards the exit. 'Wouldn't you rather sit?'

'No.'

I shook my arm free of her hand and went through the wide doors onto the street, gulping for air as a landed fish might. I leaned back against the blackened Bath stone, closed my eyes and drew the air deep into my lungs. In and out. In and out, through my nose. In and out, until, gradually, my breathing deepened and the thumping in my ears eased slightly.

Eventually I opened my eyes. The nurse stood inches from me, her glasses swinging on a chain around her neck.

'Didn't think it safe to just leave you,' she said, her expression one of concern. 'Do you feel ready to come back inside?'

My thoughts spun haphazardly through the options. The one thing I did know was that I would not risk coming face to face with her. Not with Bibby. *Think, Jetta. For God's sake, think. And quickly.*

'I'm afraid I've had some rather bad news. I need to go home.' I paused and cleared my throat. 'Perhaps you'd be kind enough to take my name off your list today and I'll phone for another appointment later.'

Without waiting for a reply, I hurried across the street, made my way along the uneven pavement crowded with late morning shoppers, and turned left in the general direction of Maddison's. There I would find a sweet pastry and a comforting hot drink. I needed comfort. I needed sugar. Most of all, I needed time to think.

Sat on the worn tan leather sofa, having forced down a Danish pastry and about to start on my coffee, I picked up a copy of *The Times* from a nearby table and spread it out beside me. I noticed the midday sun had dried the previously damp pavements and the city's inhabitants and visitors were going about their business under a cloudless blue sky. Marilyn would be a while yet, hopefully.

As I cradled the large cream mug in both hands, I felt slightly calmer. Strange, given the events of the past two days. Yet it was today's events I wanted straighter in my head before Marilyn arrived.

I could continue as if I'd never seen Bibby. As if she didn't exist. As if she'd never existed. Or I could find out more about her, such as where she lived. If I chose the latter, this would give me more options. But what was I going to do when I found out where she lived? Oh, for goodness' sake, why was I playing this ridiculous game with myself? I already knew what I was going to do. I didn't need time to make a decision. The impact of yesterday's news simply ensured a swifter verdict. That and the fact *she* was still calling herself Fellowes. I would find out where *she* lived. And then I would see to it that *she* died. It was the only way I would ever rest in peace. I would kill her. Or, to be accurate, murder her.

Murder. I allowed the word to play my pinball mind and enjoyed the feeling. It felt good. I felt good. The events of yesterday had conspired with the events of today. It was no coincidence that I'd encountered her today. Today being the day after yesterday. Synchronicity, some would call it. I called it justice. Yes, justice. Dying. Death. Kill. Murder. What matter the how? Fate had intervened with the why. It was up to me to sort out the how.

Within minutes I'd made my first decision. Retrieving a blue gel pen and my mobile from the bottom of my handbag, I rang the hospital I'd left almost an hour before. The screen displayed *Calling The Min* until a man's voice answered:

'Royal National Hospital, which department please?'

'Appointments please.'

'Appointments,' a woman said. 'How can I help you?'

'I fear there's been a mistake over my address. You see, I think you have my old address. But I've moved and therefore have a new address. But when the appointment was sent out I didn't receive the first one because…well, whatever, but really I should have told you before, but I sometimes get confused.'

A patient voice interrupted me. 'What's your name?'

'Fellowes. Mrs Bibby Fellowes.'

'And your address, Mrs Fellowes?'

I must not panic. Think, Jetta, think. 'Yes, that's right. Bibby Fellowes. Spelt B…'

'No, your address, Mrs Fellowes. What is it?'

'Yes. I have an address, thank you. Could you tell me what you have on your records as I don't think you have it correctly, you see, because when I received…'

'So you are not at 16 Cliffside Apartments, Lyme Regis, Dorset, DT7?'

'Oh, you have it correct now,' I said, scribbling the address on a paper napkin. 'I'm so sorry to have troubled you.'

I zipped the napkin into the side compartment of my handbag and gave silent thanks to my children who had insisted on buying their stubborn old mother a mobile phone, and ensuring I knew how to use it.

By the time Marilyn appeared I'd also called my surgery and made an appointment to see my doctor the following morning. Yet another part of the plan in place.

'Another coffee?' Marilyn mouthed from the counter.

I nodded, despite still having half a cup. It was going to be a long session.

'You're early,' she said, placing two full Waitrose carriers alongside me and pulling up a chair opposite. 'I thought I'd be here before you.'

After a young, dark-haired man placed the coffees on our table, Marilyn leaned towards me. 'Now tell me, Jetta. What happened yesterday?'

Her blue-grey eyes searched mine. I knew she could see the answer before she heard it from me. She was the only person who knew about my visit to the oncologist the day before. I hadn't told another soul, certainly not the family. There didn't seem any point, at least until I knew something for certain. Now I did.

'It's as I suspected, Marilyn,' I felt her hand on mine and I lowered my gaze, unable to maintain eye contact. The veins on the back of her hand raised as her skin tightened. 'The doctor said I've got less than a year. Well, six months. Nine at the outside.'

Her grip relaxed momentarily. I'd deliberately chosen to tell her in a public place. For now I simply wanted to tell someone whom I knew would be strong for me. Someone who wouldn't give me the added pressure of having to consider how my dying affected them. And as I saw the depth of sadness in Marilyn's eyes, I knew she would show strong no matter how she felt inside.

'I'm so sorry, Jetta.'

And I knew she was. I was sorry too. Life had suddenly delivered a cut-off point. No longer was there an open-endedness to my days. Last night I doubt I'd slept for more than an hour. I lay awake, hearing the church clock strike one, two and three. For the first time I could remember, reading didn't help. I read the same sentence a dozen times before getting up and pulling on my old red dressing gown. In the hope there was truth in the soporific properties of hot milk, I went downstairs and made a tumbler full whilst the cats, seemingly sensing my unease, rubbed against my legs as if to reassure me. When I returned to bed with the milk, cats and a hot water bottle for comfort, I wished, for the first time in a long while, to have someone in bed with me. Someone who would understand and place a reassuring arm around me and tell me it was going to be alright. It didn't matter that we'd both know it wouldn't.

The worst part was the prospect of telling Peter and David. Deborah too, who I loved more as a daughter than a daughter-in-law. And what about Andrea and Becky?

'Don't be so morbid, Nan,' they always said, if I ever said I wanted to leave Poplar Cottage in my box.

They knew I loathed the prospect of ending my days in a high-winged chair in a nursing home with people saying 'How are we today?' and calling me *dear* and *darling*. I simply wanted to go to bed one night, fall into a deep sleep and never wake. Yet the more I thought about it, why shouldn't I be dying? I was 80 and had to die of something at some time. Everyone does.

'My biggest concern is the family,' I said before taking another gulp of hot coffee.

'You're dying and you're thinking of how to lessen the impact on your children.'

'Because that's the one thing I can do, Marilyn. I can cry, scream, moan, say it isn't fair, ask *why me* and self-pity my way out of here, but it won't change things.'

'When are you going to tell them?'

'Not for a few weeks. There are things I need to put straight first and people I want to see.'

After receiving the news yesterday my plan had been to tell them at the weekend. Have them all over for Sunday lunch. But after fate intervened today in the form of Bibby, my plans had already changed. I couldn't risk the family taking too close an interest in me and my whereabouts before I sorted her.

'It's your choice.' I knew from her voice she didn't agree. 'What's the procedure now regarding treatment?'

'They were awfully kind at the clinic. But I couldn't take anything in yesterday. They said to continue taking the painkillers I've got and they'll arrange for me to meet with a nursing specialist later this week.' I looked from Marilyn to my skinny, liver-spotted hands. 'Another good thing is that Lawrence went before me.'

'I wish I'd known him,' Marilyn said. 'Especially if he was anything like you.'

I smiled, picked up my coffee and drained the cup, watching milk rings merge on the saucer. 'He was nothing like me. He was quiet and not a bit practical and, yes, I'm sorry you didn't get to meet him too.'

Marilyn edged her chair closer to the table. 'And what did they say at The Mineral Hospital?'

'I didn't see the doctor.'

'Why ever not?'

'There didn't seem any point. Here I am riddled with cancer and months to live. Doesn't seem worth wasting his time or mine on a slightly arthritic hip.'

'I see what you mean. But you knew this yesterday.'

'I know, but I thought I'd go. See Dr Bhalla and explain. Yet when I got there well, it didn't seem worthwhile somehow.'

Except it was worthwhile. I was obviously meant to be there at that time. When I think of all the thousands of people who come to that hospital from all over the country, what were the chances of me being there at the same time as *her*? Coincidence? Who was it said there is no such thing as coincidence?

The next rain shower came as I watched Marilyn reverse out of the drive to make the short journey to her home. The spots fell cold on my sun-warmed skin. After waving her off, I stood in the garden I'd spent so much time in over the years. It showed signs of neglect. Unruly stout weeds poked through the thin gravel every few inches and the old English rose to the left of the kitchen window needed tying back. The wavy timbered tool shed that Lawrence had built shortly after he retired remained upright. Just. He never was one for DIY and I knew instinctively that if the shed stayed upright for another winter it would be a miracle.

The thought of Lawrence and a miracle sent my thoughts flying and I fished the door keys out of my handbag and let myself into the cottage. It wouldn't do for anyone to find me stood out in the garden in the rain not in control of my emotions. Placing my handbag on the wooden draining board, I poured a glass of tap water and took two painkillers from the packet on the dresser. It was too early for a gin and tonic.

Moving through the dining room, I went upstairs to the bedroom, clutching the banister as I went. I needed to lie down, if only for a while. For some reason I felt exhausted. Placing my taupe skirt over the back of the chair and my blouse back on its wooden hanger, I lay on the double bed in my cream slip and felt the cool of the quilted eiderdown where it pressed against my cheek.

As I lay there thinking about how I would murder *her*, I heard the church clock strike the half hour and wished my body wasn't hurting so much.

Chapter Two

Swindon, Wiltshire, September 1975

It was what I had once heard an Australian refer to as a typical Pommy no-weather day. A grey blanket sky tucked into the sides of the landscape as far as the eye could see. No fog. No rain. No sun. Perhaps he was right. No weather.

Lawrence twisted the key in the ignition and once again the engine refused to start. I sighed inwardly and Peter groaned.

'I thought you were supposed to have cured the problem?' I said.

Lawrence shook his head. 'I thought I had.'

'Do you want me to take a look under the bonnet, Dad?' David asked from his position wedged between Deborah and me on the back seat.

'Either way we'll be late,' Peter said as he wound down the front passenger window. 'Anyone mind if I smoke?'

Without waiting for an answer, he drew a silver lighter and the familiar gold Benson and Hedges packet from his jacket pocket and lit up, his shoulders visibly lowering as he blew smoke and tension out of the open window.

Lawrence rattled the gear stick noisily and glared at Peter. 'Don't put that out in here.' I was reminded that there is nothing worse than a reformed smoker.

'Why don't you get something more reliable?' I said, making eye contact with Lawrence in the rear view mirror. 'I don't know why you're so attached to this damn old thing.'

He ignored me. And, as the engine clicked its all too familiar fail-to-start tune, I felt my muscles tense. Lawrence didn't have a practical bone in his body, unlike David, who seemed to have taken after me in matters practical. After several minutes, to sighs of relief from all, the Humber Hawk roared into life. Thank goodness, I uttered silently, perhaps now we would get on our way.

'There you are.' Lawrence settled back in the driving seat. 'You ought to have more faith in me.'

'No time for that now, Dad,' Peter said, drawing hastily on his cigarette before flicking it into the kerb as Lawrence pulled out of the driveway. 'I said we'd be there at three.'

I'm sure Lawrence exceeded the speed limit as he sped down Marlborough Road, something he often criticised me for, though it didn't seem the time to say.

'Never forget,' Lawrence said, patting the dashboard as he drove slightly slower along Newport Street, 'she pulled the caravan to Boulogne and back and never let us down once.'

'That was over five years ago,' David reminded him. 'Things get older. Wear out. Rust out.'

'Tell me about it,' I said, and for a few minutes we travelled in silence.

As we passed the Dancing School in Bath Road, Peter said, 'Now that we're all together I might as well tell you that I've met someone. I mean, not just someone. I was going to keep quiet for a bit longer. But now I've got the house sorted out and, well, I want you all to meet her.'

I knew immediately from the way he spoke that this wasn't simply another girlfriend. Peter was never short of those.

'I thought I'd ask her over to the house tomorrow afternoon when you're all there. What do you think?'

'I think it's a great idea,' I said, intrigued by the woman who had this effect on him. Lawrence nodded.

'Yeah, about time you stopped enjoying yourself!' David pushed the back of Peter's shoulder and laughed.

'Yes,' Deborah added, 'all the fun you have is a disturbing influence on your brother.'

A couple of minutes later we pulled into a street of red-brick terraced houses.

'Park anywhere,' Peter said, before letting himself out of the car and crossing the narrow road to where a woman in her mid-thirties stood with a clipboard and a slim briefcase. A woman who smiled at the sight of him, as most women did.

'Peter,' I called after him, 'this friend of yours, this…woman, what's her name?'

'Bibby,' he said, turning to face me. And, as if relishing the sound of her name on his lips, he said it again. 'Bibby. Her name's Bibby.'

As with the other houses in the street, a walled front garden separated 7 Newhill Street from the pavement by several feet. Some people had concreted their front gardens and placed pots either side of their front doors and windows, and one had used the space to park a motorbike.

Number seven was modernised to a high standard – according to the sales particulars – which included gas central heating, new windows, new kitchen and a new bathroom. Peter's offer, which was under the £7,000 asking price, had been accepted, and with no chain he hoped to move into the house within six to eight weeks.

Downstairs the white painted woodwork and magnolia walls gave a spacious feel to the mid-terraced house. Upstairs, a large rear bedroom had been divided to make a single room, a landing area and a bathroom. An upstairs bathroom, according to the agent, was what people wanted. Although I'm not sure the brown bathroom suite was. Opening the window of the rear bedroom, Peter pointed to an access lane that separated the long, narrow, recently turfed garden from the gardens of the houses beyond. 'I could even build a garage at the end there, safer than parking on the street.'

Without waiting for a response, he turned and pushed his floppy dark brown hair away from his face. 'Thanks Mum, Dad, I couldn't have done it without you.'

'You would have.' I circled an arm around his waist. He towered over me and, at 6'2", was several inches taller than Lawrence. 'Maybe we helped you get your foot on the ladder a bit earlier, that's all.'

'It's no more than we did for David,' Lawrence said, rapping his knuckles on the freshly plastered walls.

'What's this about me?' David walked into the bedroom, closely followed by Deborah.

Peter closed the window, shutting out the crisp autumn air. 'What do you think then, Dave?'

'I think it's great, especially now I know there's a pub at the end of the road.'

Deborah hit David's arm. 'I think it's lovely, Pete. And now with a woman to place a calming influence on you…'

'Get you under her thumb, she means!' David laughed.

I moved across the landing and into the front bedroom, leaving them to their banter. A wrought-iron fireplace, complete with original tiles, graced the end wall. Through the picture window a pewter sky was visible above the terracotta roofs of the houses opposite. It would rain before the afternoon was out.

It was true what I'd said about Peter having got the house without our help. He was resourceful, always had been. Our help meant he had a smaller mortgage, that's all. Peter would go places.

We'd always known that. We had given David the same sum of money as a deposit on the house he and Deborah shared in Cheney Manor since their marriage six months earlier. Two boys with two years between them, yet the differences were marked. David was a plodder, practical and hard-working. Peter was more of a risk-taker, creative, good with people. And thankfully they each admired the other's attributes and got on well together. In the main.

Outside a black and tan terrier ran past the house, followed by a young boy on a skateboard with a red and white Swindon scarf wound around his neck. The boy's shouts for the dog to slow down went unheeded. He hadn't learned about terriers yet. That was one of the advantages of ageing; you got to understand things and people, if you took the trouble.

'Mr Fellowes,' a voice called from downstairs. It was the estate agent reminding Peter she had another appointment at four. And time, according to her watch, was ticking fast.

That evening after soaking in a hot bath, I slid between the cotton sheets wearing a dusting of Kiku talc and a lilac scoop-necked nightgown. I'd left Lawrence downstairs in his armchair reading the *Evening Advertiser*. It was part of his nightly ritual. I visualised him: his elbows resting on the worn arms of the chair, clutching the newspaper at chest height, his face hidden behind the town's daily news. Next, he would pull out the TV plug, switch off the cooker at the wall and check all the outer doors were secure on our detached, bay-windowed suburban home. With Peter about to leave home for good, Lawrence and I would be left alone together. And I wasn't sure how it would all work out.

Lawrence was a neat, predictable man. Peter and David were not. Lawrence was quiet, I wasn't and having two boys that took after me seemed to make him quieter still. *Empty vessels make the most noise*, Lawrence would remind us. *The quiet ones are the worst*, I'd remind him. For every such phrase there was its opposite: *too many cooks spoil the broth* could be countered with *many hands make light work*. Or *great minds think alike* with *fools seldom differ*. He wasn't going to pull that one on me.

Lawrence's job as an accountant for a local garage group suited him as he was paid a regular salary for regular hours. It didn't stretch him. It was safe. And he had been there long enough to know he had a job for life.

Our married life had not been without conflict. Sometimes it was about money, sometimes it was about the boys. But more often than not it was about something indefinable – an absence of something I couldn't seem to name. Although, on occasion, I did try.

Once, in the early 60s, I'd consulted a solicitor about a divorce. But consultation was as far as it got. I made the mistake of telling my mother and she reminded me I was married to a professional with a good salary. I had a home in an area of Swindon to which many people could only aspire. And I didn't have to work. Her parting shot was that some people did not know when they were well off. 'Some people', obviously, being me. Funnily enough, she repeated most of what the elderly solicitor had told me when I visited him in his stuffy Georgian office in Old Town. Strange how neither of them mentioned David and Peter, the part of our marriage that did make it all worthwhile.

It was 10.35 pm when Lawrence came to bed and I was still reading. He stepped out of his trousers, folded them neatly and hung them on his clothes press. Same with his shirt and jumper. Without a word he went into the adjoining bathroom and emerged minutes later wearing his pyjamas and a smear of toothpaste on his bottom lip. I laid *The War Between The Tates* on the bedcover as Lawrence climbed in beside me, then I leaned over and rubbed the white smudge off his lower lip. His once black hair was now completely steel grey, yet it suited him. And he hadn't run to fat as so many men had by their early 50s. He sat, three pillows propped behind him, and I leaned into him, laying my right arm across his chest against the soft fabric of his overwashed paisley pyjamas. I wanted to ask him if he was happy. Or, if he wasn't, was there anything I could do to help make him so. Instead, I leaned up and kissed his slightly flabby jowls, patted his chest and said, 'Goodnight.'

I put my book on the bedside cabinet, turned off my lamp and curled under the covers, thinking of tomorrow and meeting Peter's girlfriend. I felt Lawrence's foot touch mine, a deliberate touch. A touch that said: *I know what you want and I can't give it to you.* And I pressed the sole of my foot back against his and I'm not sure what it said, because I'm not sure of anything any more.

The late afternoon sun cut through the leaded bay window, leaving triangles of light on the Sanderson-covered window seats and plain moss carpet. The room was warm as Lawrence had lit a fire in the sitting room and shut the sliding frosted glass doors that shut off the other half of the room. Once, there had been a wall there, but we'd followed the craze of knocking two rooms together to make one large room, though neither of the rooms could ever have been considered small. An old black and white Western played out on the television in the corner of the room and Lawrence, who'd insisted he wanted to watch it, had been asleep for the last half hour. And when he woke he would blame the heat or my giving him too much Sunday lunch, as if he needed to blame something or someone for him taking a nap.

David and Deborah were sitting on the large pale green sofa, arms entwined. I had finished in the kitchen preparing food for Pete's return; his return with Bibby. Not that there was much to

18

do. I'd decided on a cold concoction, buffet-style, mainly chicken and ham with salad, and trifle and cream for dessert.

'OK, you two, what's Bibby like?' I said.

'We haven't met her.'

'Come on, you always know what girls are in his life before I do.'

'Honestly, Mum, not this time.'

Deborah nodded in support. 'We don't, Jetta. We were as surprised as you. We thought we hadn't seen much of him lately, now we know why.'

The more I knew of Deborah, the more I liked her. She and David seemed a perfect match, if there was such a thing. Her round face with its high cheekbones was framed by a mop of wavy, almost black hair, and she was pretty in an old-fashioned sort of way.

'Well, the mystery thickens,' I said.

A loud snore from Lawrence caused his leg to jump and his eyes to open. 'Must have dozed off,' he said, straightening his pullover. 'It's the heat from the fire that does it.' He looked at me. 'I'm hungry. Hope Peter's not going to be too much longer.'

'We'll eat as soon as they arrive,' I said, and with the words barely uttered, we heard Peter's Mini pull onto the driveway.

Peter walked in from the hallway still wearing his overcoat. 'Come on in,' he said, half-turning towards the doorway, 'Come and meet everyone.'

I hadn't formed any picture of Bibby in my mind, so I'm not sure who I expected, but it wasn't Bibby. She wasn't pretty. She was stunning. I had only ever seen girls who looked this perfect in magazines. She stood around 6 feet tall in platform boots and a long black coat with silver pepper-pot buttons. The black accentuated her blonde hair, which she wore long, almost to the middle of her back with the front flicked in a way that drew attention to her oval kohled eyes and full glossy mouth. And her smile at each of us when introduced revealed teeth as perfect as the rest of her.

Peter took Bibby's coat to the cloakroom and she sat down next to Deborah, who looked as though she'd been darted with a slow-acting anaesthetic. I watched her go from open bloom to tightly furled bud, whilst Lawrence became animated, interested. Almost charming.

'Shall we eat now then, dear?' Lawrence rubbed his hands together and looked at me, his eyes bright.

'Do you feel ready to eat?' I asked Bibby.

'I'm happy to eat at anytime, Mrs Fellowes,' she said in a voice that definitely didn't hail from the West Country. 'Do you need any help?'

'No, you sit here and chat with the others. Give me quarter of an hour, then come through to the dining room, all of you. And please, Bibby, call me Jetta.'

Half an hour later we were all sitting around the oval mahogany table I'd overlaid with my late mother's embroidered linen tablecloth and napkins. Oval platters of sliced chicken breast and thinly cut ham sat in the centre, surrounded with crusty bread and dishes of my homemade chutney and coleslaw, and I'd filled the compartments of the party tray with lettuce, tomatoes, spring onions and carrot sticks.

As Bibby waited politely for food to be offered to her, I could see up close what Peter saw in her. I could see what any man would see in her. She was pre-Raphaelite, willowy, graceful, with a small, perfectly formed bosom and a flawless skin. She looked much younger than Peter's 23 years, yet there was a quiet confidence about her.

'You're not from around here,' Lawrence said, putting slices of ham on his plate, 'judging by your accent?'

'No.'

'Whereabouts are you from?'

'Now or originally?'

'Both.'

'Now, I rent a room in a house off Farringdon Road. Originally, I'm from Canada.'

Peter looked at her. 'I thought you said you were from New Zealand.'

She hesitated momentarily. 'Well, no. I said I was *born* in New Zealand. But we moved to Canada almost immediately.'

I watched Bibby. She smiled at Peter. Her full-gloss lips parted and the pink tip of her tongue appeared between her teeth. Those bright beautiful teeth. And I watched Peter. He leaned over. He kissed her cheek. That flawless blushing cheek. And for some unknown reason, my stomach lurched. And I thought how unusual it was for Peter to get details wrong.

Chapter Three

Hampton Stoke, near Bath, Wednesday, July 2006

This was the third morning in a row I had woken with a sickly feeling. Yet today was different. Today it was almost immediately replaced by a sort of excitement. Excitement at the knowledge that whilst I might be dying, I would see to it that Bibby went before me. Bibby. Simply using her name caused bile to rise in my throat.

Bibby was short for Elizabeth.

'Daddy always called me his little Bibby,' she once told us.

Little Bibby. I'd come to loathe the sort of women that hung on to inappropriate childhood names into adulthood. Way past the time when they should have known better. They were usually horribly spoiled and expected their husbands or boyfriends to provide for them in exactly the same way their daddy had. Bibby certainly lived up to that image. When she wanted Peter to agree with something, usually a purchase she didn't need but simply had to have, she would tilt her head, sweep her hair away from her face in an exaggerated gesture, and say, 'Oh Petey!' in a little girl's voice. It was enough to make any self-respecting woman vomit.

By 9.30 I was sat in the waiting room at the local doctor's surgery. I'd breakfasted, fed the cats and rehearsed my lines for Dr Harper. I sat without a magazine, more than content to people-watch.

Last time I was here I'd felt a fraud. Other people's ills had seemed considerably worse than mine. One man sat in a wheelchair and several patients used walking aids. And almost all were younger than me. But now I of all people knew how easy it was to make false assumptions. Did they know they were sitting with a murderer?

'Surely not,' they would say if asked, remembering the little old lady with the camel cardigan and the way she'd fiddled with its pearl button fastenings. 'The one with the blonde-grey rinsed hair and pale blue eye make-up? She had to be 80 if she's a day.'

That's when I truly made my decision, sat there surrounded by people with cancerous organs, diseased bones and failing hearts; people who deserved to live. I would find Bibby. And I would kill her. And nobody would suspect that a slightly arthritic old lady of 80 who'd recently been given six months to live would be capable of such a thing. That's because most people don't know that age is just a number and it's simply that the vehicle I turned up in is wearing out.

By the time I got in to see Dr Harper, it was almost 10 o'clock. Extending a strong hand, he welcomed me warmly and guided me into the seat facing him before flopping back into his own. Dr Harper and I had reached an understanding when I'd first become his patient. I wouldn't waste his time with non-essential visits and he wouldn't try my patience with non-essential platitudes. He agreed and it worked well, for us. After sympathising briefly over my test results he wasted no further time and asked what he could do for me today.

'I haven't slept since I got the news on Monday,' I told him. 'And I'd like a strong sleeping powder just so I can get a few nights' sleep. Maybe a week's worth. The hospital said I'll see someone to discuss care and…but I really would appreciate–'

I took an embroidered cotton hanky from my sleeve, dabbed at my eyes and maintained the silence.

'Of course.' He leaned forward, patted my hand and smiled before turning back to his computer.

I left the surgery clutching the prescription and drove the short distance to the chemist. Finding a parking space outside the low modern building was easy and after reversing my pale blue Citroën into it, I took a pen and notepad from my handbag and turned to a blank page. It was imperative I write things down as they came to mind; I was getting more forgetful as the days advanced.

Pills/powder
Tourist Information
Peggy/Open Minds
Marilyn
Cats
Nursing specialist
Family

Leaving the pad on the passenger seat, I locked the car door and made my way up the concrete slope. Square wooden pots either side of the chemist's door brimmed with purple petunias and scarlet and white geraniums, and a panting golden retriever lay obediently in a slice of shade, his lead tied to a metal wall ring. It was already another hot day.

When the assistant held out her hand for my prescription I asked to speak with the pharmacist; I would leave nothing to chance. A thin girl with hooded eyes wearing a white cotton coat emerged from behind a white screen and asked if she could help. She looked too young to be in charge of dispensing dangerous drugs, but I felt that about most professionals these days.

I showed her the prescription. 'My doctor's prescribed these for me, but I'm not good at taking pills, would you mind showing me one?'

She disappeared behind the screen and returned minutes later with a bright orange capsule.

'So there's powder in there?' I asked.

'Yes.' The hooded eyes opened slightly more.

'Good. I prefer a capsule. I find those large solid tablets so beastly to swallow.'

She returned to the job of dispensing the Secobarbital without another word. Usually, I would have minded her morose attitude. But today, her lack of enthusiasm for me, her day and her job was her concern. The capsules containing powder made it mission accomplished as far as I was concerned. And as far as my plans were going it was so far, so good.

I sat at the kitchen table with my list, coffee and telephone next to me, ticking the items as I completed them. There was already a thick blue line through *Pills/powder* and *Tourist Information*, the latter being easier than I'd imagined. The Lyme Regis tourist information centre had given me several numbers of hotels and bed and breakfast houses but doubted whether any had vacancies at such short notice this time of the year. I decided against bed and breakfast houses, I would be more anonymous in a hotel. Fortunately, my third call to The Admiral's House Hotel in Pound Street paid dividends. Literally minutes earlier they had received a cancellation for a double room with a sea view and I booked in for nine nights from tomorrow under the name of Francis. Mrs Jean Francis. The cost almost stopped me until I reminded myself that I had only six months in which to spend any of my meagre savings. What better cause than now? Besides, the family would have the cottage after I'd gone so I wouldn't be leaving them without anything. Peter had money of his own and David hadn't done too badly either so the cottage would be a bonus to them. I was just so unused to spending such large sums on myself.

I took another sip of coffee, draining the deep blue mug of the dark, now tepid liquid. Elevenses. Such a simple pleasure, not to be taken for granted, I now realised. *Peggy/Open Minds* was next on the list so I phoned immediately. I wouldn't give myself time to consider what to say or I'd get tongue-tied, or worse, back down.

Dropping my shoulders and taking a deep breath, I pressed the figures on the phone's keypad and leaned back into the wheel-back dining chair. Peggy answered.

'Peggy? It's Jetta.'

'Oh, how are you managing in this heat? It's too hot for me, Jetta. It's unbearable. It really is. Plays havoc with my joints.'

Sadly the wind and rain did too so there was rarely a day when Peggy's joints weren't being havocked. 'I'm sorry to hear that, Peggy.'

'And Geoff's worse than useless in this hot weather. Honestly, I never thought I'd wish for the onset of winter but his breathing's so laboured. Trouble is, I then have to worry about him getting colds and flu. Honestly, it's terrible getting old. Now I'm glad you rang because I wanted to remind you that we've got a new woman coming tomorrow night, so you'll need extra–'

'That's why I'm ringing,' I interrupted. 'About tomorrow night. I'm afraid something's come up and I've got to go away for a few days so I won't be able to have it at my place tomorrow.'

'Oh, goodness, Jetta! Didn't we say right at the outset that we would all commit to the first and third Thursday of every month, come hell or high water? You know we talked about how groups fail through lack of commitment by every member. I mean, I can't have it here. Geoff's in tomorrow night and there's some important match on the TV.'

'It is important, Peggy, otherwise I wouldn't do it.' I tried to stop her flow, but she wasn't listening.

After a few more unsuccessful attempts to get a word in when she drew breath, my polite veneer began to slip away. Peggy irritated me at the best of times. Today she was doing a grand job. No question of her asking if there was a problem or if there was anything she could do for me. No question of her asking if I was alright, or 'Don't you worry, Jetta, I know you wouldn't do it unless absolutely necessary.' No, it would be all about her arthritis, her Geoff's chest or her dog's canker. God forbid that she should have to change her routine. Lunch was always at one, grocery shopping was always on a Wednesday, and Geoff was never allowed a tea or coffee after seven in the evening because he would disturb her sleep by getting up for a pee. The man existed. He certainly didn't have a life.

'Really, Jetta, I do think as one of the founder members...' she waffled.

I was only half listening. Peggy belonging to Open Minds was a joke. The original idea had been to get together regularly with local people of all ages and backgrounds to discuss topics of interest – keeping an open mind. Something the majority of the group managed, although Peggy had always been a thorn in the group's side. 'I think you're being so inconsiderate to me, Jetta, and the others,' she added as an afterthought. It was then I realised I had wanted to say something to her for a very long time. And now was the time.

'Peggy!' I shouted loudly, causing her to pause long enough for me to add, 'Why don't you fuck off!'

My hands shook as I poured myself a schooner of sherry. I needed it. God knows what was happening to me. It wasn't even midday. What on earth had I done? It would be all around the village by noon. Leaving my list on the table, I went into the cool of the sitting room and sat in the chestnut leather armchair, putting my slippered feet up on the round footstool. I sipped the sherry slowly and watched a grey squirrel leap from the horse chestnut outside the window onto one of the swinging bird feeders. Usually I would shoo him off. Today I admired his agility.

The shaking had almost stopped when the phone rang. It would be Peggy and I wasn't going to answer. When the answer machine took over I heard Marilyn's voice: 'Jetta, pick the phone up. I know you're there. Come on, Jetta, pick up. Jetta…Jetta! OK, I'm on my way around.' and the line went dead. Of course, I should have realised that Marilyn would be one of the first people Peggy would ring. I'm not sure whether it was the sherry or not, but I felt a ridiculous sense of glee. And it felt good. I felt good. I felt mighty and courageous. I was glad I'd stood up to the self-centred old bag, who happened to be 16 years my junior. And with the thought of her face when she told Geoff that I'd told her to eff off, I began to laugh. And that's how Marilyn found me, rocking with laughter beside an empty sherry glass.

'No, I wasn't drunk. No, I've only had the sherry since speaking with Peggy. No, I don't regret it. I should have guessed she'd ring you though.' All of a sudden I had a horrid thought. 'You didn't tell her anything about…?' I left the question hanging.

'Of course not. I didn't give her a chance to say much at all, I was more interested in speaking with you.'

I smiled at Marilyn. I shouldn't have asked the question. I could trust her. A woman 21 years younger than me, with big hair and a big heart who was the antithesis of the Peggys of this world.

Within minutes Marilyn had made us coffee and we sat at the kitchen table and laughed as she suggested I take mine black.

'I'm not drunk, though I do feel rather heady. I think it's the delight at doing something I've wanted to do for a long time.'

'Which was?'

I hesitated, too embarrassed to repeat it. 'I told Peggy to eff off.'

Marilyn screeched with approval. 'It's true then! What on earth brought all that on?'

'I've decided to take myself off for a week's holiday starting tomorrow morning. In fact, I was going to ring you to ask if you'd feed the cats.'

Marilyn nodded – 'Of course, goes without saying' – and waved her hand at me to continue.

'I rang Peggy to say that I couldn't hold the Open Minds group here as planned tomorrow and she launched into a tirade of how we'd all made this commitment and how I was being inconsiderate and I simply saw red. Can you remember how many times we've all sat and listened to her self-pitying monologues? I just found it all so trivial, Marilyn. Bloody trivial. I told her something had come up, I told her it was important, but she wouldn't listen. She never listens. It was the only way to shut her up. And, what's more, I don't regret it. I'd do it again.'

'Good for you. About time somebody told her. You've probably done us all a great favour. Geoff certainly. I wish I was a fly on the wall in their house right now. So what is this about you going away? You never mentioned it yesterday.'

I knew Marilyn would be suspicious and this was the worst bit for me, lying to her. I hated it. But I could minimise the lies by only telling her the truth – unless she asked awkward questions. 'I've decided to have a week or so away, somewhere near the coast. I want to get some things straight in my mind before I tell the family and this is the way I want to do it. I need to go as soon as possible as I'll only get weaker over time.' I paused as we finished our coffees. 'Besides...'

'You're not thinking of...?'

'No, Marilyn. I'm not thinking of doing anything silly. Trust me.'

'Why don't I come with you? Tony will feed the cats.'

'Usually I'd love you to come, you know that. But this time,' I paused, 'It's important to me to be on my own.'

'Where will you go?'

'I'm heading towards the south coast and I'll stay at hotels so I won't have to do a thing. And I won't overdo it, and I will ring you. Promise. I aim to return a week on Saturday, so if you could take care of the cats until then.'

Marilyn nodded. 'I thought the family were coming over this weekend. Have you told them you're going away?'

'No, but I will. And if they call you, Marilyn, you will reassure them I'm OK? I don't want them fussing or worrying about me any sooner than necessary.'

'It's your life. You're in charge,' she said.

And for the fist time since Monday I felt I was. I might not be the final arbiter of the cut-off point, but I was the decider of how I got to live up until then. And I wasn't going to spend my time simply not dying. I was going to spend it living.

Chapter Four

Swindon, Wiltshire, Friday, February 1976

I pulled the last letter out of the typewriter, checked it for errors, and placed it with the others for Dr Euwan to sign. I typed the address on the brown envelope, licked the pale green first class stamp and stuck it on ready for posting; Dr Euwan rarely sent anything second class. 'If it's worth sending, it's worth the extra two pence,' he'd say. A way of thinking Lawrence would do well to adopt, I thought.

Tomorrow Lawrence and I were going to buy wallpaper for the sitting room. I had a fresh, delicately patterned paper in mind, in summer or spring colours. Lawrence, I knew, would look along the sale shelves and delve into the end of line bins at Fads and recommend whatever he saw there, irrespective of colour, texture or pattern. I didn't understand him. It wasn't as if we were that short of money. Not anymore. We didn't spend foolishly, oh that I could, the boys were self-supporting and I worked. Money wasn't tight, Lawrence was. Or, as he would say, careful.

I had started work at the doctor's surgery in Milton Road a couple of years before. Besides the obvious benefits of more money and greater independence, I discovered much about people and their lives. It was impossible not to. The thin partition wall between Dr Euwan's consulting room and my office was unlike the other more substantial walls of the converted Victorian house. I was fond of Dr Euwan. He always concerned himself with his patients' personal lives when making his diagnosis and as a result, there were always far more patients on his list than his partner's.

The scenario of males locking horns wasn't that unusual, I heard him tell one patient as she sat crying about how her son and husband had almost come to blows. Jealousy was one theory. It was true that Lawrence seemed better disposed towards David since David had married and moved into his own home. Maybe the same would be true with Peter. And only this morning I'd heard Dr Euwan remark to a patient who was mourning the demise of her marriage that it was far lonelier in an unhappy marriage than being on your own. I sometimes thought I should spend more time typing and less time listening.

The phone rang as I was about to leave for the day. It was Peter.

'Have you and Dad got anything planned for tomorrow evening?' Without waiting for a response he added that we were invited to his place for drinks and nibbles. 'I've just spoken with Debbie and she says she and David can make it.'

'Your father will be delighted. I've got decorating planned for this weekend so the less time he has to spend at home, the better.'

'Great. Come on over about 7.30ish.'

'Is there anything I should know?' I hesitated. 'Is this in aid of anything?'

'Come on over and find out.'

No sooner had I placed the cream handset back on the cradle than I picked it up and asked for an outside line. Then I put my finger in the two and dialled – lunch could wait. I needed to speak with Lawrence.

*

As predicted, Saturday morning's wallpaper shopping was a disaster. In the end we agreed that I would go on my own, or with Debbie, the following Saturday. Lawrence would not be involved.

'Thank God. Now if only I could do the same with the actual decorating,' he said, 'I'd be happy.'

I was working on it. I would get a quote from a professional and see what that did to Lawrence's enthusiasm levels.

By 6.30 I was sat at the dressing table, having changed into a warmer plaid skirt and a long, belted cardigan. I selected a deep pink Avon lipstick from the tray in the top drawer of the dressing table.

'Lawrence, do you really have no idea what this visit to Pete's is about?'

Lawrence pulled a navy and grey v-necked pullover on over his shirt. 'Maybe it's about nothing other than seeing us.'

'I think it's got something to do with Bibby. And whatever it is, I don't have a good feeling about it.'

'Maybe you're jealous.'

I looked at his reflection in the mirror. 'Of what?'

'Bibby. That she might have got your prize boy.'

'Shouldn't that be one of my prize *boys*?'

'No! Your prize boy. Admit it. No-one will ever measure up to Peter.'

'David does. Debbie does.' I felt I should add that Lawrence did, but I didn't.

Lawrence flopped down on the edge of the bed. 'That's because they're no threat to you.'

'Neither's Bibby.'

'Of course she is and you know it. You see less and less of him. He rings you hardly at all and he rarely drops in anymore.'

'That was inevitable once he got his own place. I'm happy that's the case. Why are you saying these things?'

'You don't mind him not doing those things, not calling over, not ringing, but you do mind Bibby. You mind her being in Peter's life, period. Go on, disagree with me.'

'I can't. I don't know what it is, call it a mother's instinct, call it what you like, all I know is that she's bad news. She's not good for him.'

'And so here we are back at the beginning. Nobody ever will be.'

I'd never heard Lawrence like this. His voice was vile, full of venom. And for the first time in 26 years of marriage, I wanted to hit him, slap him hard across the face. He was bewitched. With her. With Bibby. Bewitched. Infatuated. Obsessed.

'You're as daft about her as he is! Go on, admit it. She had you wound around her finger from the first time he brought her to this house. It was so obvious it was pathetic. Nauseating. For God's sake, man, how can you be so naïve?'

He brought his fist down onto the bedside cabinet before sweeping a cup and magazines to the floor. 'I'm not the naïve one. I recognise that everyone becomes familiar after time, however bewitching they might start out.'

I jumped up. 'What are you saying?'

'Do you think I don't know? That I don't see it at work? Middle-aged men making fools of themselves with girls young enough to be their daughters. Middle-aged women tired of their tired husbands. Questioning. Wanting something different. Of course it must appear exciting at first, yet even I've got sense enough to know it won't last. Because after the initial excitement and euphoria, everyone falls into reality. A reality that includes working daily, paying a mortgage, paying bills and, more often than not, raising kids. If they're lucky their reality will be with someone they don't have to feed emotionally, because that someone will know how much she's loved.'

My mouth was dry. 'But how, Lawrence? How will she know she's loved?'

'Because he continues doing those things day in and day out. He doesn't rejoice about doing them, because in an ideal world he would be doing something else, but he doesn't complain and he doesn't stray. And he stays.'

I kneeled on the floor in front of him. 'In that ideal world you mention, what would he be doing?'

Lawrence leaned back on the bed and his eyes glazed. 'I don't know. He doesn't allow himself to think about it, he daren't… All he knows is that he still wants to be with her.'

I rested my hands on his knees and looked into his sad grey eyes. 'Is that because he loves her?'

'Yes.'

Feeling tears prickle, I picked the cup up off the floor and took it down to the kitchen. That was the nearest Lawrence would come to saying he loved me.

Peter came out to meet us as we stepped out of the car. He looked happier than I'd ever seen him. There was a lightness to his step, a shine in his eyes and his broad mouth was set in a permanent smile.

'Bibby's here,' I said, almost to myself as I shut the car door. I could see her slim form lit through the window.

'Yes.' Lawrence placed his hand in the small of my back and steered me across the street.

Debbie and David had arrived minutes earlier and were pouring the drinks. Bibby was laying out bowls and plates of crisps, sausage rolls, vol-au-vents, nuts and was her usual charming self.

'I'll have a beer,' Lawrence said, watching David twist the tap on the party seven can of beer.

'And I'll have a glass of red,' I told Debbie, who was in charge of the wine.

'Help yourselves to nibbles,' Bibby said. 'There's plenty more.'

Within minutes we were all sat, drinks in hand, admiring the surroundings.

'I love the way you've got this room, Pete,' Debbie said. 'It's giving me ideas.'

'That's what I'm afraid of.' David squeezed her hand. 'But I can't believe for one minute our Pete did all this.'

As creative as Peter was, the room, though too modern for my taste, did seem to have the touch of a feminine hand about it. It was the attention to detail: the fresh irises, the geometric rugs, the white cube coffee tables and strategically placed matching photo frames. The wall lamps cast a warm blush onto the room and the heat from the recently fitted Baxi Bermuda gas fire would certainly send me to sleep if I drank too much.

'You're right. I can't take credit for it all. Bibby's been great. And, as you've probably guessed, we've been spending more and more time together.' He drew her towards him, slipping an arm around her waist.

It was obvious Peter was on the verge of an announcement. The way he stood while everyone else sat, the way he kept trying to get everyone settled and quiet. And we didn't have to wait long.

'I've asked Bibby to move in with me,' Peter said eventually. 'Not least because…because I love her.'

'Aahh,' David said, and we all laughed. Me, nervously.

'But also because we have another, more important announcement. We…' He looked around the room, ensuring we were all hanging on his every word. 'We…that's me and Bibby…Bibby and I. We are…expecting a baby!'

As they turned to each other and their lips met, I lost my hearing. I watched Lawrence move forward to embrace Bibby and saw David pat Peter's back. Debbie kissed Bibby on either cheek and Lawrence shook Peter's hand. The five of them swam about before me, their mouths moving, smiling, saying words I couldn't hear. I pushed my wine glass to the edge of the coffee table and moved forward; then, dragging a smile across my mouth, I hugged Peter, then Bibby.

All the time I heard nothing. I had heard enough. This was a disaster. She was having Peter's baby. He'd only known her for a few months. They weren't even married. And now he would be tied to her. For life.

Realising Bibby was offering me a sausage roll, I took it. I couldn't eat it, but it was something to concentrate on. Eventually I sat down. Taking a sip of wine, my inner trembling subsided and my hearing returned as I heard Debbie ask the question I most wanted answered.

'When is it due?'

Bibby hesitated and smiled at Peter. 'We'll let you know when we get the exact date.'

'Do your parents know?' I asked.

Bibby smiled her bright white smile at me. 'No. My parents are divorced and live abroad, so getting in touch with them isn't always easy.'

It was then I realised how little we knew about Bibby. We knew nothing about her. We knew nothing about her family. And I was certain Peter didn't either.

Chapter Five

Hampton Stoke, near Bath, Thursday, July 2006

It was 9.35 according to the kitchen clock as I did my last minute checks. Cooker off at the wall, tins of cat food and biscuits left out, answering machine on. I wouldn't turn the water off as Marilyn would be in daily to feed the cats. Both cats had been acting strange since I'd got up at six, weaving in and out of my legs and rubbing around the worn suitcase. They knew I was going away. They would miss the fresh white fish I cooked them every other day as a treat, but they'd survive.

Placing my case and raincoat on the car's rear seat and my handbag in the passenger footwell, I sat for a few minutes in the driving seat in an attempt to still myself. Ants filled my body, making me restless, unable to keep still, physically or mentally. I couldn't finish one thought before another arrived, demanding instant attention. I opened my handbag and searched for the bottle of Rescue Remedy; Debbie swore by it and God knows I needed something. Thinking of God, I knew I ought to try and sort my feelings out in that direction before much longer. Does he or doesn't he? Will I or won't I? *There I go again, more thoughts. More bloody irrelevant thoughts.*

Get a grip on yourself, Jetta. Four drops of Dr Bach's essence on my tongue and I sat back in the seat and thought of what I was taking with me. Essentials only, which included tablets –

painkillers and sleepers – plus a couple of Alexander McCall Smith's books – *The Number 1 Ladies' Detective Agency* and *Tears of a Giraffe*. I would need some of Precious Ramotswe's straight-forwardness in the coming weeks. She wasn't averse to doing what had to be done.

My only surprise regarding Mme Ramotswe was that she was created by a man, a topic we'd once discussed at Open Minds. Can a man realistically write fiction from a woman's perspective and vice versa? The only man present, Terry, the sub-postmaster, said he didn't think it was possible. A man could only write as a woman as he, a man, thought it might be like from a woman's perspective. And, he added, it must be true the other way around. I was inclined to agree. As I steered my car through the quiet lanes of Hampton Stoke towards the main A36, I reckoned the Open Minds group would have other things to discuss this evening. Not least, my outburst. And I could see Peggy now: 'It was awful, so awful,' and she'd dab a tissue to her eyes whilst questioning whether I was suffering from the onset of dementia or Alzheimer's. Never would she believe my outburst had any-thing to do with her.

As most of my driving over the last year or two had been lim-ited to places less than 30 miles from my home – Bath, Warmin-ster, Stourhead, Bradford upon Avon, occasionally Salisbury – I wasn't looking forward to the drive to Lyme Regis. But I wouldn't let it deter me. I would do it in chunks, which was the way to get through most things, I reminded myself.

The first chunk went well and finished with me stopping at the Little Chef near the Podimore roundabout on the A303 for a welcome shot of strong mid-morning coffee. The second chunk was uneventful and ended with me pulling off for petrol at a service station near the Ilminster bypass. The third chunk wasn't so good. The driver of a black saloon, in his 40s, blared his horn and shook his fist at me as he overtook on the road between

Chard and Axminster. I think he was insinuating my driving was too slow. My instinct was to give him the V sign; instead I raised my hand, smiled sweetly and put on my best little old lady act. It doesn't do to attract attention or trouble when you're about to commit murder.

On arrival at the Admiral's House Hotel, I eased my stiffened joints out of the car and stretched. I felt 90. Immediately, I knew the hotel was a good choice. It appeared quiet, dignified and the narrow herbaceous borders surrounding the front were well tended. The purple delphiniums, red hot pokers and baby's breath were tidy, but not too neat. Not always easy with such plants. To me, neat not regimented was a good sign. Part of the small things that made up the whole.

I left my car alongside a curved gravel pathway that led to the rear of the hotel, walked up the wide entrance steps carrying my raincoat and handbag and through the white painted double doors into the red carpeted hall-cum-reception. A small brass plaque beside a brass push bell read: *Please ring – thank you*. I did.

A smiling young man came through a panelled door at the end of the hall. The badge pinned to his white shirt told me he was Matthew, Trainee Manager.

'Mrs Fell–' I caught myself in time. 'Francis. I've got a reservation. Mrs Jean Francis.'

After checking me in, Matthew collected my case from the car. 'If you'd like to follow me, Mrs Francis, I'll take this up to your room. And if you give me your car keys, I'll move your car for you as well.'

'Oh dear, have I parked badly?'

'Not at all, you've done it well. It's just that our parking is somewhat limited and not all our other guests are as good at parking as you. I think you'd be better tucked around the side, nearer to the wall, if you want to avoid someone clipping your bumper.'

I handed him my keys. Matthew would get on. I only hoped he wouldn't notice that the car registration number I'd given him was incorrect. Hopefully it was near enough to the original, with the first and last letters being true, not to raise his interest.

Once alone in my room, I began to wilt. The drive had taken more out of me than I wanted to admit. Unpacking was too much like hard work and the pains in my body were not going to leave without help. I took two round painkillers, removed my cardigan and shoes and lay on the king-size bed, propping myself against the plump feather pillows. My muscles sighed and my bones thanked me.

As I lay there feeling the cool of the cotton pillows and the warmth of the midday sun, I could, without moving so much as an inch, see across Lyme Bay. From its long serpentine break-water, to where it met the grey and golden cliffs of the Jurassic coastline, and beyond to where it merged with the sun-filled sky. And the last thing I remember before sleep and peace arrived was watching a petal fall from the fresh rose onto the mahogany writing desk as a warm breeze fluttered in through the open window.

It was essential I blended in, became part of Lyme's wallpaper. Fortunately for me, the town's charm meant there were always hordes of visitors and holidaymakers to keep people's attention diverted from yet another grey lady enjoying one of the Dorset coast's jewels.

The Admiral's House Hotel was situated close to the town centre. I could step out of the front door, turn right and within minutes be in the centre of the main street, or Broad Street, as it was known. After a lunchtime snack at the hotel, I took a walk down the hill, past the painted blue and white period cottages with their red geranium-filled window boxes, The Regal Cinema and an eclectic mix of shops. The return journey up this historic street would be uphill. Something I must remember.

The next part of my plan called for a map. Halfway down Broad Street I found a newsagent selling maps for fossilers, walkers and drivers. And, for £1.99, a town street map.

The kitten-heeled shoes I was wearing pinched my corns and I remembered seeing a Boots chemist on the other side of the street near Woolworth's. I would get plasters there, and a toothbrush, which I had forgotten to pack. Crossing the street was easy as traffic was stopped in both directions whilst the driver of a large white van, double parked outside Lloyds bank, made his deliveries. I paused outside an antique and bric-a-brac shop. An ornate painted milk churn and flower tubs stood sentry at the open door, next to a rectangular blackboard on which was painted in bright white letters:

Psychic Readings
with Nomad & Mary
Every day except Wednesday & Thursday

Psychic readings; I didn't need a psychic to tell me what my future held. I was facing death or jail. Or both. That was it. Those were my options and I didn't need a crystal ball or Tarot cards to work it out. But I didn't care. It would be worth it to leave my family in peace. Oh, so very worth it, I thought, suddenly feeling light-headed with satisfaction.

Noticing a solid pine trunk immediately inside the door, I sat down on it, out of the direct sun. I hadn't been there more than a minute when I felt a hand on my shoulder.

'You all right, m'dear?' A man with big hair and kind, shining eyes looked down at me.

I made to stand up, but his hand stayed firmly on my shoulder. 'Yes…yes, it's these hills you know. I'm not as young as I was.'

He laughed. 'None of us are. Why don't you come through and sit on a proper seat. I've even got a cushion!'

This time I did stand up. I wasn't here to have people meet me, know me. I was here for one thing. Murder. *Get a grip of yourself, Jetta,* I told myself. *Get a grip.*

'No…no…I must be going.' And I backed out of the doorway into the warm bright day.

'Don't worry,' he smiled and inclined his head towards the blackboard. 'I wasn't going to force you into a reading. Besides, we don't usually do readings on a Thursday; I simply thought you looked as if you could do with a sit down.'

So this was Nomad. Yes, I could see that. I could see that this was someone who would know things. It was written in his face. It wouldn't do for us to spend any time together.

'No, it's not that, really. You're kind to offer. But I have to go.'

'Before you do,' he moved close and almost whispered, 'I feel compelled to tell you something.' I stopped, but didn't speak. 'You're searching,' he continued, taking a hand-rolled cigarette from his trouser pocket. 'And I'm to tell you that your search will bear fruit.'

I didn't wait to hear more. I turned and made my way up the street, threading between holidaymakers and locals. I didn't look back. Couldn't. Wouldn't. What did he mean, searching? What could he mean? It was nonsense. All nonsense, of course it was. Except he was right. Of course I was searching. And when I found her… I smiled as I recalled him saying my search would be successful. Or, as he put it, bear fruit. Now that was encouraging. Yes, most encouraging, I thought as I chose a maximum cleaning toothbrush in Boots.

Back in my hotel room, I spread the map out on the desk and located Cliffside Apartments. It wasn't difficult, Lyme Regis wasn't a big town. And less than 15 minutes later, with the map open on the passenger seat beside me, I manoeuvred my car onto Pound Street. The traffic was slow and with cars parked on the left of Broad Street and vans unloading on the right, the journey down through the town centre to the traffic lights took longer than if I'd walked. I wished I wasn't at the head of the traffic queue as the lights changed to green; I needed to drive slowly to look for the turning as I left town on the road towards Charmouth.

Some way past the car park I saw Cliffside Road on the right, indicated and turned. According to the road sign it was a no through road. I understood why when I reached a left-hand bend. On the right stood a four-storey apartment block set back from the road and surrounded on two sides by car parking. A peeling painted sign read:

Cliffside Apartments
Nos 1–16
Private Parking
Residents and Guests Only

It was obvious that the road had at one time continued round to the left, onwards to the golf course, and that the apartments had once been surrounded by spacious grounds. Coastal erosion had changed all that. Nature had played its hand. The apartments would once have been highly desirable with their outstanding coast and country views and most with sea-facing balconies. Now it looked as if many were empty. By my reckoning, if there were four floors and 16 apartments, she lived on the top floor.

There was a solitary red estate car parked in one of the parking bays and, not wanting to draw attention to myself, I decided to return to the hotel. So far everything had gone to plan; I couldn't afford to make any mistakes. It was so far, so good. Tomorrow was the problem. I would need to plan well. For tomorrow, I would have to locate Bibby.

Chapter Six

Swindon, Wiltshire, April 1976

I perched on the edge of the Bradstone wall waiting for Lawrence to return with the wheelbarrow. Spending Sunday afternoon in the garden together, raking, clearing and planting, had been his idea. He knew how much I enjoyed gardening, and I knew how much he didn't. It was a sacrifice on his part. A way of us forgetting about or at least not discussing last night's visit from Peter. I was going to suggest we went to a film matinee. *Ten Rillington Place* was the last film we'd seen together, which must have been at least four or five years earlier. But I decided against it. Whenever I suggested a trip to the cinema, whether it was to see *The Sting; Jaws* or *One Flew Over The Cuckoo's Nest*, Lawrence would invariably say, 'I'd rather watch something in the comfort of my own home.' Lawrence would, if he wasn't careful, get old before his time.

A thin spiral of smoke rose from behind the potting shed and eau de bonfire filled the cold damp air. I pulled the collar of my nylon waterproof higher and tightened the knobbly woollen scarf around my neck. The rhythmic squeaking of the wheelbarrow told me Lawrence was returning. I crossed the lawn, circling the horse chestnut and skirting the larch lap fence where the garden would produce its next show of colour. The snowdrops, bluebells and crocuses had bloomed and left, and now it was the turn of the daffodils. Once again they would push through the earth, reminding me that there is a cycle to all things. Maybe even marriages.

The sight of Lawrence coming back up the path pushing the rusting barrow caused my chest to fill, but I don't know what with. Was it love? Pity? Longing?

'Do you want me to put the old garden bench back under the tree?'

I nodded. The forecast was for a long hot summer, we'd need shady seating. 'I'll give you a hand when you're ready.'

'OK,' Lawrence said, and as he continued I heard the faint echoes of *Save Your Kisses For Me* from the wireless in the kitchen. I don't think I'll ever hear that song again without being reminded of that evening.

Debbie and David had called over to watch the Eurovision Song Contest with us. We watched it every year out of some sort of perverted loyalty, I suppose. Hosted in the Netherlands, Mike Aspel was commentating and we all sat nibbling and drinking and scoffing at the usual bizarre mix of songs and talent. Just as Brotherhood of Man took the stage, I heard a noise in the hallway.

'You're imagining things,' Lawrence said, and David nodded in agreement as *Save Your Kisses for Me* filled the room.

'I'm going to the toilet anyway, so I'll check.' I was certain I'd heard something.

Fumbling for the hall light switch, I pushed it down, flooding the hallway and stairs with light. Peter was sitting on the second from bottom stair, his coat wrapped tight around him, his face buried into the collar.

'Pete.' I put my arm around his shoulder. The warmth of my hand noted the cold of his coat. His thick dark hair was untidy, uncombed. So unlike him. 'Pete?'

He looked up.

46

'What is it, what's happened?' Then I remembered how Dr Euwan always made people comfortable before he asked questions. 'Come on, let me have your coat, and we'll go into the kitchen and get a hot drink. Or something stronger if you like.'

Peter stood up and let his coat slide to the floor. We went into the kitchen, ignoring the voices and singing coming from the sitting room. Neither of us said a word until, sat on one of the kitchen stools, leaning an elbow on the worktop and clutching a mug of steaming black coffee, Peter's words speared the silence.

'It's Bibby.'

Of course. It had to be. I knew it would be. But I never said a word. I never let a word through my lips, I kept them sealed tight. I simply nodded. And waited.

'It's Bibby, Mum. She's…she's…' And he put his hand to his mouth as if to stop the words coming out. Then he bowed his head. 'She's lost the baby.'

I looked up. Lawrence stood in the doorway.

'I'm so sorry. Is she in the hospital?' I asked.

'No. That's just it. This happened on Thursday and she's acting as if nothing ever happened. She won't even explain anything. It's as if we were never having a baby. She's just her bouncy, life-living self. She can't seem to understand my concern. I go off to work Thursday morning and she's expecting. I come home Thursday evening and it's all over. She said she'd lost the baby. Miscarried. And when I asked her what happened – where, how? – she says she doesn't want to dwell on it. That's she's fine and that's it and let's get a take-away for supper.'

Lawrence came and patted Peter's shoulder. 'I'm sorry, son.'
Peter nodded.

'People react in different ways to things,' I said. 'Maybe she thinks this way is less painful.'

'Good for her. But guess what? That baby had two parents. One moment I'm a father-to-be, decorating a nursery and making

47

plans to get married, next it's all over. Forget it. Nice idea but it ain't happening. So let's not talk about it. Let's get a take-away.'

Nothing we could say consoled him. Lawrence offered to drive him home after he refused our offer of staying over, but he preferred to drive himself, he said.

'I'll have a chat with the nurse at the surgery when I get to work on Monday. She'll know about these things, about how people react. I'll let you know what she suggests.'

'Thanks, Mum,' Pete said as he left. 'Sorry to have spoiled your night. Apologise to Dave and Debs from me.'

'There's nothing to apologise for,' I said, staying to watch his red tail lights disappear into the dark of the night. Before returning to the others I took gulps of the chilly night air. Shame flooded me. I never wanted Pete to hurt this way. Never. Never in a million years. But the news that Bibby was no longer carrying Peter's baby brought me only the greatest sense of relief. Relief bordering on joy. Yes, joy.

May God, if he exists, forgive me.

The car almost started.

'Try it again,' Lawrence shouted to me as he closed the garage doors.

'I've got the choke pulled right out. I don't want to flood the engine.' I sat back against the cold red vinyl of the driver's seat. This was the trouble with cold mornings.

'If you can't get her started, I'll drop you off,' he said, pulling his car alongside mine.

'No, honestly, Lawrence. You'll be late. Carry on and if I can't do anything I'll catch a bus.'

'If you're sure.'

I nodded and he waved as he drove off in the direction of Coate Water. Reporting, I reminded myself, for another week of duty.

After a couple more failed attempts, I lifted the rusting bonnet of my old Vauxhall Viva and gave the engine a spray of WD40. It worked and within less than half an hour I was standing in the reception at work.

'I want to have a quick word with Gladys when she has a moment,' I told Theresa, our receptionist.

'I'll tell her, Jetta. Though you know what it's like on Mondays.' At the sound of a buzzer, Theresa swivelled her chair towards the two-door wooden hatch that opened into the crowded waiting room. 'Mrs Walsch,' she called. 'Mrs Walsch, Dr Euwan will see you now. Yes, that's right, down the stairs, last door on the left.'

'Thanks.'

'Are you alright, Jetta? You don't seem your usual self.' Theresa raised her eyebrows and smiled as another buzzer sounded. 'Mr Sanders. Mr Sanders. Dr Markson will see you now.'

'It wasn't the best of weekends.' I was interrupted by the telephone ringing.

'Monday mornings!' Theresa said in mock horror for in truth, nowhere would we or anyone find such a good-natured receptionist.

'I'll see you later,' I mouthed as I went into the waiting room, down the half dozen carpeted stairs and through the second door on the left marked: *Private. Staff Only.* The inner sanctum.

Gladys found me there two hours later. Two no-shows, one for a smear test and one for a dressing change, meant she had a few spare minutes. I enquired about her weekend.

'I feel terrible. John had a 30th birthday party and I don't know who it was that said you can't have too large a party, but that's my John.'

I laughed. 'I can't imagine being married to a man who'd want a huge party.'

'Thank your lucky stars, Jetta, believe me! On Saturday night I'd have given anything to have been married to a pipe and slippers man. I've still got the headache now. John's remedy is to have a hair of the dog. Me? I'm amazed at what a couple of paracetamol can do.'

'You should know.'

'Now,' she said, peering down at the watch pinned to her chest. 'Theresa said you wanted a word.'

I filled her in on Pete's situation and answered as many of her questions as I could. It might have been 1976, yet I still didn't feel comfortable admitting that Peter had been having a baby out of wedlock. But if Gladys was surprised, she didn't show it.

'Our first concern has to be her health, but if you don't know if she was attended to at the hospital or the doctor's...'

'I don't think she went to either, from what Pete said.'

'I tell you what,' Gladys said in her 'now don't you worry about a thing' voice I'd heard her use so often with patients, 'I'll make a few enquiries – with the doctor first, then with the hospital if necessary. There's a place on Victoria Hill too, private. I'll be discreet, don't worry. I know a few people.'

After Gladys left I picked up a piece of blue carbon paper, slid it between the blank white back sheet and headed top sheet, rolled it into the typewriter and typed:

5th April 1976
Our ref: DAE/JF

And as my fingers continued with Dr Euwan's correspondence, I considered how fortunate I was to have this job. If only because it opened my eyes to the fact that much goes on between heaven and earth. And I realised one could never be certain when some of that much was going to happen to you.

*

I was about to pull out of the parking space allocated to me at the rear of the surgery when Gladys appeared at the back door.

She waved to attract my attention and came running over to the car as I wound down my window.

'Have you got a minute?'

'Of course,' I said, 'do you want to sit in?'

She shook her head. 'I can't be a minute, my John's picking me up tonight and with the yellow lines out front he gets narked if he has to keep doing circuits to avoid the traffic warden. No, it's just that I've got some news.' She opened her mouth to speak and then hesitated.

'Whatever it is, you can say…honestly, Gladys.'

'No doctor or hospital has a record of your um…daughter-in-law-to-be having a pregnancy test, positive, negative or otherwise. No doctor or hospital has a record of her having ante-natal check-ups. And no doctor or hospital has a record of her being attended to for a miscarriage. That's to say, no hospital she would have been likely to attend. But her doctor's records do show that she's continued to order and collect repeat prescriptions for her contraceptive pills. The last time being a month ago. If you want my opinion, Jetta, I don't think she's miscarried your son's baby. Because I don't think she was ever pregnant. In fact, I'd almost guarantee it. I've come across this before.'

'But why would she…?'

'That's a whole new other question,' Gladys said, putting her hand on my arm. 'I'm so sorry, Jetta.'

'It's not for you to be sorry. I'm really grateful.'

From across the rooftops and the roar of traffic into the still of the damp early evening air came the sound of a car horn.

'That'll be my John,' Gladys smiled, stepping away from the car. 'He's an impatient bugger. We'll talk some more tomorrow.' And she disappeared through the rear door back into the surgery.

I drove too slowly along Farnsby Street because I had no idea where I was headed. My knee-jerk response was to go to Bibby. To hear what tale she came up with before I confronted her with the truth. But I knew that wasn't the answer. No. Not yet.

By Wednesday I'd made my decision. I would tell Peter what I'd learned. It was the only right and proper thing to do. So far, I hadn't told another soul, not even Lawrence.

After we'd eaten supper I sat at the telephone table in the hall while Lawrence sat in the sitting room watching *Nationwide*. Picking up the green handset, I dialled Pete's number. I felt queasy and only hoped Bibby didn't answer. I didn't want to make polite conversation with her.

'Hello.' It was Pete, sounding brighter than when I'd last seen him.

'It's Mum. I'm just ringing to see how you're doing.'

'Yeah, I'm good, Mum, Bibby too. In fact when she comes in I was going to suggest we call over.'

I closed my eyes and wished I had a gin and tonic handy. I wasn't looking forward to this, but at least he was on his own so I could talk freely.

'Before you do I wanted to tell you something I found out earlier in the week. You know after you called on Saturday I said I'd make some enquires?'

'Aw, Mum, that's good of you, but that's all sorted now. Bibby and I have talked and talked since I got back from you. And we understand why she couldn't discuss it. It's a sort of suppression thing I suppose that some people use initially to help them cope with loss. But she explained exactly what happened and how everyone was with her and–'

'When you say everyone, Pete, who do you mean?'

'Well, everyone. A friend, nurses.'

'Where was this exactly?' My head was whirling with thoughts that made no sense.

'At the clinic.'

'Private clinic?'

'Don't be silly, Mum, on my pay? No, Princess Margaret's Hospital, of course. Why?'

'Because I promised you on Saturday that I'd see what I could do for you both. Make some enquiries. And I did.'

'That's really good of you. And?'

'And…I don't know how to say this to you Pete, but according to the lady I spoke with…well, she said that Bibby…' I paused.

'Bibby what? Mum, what's the matter? It's not Bibby, is it?'

'She says that Bibby never was pregnant.'

There was a short silence. 'She said what?'

'That Bibby never was pregnant. She never was expecting a baby.'

'How bloody ridiculous! How can she say such a thing? How?'

'Because it's true, Peter. Because–'

'Stop! How can you be so wicked? So bloody wicked and cruel? Have you no idea what that baby meant to us? And what right do you have to go discussing our private lives with your cronies? How dare you!'

'I told you I'd try to find something out for you. You agreed.'

'Yes. I agreed for you to help us. Not so you could come up with some fantastically ridiculous tale about Bibby. Some fantasy about her never even having been pregnant. Christ!'

'It's not like that, I–'

'Come off it, Mum, you've never really liked her, have you?'

'That's not true!'

'Of course it's true. And the first time I come to you for help, you use it against her. Against us. Because whether you like it or not, she's part of my life and always will be.'

'Peter I'm not making this up. Please hear me out.'

'I'm not listening to another word you've got to say. The woman I love has lost our baby and all you want to do is use the opportunity to pull us apart. You really have got it wrong this time. So completely wrong. Maybe you ought to get yourself checked out.'

The green longcase clock across the hall struck seven. And I was left listening to a dialling tone.

Chapter Seven

Lyme Regis, Dorset, Friday am, July 2006

Nine o'clock. I pushed back the bedclothes hurriedly and put my feet flat on the floor, immediately reaching for the glass of water on the bedside table. My mouth was dry and I felt slightly groggy – the after-effects of the sleeping tablet, no doubt. The tepid liquid revived me somewhat as my mind began to fill with the do's and don'ts of the day. It was too much and I swung my legs back up on the bed and lay there, at that precise moment wishing I had someone else's life. Recognising this as the self-pity it was, I spoke sharply to myself. If there was one thing I found insufferable, it was self-pity; which wasn't to say I hadn't engaged in it on occasion.

Dying for a wee, I staggered into the bathroom unable to remember the last time I'd gone a whole night without getting up to use the toilet. The sleeping tablets obviously worked. And I'd only used one.

I had decided to take a sleeping tablet around midnight. My mind was far too active to let me sleep and this would let me test the pills' effectiveness. I placed the 'Do Not Disturb' sign on the outside of my door, swallowed the orange capsule with half a glass of water, lay down and began to re-read *The Number 1 Ladies' Detective Agency*. And that was the last thing I remembered.

I plugged the kettle in for my not-so-early morning cuppa, and considered the plans I'd made the previous evening. Today, after breakfast, I would drive to another town and buy myself another mobile phone. I'd watched enough *Inspector Morse* and *Silent Witness*, and read enough Graham Hurley and Ian Rankin to have some idea of police and forensic procedures. Calls from mobile phones could be traced, so I would buy a new phone and dump it when I'd finished.

Finished. The word hung cloud-like in my head. Because finish her I would. Finish Bibby. There, I'd said her name. I would finish Bibby in the way she had first finished Peter, then Lawrence and, by default, me. And, an untraceable mobile would be one clue less.

I'd narrowed my choices of other towns to Honiton, Bridport or Chard, eventually choosing Honiton. Not for any reason other than I'd performed 'Ip dip sky blue, who's it, not you' on all three towns and Honiton had remained. It seemed as good a method as any.

Remembering the hotel stopped serving breakfast at 9.30 on weekdays, I quickly dressed and went to the still busy dining room where I enjoyed smoked kippers and tea at a corner table. Declining more tea, I went to reception in search of Matthew.

'I want you to check something for me,' I told him.

'Of course.'

'If I choose to stay longer than the nine nights I've booked, is that a possibility?'

Matthew went behind the desk and consulted his books. 'Sorry,' he apologised after a few minutes. 'We're still not computerised yet, they keep threatening, but...'

'I'm in no hurry,' I lied, somehow pleased to know they still relied on handwriting and not computers. That always left room for error.

'The thing is, your room is booked so you would have to

change rooms and all we've got free for the following week is a single.' He looked at me apologetically.

'That would be alright. Can you pencil me in?' I said, having come to the conclusion that giving myself a week in which to complete my mission had perhaps been overly optimistic. It might require a few days more.

'I will, Mrs...' He hesitated and looked down. 'Mrs, er, Francis. But if someone wants to book the room, I'd have to get an immediate yes or no from you as to whether you wanted it or not. This time of year, it's unlikely to remain vacant.'

'Of course,' I said and walked out into what was already another hot summer's day.

The drive to Honiton was straightforward. The A35 wasn't too busy and within less than half an hour I was in the town's busy High Street. Seeing a car pull out of a space, I immediately indicated and pulled in alongside the kerb. Before getting out of the car I took my mobile from my bag and dialled Marilyn's number.

'Jetta! I'm so glad you've called. You promised to ring yesterday.'

'I know, but it got late.'

'Where are you?'

'Honiton. I stayed at a hotel last night.'

'Which hotel?'

'Oh,' I looked around for inspiration. 'The Carlton, I think it was called, or something similar,' I said, seeing I was parked outside The Carlton Inn. 'I'm about to have a coffee and set off again. And, before you ask, yes, I feel good.'

'So are you staying in Honiton?'

'No. I'm moving on, but wanted to see how you are first and to thank you for looking after the cats.'

'Don't worry about me, I'm fine. Tony's got hay fever, he reckons, but I think it's a summer cold. And the cats are fed, watered and happy.'

'Good.' I paused. 'How did the Open Minds session go?'

Marilyn laughed. 'We held it at mine after all. And would you believe it, Peggy couldn't come! Something about the weather playing havoc with her joints.'

'So much for committing come hell or high water,' I laughed, and after a few more pleasantries added, 'I'll give you another call in a few days.'

According to the young waitress in the coffee shop I called into, there were two phone shops in the town that she knew of. One the other end of the High Street towards the traffic lights and one in New Street, the latter being nearest. Less than an hour later I returned to my hotel with a new pay-as-you-go phone, complete with £25 credit. I paid for it as I would for the hotel, in cash, thankful there had been some advantage to my squirreling cash away over the past 20 odd years. A few pounds here and there had amounted to a reasonable sum which I was certainly glad of this week.

I automatically put the kettle on once back in my room and tipped a half-sachet of coffee into my cup. Sitting in a chair by the window, I thought how spacious and pleasant the room was to return to. The half-tester bed was covered with sumptuous fabrics, as were the upholstered chairs. A television sat discreetly in the corner and a pre-tuned wireless on the desk. In the garden below, I could see guests sitting around ornate iron tables, umbrellas shielding them from the sun's increasingly hot rays. I recognised one couple from breakfast who I thought might be on their honeymoon. Which, for some reason, made me think of Peter and why I was here. As if I could forget.

Coffee was, according to the booklet in the room, served in the conservatory or garden between 10 o'clock and 12, but I would make mine here in the room today. I'd borrowed a local telephone directory from the hallstand downstairs and once I had made my coffee and got myself comfortable at the desk, I turned to the listings. She wasn't difficult to find. Fellowes, E. 16 Cliffside Apartments, complete with telephone number. I copied the number into my notebook and closed it with a sense of satisfaction.

Relaxing deeper into the chair, I picked up the local tourist guide and flicked haphazardly through its pages. There was much to see and do in addition to the usual coastal activities. Churches, museums and mills, a theatre in the town and, a short drive away at Abbotsbury, a swannery. They were the sort of places I'd normally visit. But I reminded myself I wasn't here to holiday.

And that's when I noticed something even more interesting. I'd almost missed it. It was set below an advert for deep-sea fishing trips where bass, shark, huss and conger were regular catches, if the advert was to be believed. It had to be her. How many Bibbys could there be in a town this size? This was no coincidence, I was certain of that. And I had reason to recall the man yesterday saying, '...your search will bear fruit.'

Chapter Eight

Swindon, Wiltshire, August 1976

Situated between Commercial Road and the Brunel Centre, Tea for Two was a café I'd used on several occasions. The owner – a lady with suitably doughy cheeks and coffee-coloured hair – ran, as Lawrence described it, a tight ship.

Giving me a personal greeting and handing me a menu as soon as I was seated, she said one of her girls would come and take my order.

'I'm waiting for someone,' I said. 'There's no hurry.'

She nodded. 'Certainly, madam,' and returned to her post behind a trellis-covered counter, most of which was hidden beneath plastic variegated ivy.

The teapot-shaped clock on the wall told me I was on time. Bibby was late. As I watched for her through the plate glass window, a young couple passed by wearing ripped black T-shirts, chains and piercings. Her black tights and his black trousers were full of holes and safety pins and their heads were shaved except for a lengthy ridge of hair across the top, glued into stiff spikes. Her hair was scarlet, his lime green. What was the world coming to? Oh my goodness, wasn't that what my departed mother would have said? God forbid, if I wasn't careful I'd end up sounding as miserable as she did. Times were moving and I had to move with them.

I leaned back in my seat and let my arms flop down beside me. Perspiration began to trickle between my breasts and bead across my brow. As if it wasn't bad enough that we were in the middle of a heatwave, I was being plagued with hot flushes. I removed my cardigan and hung it across the back of my chair, leaving my sleeveless cotton top clinging damply to me.

Closing my eyes, I fanned myself with the menu until a voice said: 'Here you are, madam.' I opened my eyes to see the doughy-cheeked lady place a tumbler of iced water on the table. 'Thought you might be wanting this,' she said, a faint Irish burr to her words. 'I have them meself.'

Before I had a chance to answer, she'd gone. How considerate, I thought. I'd leave a good tip today by way of saying thank you.

At five and twenty to one, there was still no sign of Bibby. I drained my glass of water and ordered lunch. Maybe she wasn't going to come after all. Part of me was relieved; part of me was anxious. It had cost me a lot of effort to get back to a situation with Peter where he wasn't being hostile. Not that he ever let Bibby know anything of our hostilities, thankfully, and I didn't let anyone know what had gone on with us either. It seemed best if we had any chance of being reconciled.

It had worked, sort of. Peter and I weren't as easy with each other as we had been, but we were getting there. Today, inviting Bibby to meet me in my lunch break was another of my attempts at good relations.

I cut into my piece of haddock and was about to take a bite when I heard a voice call: 'Mrs Fellowes?' I looked up. 'Is there a Mrs Fellowes here?' The café owner stood behind the counter, her hand held over the telephone mouthpiece as she scanned the faces in the café.

It must be Bibby. Who else knew I was here?

I took my cardigan off the back of the chair, slid an arm into the sleeve and approached the counter. The lady held the handset out to me.

'It's a young woman. Sounds as if she's got a bit of an emergency at her end.'

My body was electrically charged. 'Hello?'

'Jetta. It's me, Bibby. Please, please, you've got to come.'

It was obvious she'd been crying and she sounded desperate.

'What's happened? Where are you?' I held my breath. I didn't want the answers, yet I did.

'I'm in the hospital, Princess Margaret's.'

Oh my God. It must be Peter. The lady behind the counter was a mind-reader. She pushed a stool behind me and urged me onto the seat. I must have looked as I felt. My legs wouldn't hold me.

'What's happened?'

'It's me, Jetta, I need you. Please come. I haven't got anyone else. Please say you'll come. I've got…I've got cancer…and I'm going to die.'

'Bibby.' The sound of repeated pips told me Bibby would soon be cut off the payphone. 'Look, don't put more money in. Just tell me which ward you're on and I'll be there in half an hour. Promise.'

The café was within easy walking distance of the surgery. Usually it was a 10 minute stroll but today I did it in five and felt light-headed as I opened the door into reception. Hearing my news, Theresa shooed me off, saying she'd explain to Dr Euwan where I was. Theresa was a saint.

I couldn't believe this was happening. Bibby was too young, surely this couldn't be right. Cancer? At her age? And where? How had they known? Oh, so many questions, none of which would be answered until I arrived.

The dark news didn't fit the bright day. I wound both front windows down, but the incoming breeze made no discernible difference. I was travelling in a greenhouse. People idled along the pavements with panting dogs and a young mother pushing a pram stopped for breath near the top of Kingshill. Everyone was fatigued by yet another sweltering day.

By the time I turned left off Okus Road into the hospital, it was approaching two o'clock. And all I know is that at that moment any malice I might have had for Bibby evaporated. She was a vulnerable young woman, faced with the most difficult thing she'd have to face in her life. And apart from Peter and us, she had no-one. Well, I would have it be different. Whatever had gone before, there was now a clean slate. She would have us.

I headed straight to the ward lifts, passing the shop on ground level. I would come back down to get Bibby anything she needed. My priority was to get to her.

Once I was in the ward the clerk confirmed Bibby was there.

'Can I see her?'

'Of course.' She pointed to a bay of beds. 'She's on the right, the corner bed by the window, the one with the curtains drawn around.' And, sensing my next question, she added. 'You can see her, there's no one there. She just prefers having the curtains around her, it seems.'

Given Bibby's situation, I was sure I'd feel the same. I peered around the edge of the pale striped curtain. Bibby lay in bed, her red silk Japanese style pyjamas a striking contrast against her pale skin and the white cotton hospital sheets. Her halo of hair spread over the pillow. It was obvious she'd been crying and the white wastepaper bag elastoplasted to her locker was full of used tissues. A box of opened hospital issue tissues sat on top of her locker alongside an empty glass and a blue lidded jug full of water.

Where was Peter?

I steeled myself. 'Bibby, I got here as soon as I could.'

Bibby looked at me, but didn't sit up. And immediately she pressed a tissue to her eyes.

'Jetta, I didn't know what to do! Who to call. I've been in such agony and now it seems…well, now it seems…'

I sat on the edge of the bed and took her hand. It was warm, smooth and her long slender fingers gripped mine, her hands, immaculate with their opal painted nails and perfectly shaped cuticles. It was the first time we'd sat so intimately. Tears beaded on her thick lashes before coursing their way down her unblemished cheeks. Was there anything about this young woman that wasn't physically perfect?

'Where's Peter?'

'At work. I haven't told him. I haven't told anyone yet except you. I didn't want to worry him, Jetta. I couldn't, not until I knew for certain. Something for sure.'

Her tears dropped, leaving ruby red spots on her pyjamas. More than anything at that moment, I wanted to put Bibby together again.

The ward sister poked her head around the curtain, smiled without revealing teeth and picked up Bibby's chart from the end of the bed.

'Mr Chesterton is doing his rounds and will be here shortly.' I stood up and the sister drew her hand across the counterpane, straightening it in a way she'd obviously done countless times before. 'You can come back in as soon as he leaves,' she said directly to me. And before I had a chance to ask anything, she had gone.

Mr Chesterton arrived sooner rather than later, with an entourage worthy of royalty. But if he were king, seeing Bibby sat upright in bed, there was no doubt who was queen.

I slipped from behind the curtain after reassuring Bibby I'd wait in the day room and return when he left.

'Excuse me.'

I turned as I was about to leave the ward. A frail-looking lady in the bed next to Bibby's gestured to me, her weak voice barely audible. I went to her bedside, careful to step around the drip stand that held the blood leading into her thin arm.

'Do you need something?'

'I've dropped my glasses.' She lifted her head from the pillow and pointed to the narrow space between her bed and locker. 'I was wondering…' Her head fell back on the pillow.

'Of course I'll get them for you. Don't worry.' I raised my hand to stop her talking more. She looked exhausted.

Making my way around her bed I could hear the voices behind Bibby's curtain. It wasn't difficult. Putting a hand on the woman's bed to support myself, I leaned down into the gap, but couldn't feel anything there. Getting down on my knees, I saw her glasses under the bed, but needed something to drag them out. A knitting bag sat in the top of the locker and I borrowed a needle from it to try and bring the spectacles nearer. Several tries later, it worked.

The lady nodded and smiled her thanks. I patted her hand and smiled back. 'You're welcome.'

The voices behind the curtain grew louder.

Bibby was shouting now. 'Why are you sending me home?'

'You're being discharged because there's nothing wrong with you,' Mr Chesterton was saying in a loud voice. And with that he appeared, red-faced, through a gap in the curtain, followed by the sister and a ribbon of acolytes who followed him out of the ward.

Immediately I went to Bibby. 'What's going on? What's the matter?'

There were no tears now. They had been replaced with undis-guised raw anger.

'I'll tell you what's wrong. They're useless at their bloody jobs, that's what's wrong.'

'But Bibby,' I said, wishing she'd keep her voice down, espe-cially if she was going to swear. 'What about…what about the… the cancer?'

She yanked open her locker door and pulled clothes, hair-brush and a wash bag out onto the bed. Unashamedly she took off her pyjamas and, not bothering with underwear, pulled on a pair of blue, wide-legged trousers and a skin-tight white T-shirt. She stuffed everything else, including her pyjamas, into a Kwik Save carrier bag.

'There is no cancer.'

'What do you mean, there is no cancer?'

'Exactly that. According to the great doctor there is no cancer. He says I'm perfectly fit, so that's that.' And slipping her shoulder bag over her arm, she lifted the carrier and pushed back the curtain. Everyone else in the ward could see us now.

'What do you mean, that's that?' I tried to keep my voice low. 'You ring me. Tell me you're dying of cancer. I drop everything and race here for you to say that's that! What's going on?'

'Well, I'm sorry if I interrupted your schedule.'

I followed her up the ward. 'I didn't mind coming here for you, Bibby. But you told me you had cancer. You said you were dying!'

'Well, please forgive me. I should have thought the fact that I wasn't dying would please you.'

Bibby carried on down the corridor and I saw her pause at the trolley payphone and lift the receiver.

Seeing the nursing sister sat at the ward desk, I stopped.

'Sister. Please may I have a word? It really is urgent.'

She laid her pen down and stood up, manoeuvring me to one side of the desk. A porter and a nurse wheeled a male patient past, x-rays and other notes lying at the foot of his bed. Somewhere a buzzer sounded and a red light appeared on the board behind the sister's head. A passing nurse cancelled the button and went through a door to a side-ward, after pulling on a cotton gown and a paper face mask. And I could still see Bibby, talking into the telephone.

'How can I help?'

'It's Bibby, I mean Elizabeth. You're sending her home, yet she called…'

She held up her hand. 'Are you related to Elizabeth?'

'I'm her…future mother-in-law.'

'Then I cannot discuss this with you.'

'But she has no-one else, except my son and he can't be here. And her parents live abroad.'

'It makes no difference. Besides, she's no longer a patient. She's been discharged.'

'But that's just it. I don't understand. She rang me not an hour or more ago saying she has terminal cancer and now you say she's fine and are letting her walk out of here?'

'Mrs…?' The sister laid a hand on my arm.

'Fellowes.'

'Mrs Fellowes. Despite what you might hear, we are still a caring profession. All I can say is that if we thought your future daughter-in-law needed to be in hospital, we would keep her here. The fact that we're happy for her to leave should reassure her and yourself.'

I shook my head. 'But why would she call me and say those things if they're not true? She must be mad then, or unaware of what she's doing.'

'I can assure you, Mrs Fellowes, Elizabeth isn't mad. And in my experience I would guess she knows precisely what she's doing.'

I turned to find Bibby gone. She was nowhere to be seen. I didn't know what to think. Taking the lift to the ground floor, questions flooded my mind. When had Bibby gone into hospital? Where was Peter? And, at this precise moment, where was Bibby?

I stood outside the hospital wondering where I'd parked my car. Was this a sign of premature senility? I forgave myself on the grounds that my mind had been full of other concerns on my arrival. Eventually I found my car parked between a Hillman Minx and a bottle green Vauxhall 101. The vinyl seats stuck to my legs as soon as I sat in the driver's seat, and even with both front windows wound down fully, no breeze entered. There was no breeze. Putting my cardigan onto the passenger seat and selecting reverse, I backed out of the space. I couldn't go back to work. I would go home and call Theresa. Then I'd have to decide what to do.

I was tired. Tired of the heat and tired of having to think my way out of situations I didn't feel responsible for getting into.

The blue corporation bus stood outside the hospital and a queue of people filed on as I drove past. But there was no sign of Bibby. Driving down Okus Road, my mind was in such a whirl that I almost missed her. But it was definitely her getting into the passenger seat of a smart Ford Consul that pulled up beside her. The young man driving looked about Peter's age. But it wasn't him. His hair was as blond as Peter's was dark. After a couple of engine revs the car pulled away. Fast. Too fast. And I felt sick to the pit of my stomach.

I considered following them, but what purpose would it serve? They were already a long way ahead and if I did catch them up – what would I do? What would Bibby do? Besides, I already felt drained, exhausted. I forced myself to concentrate on the road. The last thing I needed was to damage my car. No. I would go home, keep myself busy and wait for Lawrence to come home from work.

It was time he knew about Bibby.

That evening I added fresh tomatoes and a lettuce from our garden to a salad, and roasted chicken breasts. Not that I could eat a thing. But I let Lawrence enjoy his supper before leading him into the sitting room.

I told him about Bibby's 'miscarriage'; the ensuing fall-out with Peter, the phone call that day from Bibby and the scenes that followed at the hospital. Up to and including where she'd driven off with the young man in the car.

For a long while after, Lawrence sat fingering his collar and said nothing. I couldn't read him. I had no idea what he was thinking.

'Why didn't you tell me any of this before?'

'I wanted to keep my relationship going with Peter at all costs. After his blow-up over the miscarriage business, I thought I'd be more help working from the inside, so to speak. Keep it to myself. If I'd told you, David and Debbie, maybe you would have all tried something that would have driven him further away. So I decided, for Peter's sake, to try and build a relationship with Bibby. That way I could maybe see or understand what was going on. But most of all, because I would still get to see our son.'

The concern on Lawrence's face was apparent. 'I'm going to call him.'

I went to the window and drew the curtains around the bay, keeping my back to him.

'Please, Lawrence, whatever you do—'

'Don't tell me how to handle this, Jetta.'

Through the sitting room wall, I could hear Lawrence's occasionally raised voice but not what he was saying. When half an hour or more had passed and I hadn't heard him speak in a while, I went into the hall. He looked up from where he was sat next to the phone, the handset back on its cradle. His face colourless. Expressionless. A bolt of fear lodged painfully between my heart and stomach. I knew as sure as my name was Jetta Fellowes that our life had taken an irreversible turn for the worse.

I wasn't wrong.

Whilst Lawrence was on the phone, Peter had asked Bibby if any of what I'd said was true. She'd denied having even seen me that day. She denied we'd arranged to meet for lunch. She denied telling me she had cancer. She denied getting in a car with a man on Okus Road. And now Peter had spoken. He denied us as his parents. He wanted nothing more to do with us.

'Christ, Jetta, what's going on?' Lawrence stood up, colour suffusing his face. 'What the bloody hell's going on here?'

My breathing quickened. 'What do you think is going on? She's succeeding in turning him against us. Against me.'

'But why? Why would she?'

'How the hell do I know? I'm as baffled by her actions as you are. But…oh, hang on a moment, I see where this is going. You aren't convinced either. Like your son, you'd rather believe that lying little bitch than your own wife!'

'Don't be silly, Jetta, I never said that. I simply asked why?'

But I wasn't going to stand here and listen to this.

'Isn't it bad enough that Peter believes I'm a liar? Now you think… Hell, I don't know what you think! I've never known what you think.'

'Jetta…'

I screamed at him to shut up and went into the kitchen and over to the dresser. To the collection of blue and white. Oval meat platters, dinner plates, gravy boats, milk jugs, sauce boats, tureens, ladles… And one by one I lifted them high over my head and smashed them down onto the quarry tiled floor. I smashed them. Smashed them. Smashed them. With a brute force I didn't know I possessed. Until now.

Chapter Nine

Lyme Regis, Friday pm July 2006

The hat caught my attention as I passed the Joseph Weld Hospice charity shop. It lay between a hundred-piece jigsaw puzzle of the Eiffel Tower and a gift box of pink rose-shaped soaps. I hadn't thought of a hat, but it might prove useful. A silky piece of fabric in a mix of pale green and cream was tied around the brim; it matched my green blouse and cream pencil skirt exactly. I would buy it.

A tall handsome woman greeted me as I walked in, commenting on how fortunate we were to have yet another sunny day. 'But if it rained at night it would help,' she added. I agreed.

'The sun hat in the window,' I asked. 'How much is it?'

'I can soon tell you.' She came from behind the counter and leaned stiffly into the window display. 'It's £2.' She lifted the hat from the window, smiled and handed it to me. 'I've only just put it out.'

I pulled on the hat and, feeling it fitted, said I'd take it.

'There's a mirror over there,' she said, pointing an arthritic index finger towards the middle of the shop. 'It suits you and it matches your outfit.'

'Thank you. I'll take your word for it.' I didn't need a mirror. I wasn't buying it to enhance my looks.

'Do you want a bag?' she asked, removing the price from the hat.

'No.' I handed her a two-pound coin. 'I think I'll wear it.'

Sensing this was a lady I would usually make conversation with, I left the shop. My natural way was to chat and I had to stop myself. It wouldn't do for people to remember me.

Making my way down the street, I skirted a family of five stood chatting outside the Lemon Tree, oblivious to anyone squeezing past. I was pleased at the town's popularity, seemingly with visitors of all ages, as it certainly made it easier for me to blend in. I paused only once before reaching Bell Cliff and that was to look in the window of the bookshop. Books were my weakness. But if I were to buy a book I would try the charity shop first. This week was already costing a small fortune. Yet why should I worry? I no longer needed to consider finances. No more eking out. No more… *Oh my goodness, Jetta, stop there, don't let your thoughts go down that route.*

The view at Bell Cliff was enchanting and, seeing a bench by the old canon, I was tempted to take a rest. There was a gallery there too which, under normal circumstances, I would have looked around. But I didn't stop. I had to make the best use of my time.

As I went down the steps overlooking the car park, I checked the time. My watch said it was 3.35, but the clock on the tower showed the time as 3.30, which, if correct, made my watch five minutes fast.

Once on Marine Parade I weaved between racks of postcards and groups of holidaymakers lolling on white plastic chairs, gazing out to sea as they sipped the tea and coffee they'd bought at the kiosk. On my left, beneath the black railings, people strolled along the narrow road that ran parallel to the beach and sea. Cars, it seemed, could park there if they had a blue badge, although the turning space at the end looked tight. I reckoned it would call for a three or four-point turn at least – not something I'd like to try with an audience.

The sight of her name in large lettering over the well-kept premises caused me to freeze. I had no idea what I was going to do now I was here. I hadn't thought this far ahead. I didn't have a plan. I was making it up as I went along. I had been doing things as they came to me in the hope that eventually everything would come together. The overall plan was clear: to get rid of Bibby. To once and for all put her where she could never cause pain and destruction to a family again. Certainly not my family. And the only way I could guarantee this was murder.

'Excuse me!' A loud voice interrupted my thoughts and I turned to see a middle-aged, red-faced woman shaking her head impatiently. She stood tall and wide, with what looked to be her granddaughter in a pushchair and an energetic young black Labrador straining on a short red leash. Beside her, looking equally harassed, was her husband, I presumed, trying to keep hold of a young boy struggling to run free. 'Do you mind if we get past?' she added, irritably.

'Sorry.'

'Bloody people!' I heard her say as they continued up the parade, struggling with their charges. 'Just stop in the middle of the pavement with no regard for others…' She obviously wasn't a happy woman.

I pretended to read the menu that hung in the window of Bibby's Café and Gifts. There was a central door that led directly into the cafe and I could see an arch on the left leading into the gift section. The café was spacious and I estimated there were around 15 or more tables with only one empty. A hanging sign said that during the summer the café was open seven days a week. To the rear of the café there was a counter with a door beyond, presumably to the kitchen. I could see waiting staff, but I couldn't see Bibby.

I moved along to the left hand window, my heart racing as if I'd been running, and looked into the equally spacious gift section. The gifts were tasteful, not vulgar, as I might have imagined. But then Bibby always did know how to spend money, so I shouldn't have been surprised.

Oh my goodness! It was her. I glanced down, noticing the fabric of my blouse visibly rising and falling rapidly with every heartbeat. And now she was looking in my direction and smiling. Even through the distortion of the glass, I could see that wide perfect smile and despite the heat of the day, I shivered. But she wasn't smiling at me, her smile was for a customer holding a coloured glass cat aloft.

I hurried away, past pink-washed cottages with cream ironwork and came upon a blackboard outside a hotel offering cream teas. I could either sit out in the sun facing the water or go inside. I chose inside and for the next hour I sat on a two-seater sofa in the corner of The Bay Hotel, eating Dorset apple cake, drinking tea and thinking. I did plenty of thinking.

I came to several decisions. The first was that Bibby having the café was useful to me. It gave me a better chance to watch her, to find out more about her and to see if she had a routine. It also ensured she was out of her home more. I don't know why I felt this was good, but instinctively I was sure it gave me more choices. I also realised that whilst I was looking for Bibby, I should remember that Bibby wasn't looking for me. She wasn't expecting to see me. And I doubted whether she would recognise me even if she did. The last time I was with Bibby, she was in hospital with 'cancer'. That was almost 30 years ago. I was 50 and she'd been about 19. But unfortunately for me, out of sight hadn't meant out of mind because the repercussions of her actions continued to destroy those I loved long after.

I paid my bill and left The Bay Hotel, my feet complaining every step of the walk back to my hotel. They were hot, sore and stinging. The closed-in shoes I was wearing didn't help in this heat, but I wasn't about to buy open-toed sandals. My bunions were far too ugly. Back at the hotel, all I wanted to do was go to my room, soak my feet and take a nap before dinner.

Instead, I collected my car, drove to Cliffside Road and parked in a deep lay-by within sight of the entrance to Cliffside apartments. *The Lyme Regis News* I'd taken from the hotel lay on the passenger seat. A cliché it may be, I thought, but I couldn't think of a better way to hide myself, should it become necessary, than behind a newspaper.

The lay-by, it seemed, was a favourite spot for dog walkers, as several people parked there and disappeared into the thicket with their dogs, returning some time later and driving off. This was good for me, I thought, as people would be used to seeing cars parked here.

What was I expecting to find out today? What time Bibby got home, maybe? Was she alone? What did she drive? Whatever, there was nothing to do but to wait.

At 6.35 a white taxi pulled up to the apartments' entrance, the driver's side facing away from me. The driver got out, opened the rear passenger door and leaned inside. Because of the way he'd parked it was difficult for me to see what was happening, but as he walked towards the entrance carrying a couple of heavy bags, I saw Bibby get out of the back of the taxi. I could only see her head, but it was definitely her. Blonde hair swinging neatly onto her shoulders. I closed my eyes. I couldn't look. My chest was swelling. Swelling as if it would become so large there would be no room for my lungs to draw breath. I had to get over this. I couldn't feel this way every time I saw her. It would immobilise me.

By the time I looked up, she had disappeared; the taxi driver too. I waited. He emerged from the apartment building minutes later and drove off. So, Miss Bibby could afford to be driven around in taxis. Miss Bibby even had the taxi driver dancing in attendance. It was no more than I should have expected. Men would always be silly where a woman like her was concerned.

From where I was sitting I could see the road-facing side of the apartment building and the end overlooking the car park. I scanned the top floor windows, constantly hoping to catch a glimpse of her passing a window. But ten minutes later, still nothing.

I turned the key in the ignition and selected first gear, intending to drive back to the hotel. Instead I drove into the car park and reversed into a space between two large vehicles. From here I could see the rear of the apartments. But there was still no sign of her.

As I was about to leave, French doors opening onto a top floor balcony caught my attention. It was the corner balcony, at the far end, the only one that wrapped around the corner of the building, and through the doors walked Bibby. Struggling to see past the balcony's ornate metalwork, I watched her flop onto a lounger, recline and put her legs up on a table. She took a sip from a wine glass.

Twenty minutes later she hadn't moved. Neither had I.

I was hypnotised. Transfixed. Mesmerised. It was surreal. After all these years, that I should be here watching her. Watching that woman. The woman who had caused...

No, I wouldn't go there. I put my hands to my ears and shook my head from side to side. There was no point replaying it time and time again. I knew what she had done. Lord knows I knew. And I knew what had to be done. My next challenge was how.

Chapter Ten

Swindon, Wiltshire, May 1977

The Radio Times stared back at me from the coffee table. I'd read it from cover to cover. From the detailed colour feature on Badger Watch and Patrick Moore's piece about a UFO documentary, Out of this World, to the Annan Report on the Future of Broadcasting. The latter showing that people thought the standard of BBC TV was declining. I wondered how many thousands of pounds it had cost to come up with that little gem when I, or any viewer for that matter, could have told them for free. I would write and complain.

Was this what my life had come to? Leafing through a 12p TV magazine, judging the success of a night on what the TV could come up with. Obviously it had.

'There's a play on tomorrow night I'd like a look at,' I told Lawrence. 'It's part of a series marking the Queen's Silver Jubilee.'

He shifted in his armchair. 'Since when have you been a Royalist?'

'You know how I enjoy a good play. Besides, these reflect life in the past 25 years, they're not necessarily about royalty.' And then I said, 'I'm bored.' I don't know where the words came from. I'd obviously thought them or else they wouldn't have been there, poised, as if on the edge of a diving board, straining to leap into the pool of conversation. But I certainly hadn't intended to voice them now.

Lawrence looked at me. 'What side is the play on?'

'BBC1.' But I couldn't leave it there. I'd started, deliberately or not, so I'd finish. 'Lawrence, why don't we book a holiday?'

'Where and when do you have in mind?'

'Next month. Or July maybe? Somewhere we haven't been before. On an aeroplane. A package tour. Anything, Lawrence, that'll take us out of our daily lives for a week or two. Anything.'

And when Lawrence said, 'Yes. Alright,' almost immediately, I nearly fell out of my chair. 'You get some brochures and we'll take a look and book something.'

I stood up. 'Lawrence! Do you mean it? You're not going to suddenly change your mind or anything, are you?'

As he shook his head, I wanted to hug him. Instead I went to the sideboard and poured us both a large gin and tonic complete with ice and lemon. We chinked glasses and I noticed a smile on Lawrence's face. The first smile I'd seen in a long while.

A holiday. This would be something to tell Theresa tomorrow.

The last time I'd been in the Tea for Two café was that fateful day back in August when Bibby had called me from the hospital. Today I was having lunch there with Theresa and, as it was the nearest place to work that we both liked, it seemed silly to avoid it. Besides, I'd decided the previous evening that I would start getting my life back together. For too long I'd let the fallout of Bibby's actions dominate my life.

I left the travel agents in Havelock Street laden with holiday brochures. France, Spain, Italy, Channel Islands, coach tours, package tours, full board, half board, bed and breakfast; I would make certain there was something there that Lawrence and I could agree on. Theresa had managed to get us a table at a quiet spot in the far corner of the café and we decided on homemade chicken soup, buttered crispy rolls and coffee. We had less than an hour and I knew that Theresa wanted to know how everything was in the Fellowes household. We might work with each other, but rarely did we get an opportunity to talk in any depth. There was always someone around or something happening at the surgery.

Theresa leaned forward, her arms folded on the table. 'I have to say, Jetta, you look more like your old self than I've seen you in months.'

'Good. I am more my old self today. For months now I've been going through the motions and I know you've always talked about time being a great healer, but there've been days when I've wondered if I'd ever feel right again.'

I remembered the weeks following my china-smashing outburst. Though I wasn't sure I really did remember. It was all such a blur. There were many days I didn't get to work, days I simply couldn't face it. Pretending all was normal when our lives had fallen apart. Peter would have nothing to do with any of us and to discover that my own husband doubted me was more than I could bear. He insisted he didn't doubt me. But I'd seen it in his face; heard it in his voice.

'I know, it does sound such a cliché, but I know from my own experience, time does allow things to heal.' Theresa broke a piece from her roll and dipped it into the thick creamy soup.

'Peter still won't have anything to do with any of us, not even David or Debbie. That hurts. And as far as I know, he still believes that I made it all up to stop him being with…her.' I still found it difficult to say her name. The thought of never speaking with Pete again caused me to feel queasy. Maybe it wasn't such a good idea to be talking about it. It was such a ghastly situation.

'It'll be alright, Jetta. I really believe that. She won't be able to keep her pretence up forever. At sometime, she'll do something that will have him see her for what she is. Hold on to that thought. Be patient. And be ready to pick up the pieces.'

'I hope you're right. Goodness, even saying that makes me sound beastly.' I placed my soup spoon on the side and leaned towards Theresa. 'But I have seen her.'

'Bibby?'

'Yes. I saw her in Old Town on the corner of Devizes Road and Newport Street one morning a few weeks ago. I was on my way to work. I haven't said anything to anyone because, well, it seems I've already said too much. But she was with a man. A tall blond-haired man, definitely not Peter.'

'Well, if she's being so brazen she's going to get caught out.'

'I know but...'

A hand on my shoulder caused me to look around. It was the café owner. 'Sorry to interrupt,' she said. 'It's just that ever since you came in I've been puzzling where I've seen you before and I've just realised. You were in here some months ago and got a phone call from a young woman, an emergency, by the sounds of things. I thought about you a lot after that. You looked so worried and ill when you left here. Still, I'm glad she's alright now.'

'Thank you. That's considerate of you,' I said, returning to another bite of soup-dipped roll.

But before she was back behind the counter, I realised what she'd said.

'Excuse me. You said you're glad she's alright now. How do you know she's alright?'

Her expression softened. 'A man told me. He came in making enquiries, asking whether a lady lunching here, a Mrs Fennows or something like that, had taken a call from a young woman. Well, I didn't think it would do any harm to say, so I told him. And quite hysterical the young woman on the phone was too, I told him.'

I pushed my soup away from me and swivelled in my chair to face her. 'This man, can you describe him?'

'Tall. Dark hair. No older than 30, I'd say. Good looking. But then at my age...' She broke off and smiled.

'I don't suppose he gave his name?'

'No. Anyway, nice to see you again, but I'd best get on...'

And before she reached the counter where a customer was waiting to pay, I had already narrowed the man's identity down to one of two people.

'It has to be Peter or David. One of my own sons thought fit to go behind my back and question my version of events.'

Theresa wiped flecks of soup off her mouth with a napkin. 'Think about it, Jetta – if it was Peter checking up, that's good because it must mean he has doubts about Bibby, otherwise why would he bother?'

She was right. I mustn't jump to conclusions. Besides, it would be simple enough to find out. All I had to do was ask David.

By eight o'clock that evening, Lawrence had agreed on two weeks in Italy. It was nothing short of a miracle. Two weeks full board in Tuscany at the family run Albergo Bella Vista, complete with its own pool and bar. According to the brochure, there were optional trips available to a local vineyard, the walled city of Lucca, a health spa and Pisa's leaning tower. All we had to do was let the hotel proprietor know which we wanted when we were there and he would book the trips for us. Gathering up the brochures from the coffee table and the floor, leaving out only the one I needed, I bundled them into the dustbin, feeling guilty at the waste.

Lying back on the settee I realised that, for the first time in what seemed an age, I felt hope. Hope for Lawrence and me as a couple and hope for us as a family. Tomorrow I would book our holiday. At the weekend we were going to a show with Debbie and David. Lawrence was reading books again, listening to music too, though never anything from the hit parade. That would be expecting too much. All I knew was that a corner had been turned. And I could relax more. Be with my thoughts occasionally instead of doing anything and everything to avoid them. Because Theresa was right – sooner or later Bibby would slip up. She had to.

I looked across at Lawrence. There was an air of contentment about him as he leafed through his newspaper. I wondered if I should tell him about the lady in the café, but decided against it. Not tonight.

It was then I saw his face contort. I heard him gasp. It was if someone had punched him in the stomach, expelling the air from his lungs. I stood up.

'Lawrence… Lawrence what is it?'

He never said a word. He leaned forward, laid the open newspaper on the coffee table and swivelled it to face me. And I saw it immediately.

'Oh my God, Lawrence…'

My insides drained. I was numb. Hollow. Luckily Lawrence caught me before I hit the corner of the coffee table, scattering the newspaper across the floor.

As Z Cars sprang to life in the corner of the room, staring at me from a page of newsprint was a picture of Peter and Bibby. And a notice.

Sherman – Fellowes

On Saturday 30 April 1977 the marriage took place between Elizabeth 'Bibby' Jane Sherman and Peter Lawrence Fellowes at Swindon Register Office. The bride, who wore a white taffeta gown with a freshwater pearl and diamante tiara, was given away by John Ellis, a friend of the groom. The best man was Kevin Harrison. A reception for close friends followed at the Blunsdon House Hotel before the couple left to honeymoon in Paris. Peter and Bibby thank all those who shared in their special day.

Chapter Eleven

Lyme Regis, Dorset, Saturday, July 2006

The dining room was light with plenty of room between tables and I was enjoying a smoked kipper with a piece of wholegrain bread when Matthew approached.

'Sorry to interrupt your breakfast, Mrs Francis, but someone wants to rent the single room you asked me to hold, so I need to know now whether you wish to take it.'

Blast. I had hoped to delay the decision longer. Staying here was expensive and I didn't want to pay out unnecessarily. But there was nothing for it. It wouldn't be easy to find another hotel room in the locality, especially not somewhere as handy and as comfortable as this one. And I hadn't come this far to back out now.

'Yes, I'll take it.'

'Thank you,' he said. 'I'll go and let the gentleman know.'

'Oh well,' I said aloud, as he walked off, 'whoever said in for a penny in for a pound must have had me in mind.'

Behind me, the waitress laughed. 'I thought exactly the same thing last week when I treated myself to a pair of new shoes,' she said in a low voice as she passed. 'Sadly, my husband doesn't have the same thinking.'

'They rarely do,' I called after her, thinking she didn't look old enough to have a husband.

83

In a peculiar way, I realised, I was enjoying myself. The staff at the hotel were friendly and under usual circumstances I would have enjoyed getting to know them better. I would have been chattier, found out more about the town, its people, its history. I didn't usually have to go searching. People always seemed to find me. But that wasn't why I was here. Still, as I was here, I would enjoy the bits I could without drawing unnecessary attention to myself or my activities.

As I returned to my room, I was still considering whether to take today or tomorrow off, as it were. I knew what I had planned for one of the days; it was a question of whether to do it on Saturday or Sunday. I'd felt so stiff on waking, I was tempted to spend the day in bed, but eventually decided that with Sunday being the traditional day of rest, so it would be with me.

What irony – being so traditional as to take a rest on the Sabbath only to use it to plot a murder.

Firstly, I needed to get over the reaction I had every time I saw Bibby. I remembered seeing a book on Debbie's coffee table: *Feel The Fear and Do It Anyway*. It had stuck in my mind and I decided now was the time to do just that. The only way to overcome the fear was to meet it head-on. I would have to be in close proximity to Bibby and not fall apart physically, emotionally or any other way.

Not wishing to waste any time, I picked up my hat and the phone directory I'd borrowed previously and left the hotel, stopping only to return the directory to reception. The agreement I made with myself on the walk to Marine Parade was that I wouldn't hesitate outside Bibby's café. He who hesitates is lost.

So I didn't. I walked straight in and made for an empty corner table tucked to the right of the counter and the rear and side wall. With my back half-turned to the counter, I positioned myself where I wouldn't be seen full face, and put my handbag on the seat beside me. I picked up the encapsulated menu and stared blankly at row after row of offerings as the coffee machines hissed and steamed on the counter and the smell of fresh baking and roast coffee filled the air. There was an extensive choice of pastries, light lunches and beverages. And I wasn't in the least bit hungry. My stomach churned.

A young waitress approached me, wearing black trousers and a white blouse with 'Bibby's Café and Gifts' embroidered across the breast pocket in royal blue.

'Good morning,' she said. 'Are you ready to order or would you like more time?'

'I'd like a coffee, please.'

'Will that be a regular coffee, decaff, latte, espresso, Americano or cappuccino?'

'Regular, please.'

'A cup or a mug?'

'Mug, please.'

'Anything else?'

'Not at the moment, thank you.'

'I'll bring it right back,' she said, scribbling a note on her pad.

True to her word, she returned within minutes with a tall royal blue mug of coffee, complete with wrapped mint biscuit and a paper coaster on the saucer bearing the café emblem and telephone number.

'Are you Bibby? Is this your café?' I asked, seizing a chance to find out more as she placed the coffee in front of me.

'I wish!' She laughed and put her hand to her dark hair, which she'd pulled into a glittery-blue ponytail band. 'No, I just work here on a Saturday and sometimes Sunday in the summer.'

'Oh, I thought you might have been…'

'No. Besides, Bibby doesn't work in the café. She only works in the gifts section now. Not today though, she's having a day off. But she'll be in tomorrow; Sundays are one of the busiest days.'

'I suppose everyone wants at least one day off at the weekend with their husband.'

'Oh, I don't think she's got a husband,' the young woman said as she left to take the order of a couple sat at a window table. 'I know for a fact she lives alone.'

For the next hour, the bell over the door rang frequently as customers came and went, and I drank my coffee and a refill. I felt more comfortable knowing Bibby wasn't on the premises, although every time the bell tinkled my heart lurched in case it was her. I didn't wear my sun hat inside the café as I felt that made me more conspicuous, not less. Without it I was just another grey-haired old lady visiting the seaside.

The café was well thought out. Comfortable chairs, fresh flowers on all the tables, walls tastefully decorated with words and images relevant to the area, and the view of the bay was stunning. As much as I would have liked to, I couldn't fault it. Even the young staff were plentiful, friendly and efficient and all wore the café uniform of black trousers and white blouse or shirt. I wondered if Bibby had built the place up from scratch or bought it. If so, when? Not that this mattered a jot to my plans; it was simply curiosity on my part.

Eventually I left the café, freeing up the last available table, and stood outside fanning myself with the sun hat whilst I considered which direction to take.

The walk back to the hotel exhausted me. I looked in several shops on the way up Broad Street, and spent too long browsing amongst the paperbacks in the charity shop. Eventually I left with Andrea Levy's *Small Island*. I was sure I'd read good reviews about it.

I bought a pasty to have with a cup of tea, yet once in my room I didn't have the strength to make a cup of tea without resting first. I reminded myself, yet again, that I needed to take the hills into account when I planned my days. I didn't want to walk up them more than was necessary. I must use my energy wisely.

The painkillers were on my beside table, but even the thought of getting up to get a glass of water sapped me. I was told to take the painkillers regularly, but I only took them as I felt necessary – such as now. Maybe I ought to be more sensible about this. I could not, would not, have this whole visit prove futile.

I closed my eyes, but the pains didn't ease. It was no good, I would have to get up. Forcing myself into an upright position and eventually pushing myself up off the bed, I fetched a tumbler of water from the bathroom and pushed the white pills through their packaging. I took them one at a time, hastily gulping down the water lest the pills should begin to dissolve on my tongue. I hated that. There were times when everything seemed, such as now, an uphill struggle. I laughed. Yes, literally, an uphill struggle. Oh well, I might be about to let go of life, but I must hang on to my sense of humour. And I lay back on the bed and waited for the pills to do their job.

The pasty was cold by the time I got up, but as I bit into the meaty interior I thought of the quote: Hunger is the best sauce in the world. Though I couldn't be sure who said it. Cervantes? I missed having my books around me to check such things. To-night I would have fish and chips as it was far too expensive to eat dinner in the hotel every night. I would drive the few miles east to Charmouth, park facing the sea and eat a traditional British seaside supper with my fingers. Matthew said there was an excellent fish and chip shop there.

And after I'd eaten, I would pull together my thoughts. Thoughts about the sign outside Bibby's Café and Gifts, for instance, where, at the bottom left hand corner, in small royal blue lettering, it read: *Proprietor E J Fellowes.*

It worried me that she still used the name Fellowes. It truly did. It worried me a great deal.

Chapter Twelve

Swindon, Wiltshire, November 1978

Lawrence lit a fire in the sitting room when we returned from our Sunday afternoon walk whilst I made lamb sandwiches with the leftovers from lunch. Tired and full, I sat on the hearth rug, hypnotised by the purple red flames and the hiss of the glowing coals. The heat made my eyes water, but I didn't move. I needed its heat. I noticed Lawrence's head drop forward almost onto his empty plate, then back again, finally settling on one side. He was asleep.

I was thankful we had opted for the day's walking tour on our Italian holiday as it had sparked Lawrence's interest in walking. And whilst Swindon wasn't Tuscany, the Wiltshire countryside held many delights. Today we'd driven to Wanborough and walked for almost two hours, stopping only once at the edge of a copse to watch a twin-engined Cessna cross our bit of sky. The fields were steep in places and often I would turn and look back at some grassy rise I had just climbed to see Lawrence far behind, his breath visible puffs in the cold, damp afternoon air.

'Nearly there!' I shouted when I neared the car. 'And I've got a flask of tea in the boot.'

And he put his hand up, too short of breath to reply.

Back at the car I poured tea into the thermos' cups and placed them on the dashboard. By the time Lawrence flopped into the driver's seat, the windscreen and quarter lights were steaming up nicely. Despite having the hot tea, I didn't remove my gloves and wool hat. The temperature seemed to have dropped a few degrees.

I wasn't any warmer by the time Lawrence drove over the flyover from Wanborough into Covingham.

'It'll soon start to warm up,' he said, reading my thoughts, as we passed the self-build houses in Merlin Way, 'and then you'll complain of the heat.'

This was true. Unlike Lawrence, I would have slid the heater switch to the maximum red setting when we first got in the car. I would quickly get too hot, and then turn it down to midway between red and blue. It made sense to me. It made Lawrence despair. We had different ways of doing things. He would say he was more methodical, more patient. He was more willing to suffer, I thought.

When we reached Queen's Drive, I slid my calfskin gloves off and removed my hat. And by the time we were in Old Town I was ready to take my coat off, but said nothing. In less than a mile we'd be home.

I watched Lawrence's chest rise and fall as he sat sleeping in the chair. He was a strange man and I wasn't sure I would ever completely understand him, if at all.

I looked up at the invitation propped behind the delicate carriage clock on the mantelpiece. It was my idea to put it there. Lawrence would have hidden it away somewhere as if it didn't exist. In fact, if the invitation hadn't arrived by post, I doubt I would have known about last evening. But the handwritten cream envelope had landed on the mat many weeks ago and was addressed to us both:

Mr and Mrs L Fellowes,
The Gables
7 Marlborough Crescent
Marlborough Road
Swindon

Inside was an invitation card, bordered in gold, which began with the words:

The Directors of Marshwood Engineering Limited, Stratton Road, Swindon request the company of Lawrence and Jetta Fellowes at their Celebration Evening on Saturday...

This was unusual. In all the time Lawrence had been at Marshwood Engineering, never before had we received such an invite. Yet when I mentioned this to Lawrence, he seemed evasive, which led me to suspect that there had been others. He wasn't a social man at the best of times and certainly didn't believe in mixing anything with work, least of all pleasure. But, at my insistence, we had gone to yesterday's Celebration Evening and Lawrence was presented with the engraved clock in honour of 25 years' service. Service during which he had never had a day off sick.

'Such an achievement,' the Managing Director said, shaking Lawrence's hand vigorously as cameras flashed.

Yet I knew Lawrence found it easier to go to work than not. It was structured. It was his safety net. It was where he was in control. Figures add up. Incomings minus outgoings result in profits or losses. Pay as You Earn is tangible. And any oversights in these areas could be traced. Traced. Recalculated. And put right.

Not so with life.

Yet, everything considered, I thought, feeling the warmth of the fire draw me towards sleep, it had been a good weekend. As good as it ever could get bar a reconciliation with Peter.

The only light in the room when I woke was provided by the fire. I unfurled, hot and thirsty. Leaning across the floor, I switched on the standard lamp at the wall. Lawrence was still asleep. Standing up, I glanced in the mirror over the mantelpiece and saw the imprint of the hearth rug on my cheek. Noting it was already five and twenty to eight, I decided I would wake Lawrence with a cup of tea. But the phone got there before me.

'Don't worry, I'll get it,' I said, walking through to the hall. 'It'll probably be David or Debbie this time on a Sunday.'

'Hello, I told Dad it would probably be you,' I said, hearing David's voice as I sat down in the hallway, pleased the radiator was on.

'Yeah, I'll get straight to the point, Mum. I'd like you and Dad to come over to my place, this evening. Now.'

I sighed inwardly. I was too tired to go out again and knew Lawrence would feel the same. 'I'm sorry, David, we're tired. You come here instead.'

I sensed there was something wrong when David paused before saying. 'What I mean is, I need you and Dad to come over.'

'What do you mean need?'

'It would be better if you just came, Mum, and we can talk about it when you're here.'

I sensed something or someone wasn't right. 'Are you alright, David? And what about Debbie? It isn't Peter, is it?'

'Mum. We're OK, but we do need to see you. You know I wouldn't ask unless–'

'For Chrissakes, David!' I raised my voice. 'Be more specific. I can't take many more shocks.'

'Put Dad on.'

'No. Tell me. For goodness' sake, tell me.'

'Put Dad on.'

'No. I won't put Dad on. Tell me.'

'Then will you come?'

'Yes.'

'OK. It's Peter.'

'Is he…?'

'He's here, Mum. And he needs to see you and Dad.'

'Did he say that?'

'Yes.'

I felt myself give way at my middle and flop forward as if someone had removed my spine. I clutched the phone. 'We'll be right over.' And I dropped the receiver onto its cradle as Lawrence came through into the hall.

I stepped out of the car into the gutter, almost slipping on the damp leaves the rain had collected there. Regaining my balance, I caught hold of Lawrence's offered arm as he came around to the passenger side of the car. Together, arm in arm, we made our way towards David's front door. We'd left home immediately following his call, stopping only to put the fire guard up and to pull on our coats.

Under the glow of the streetlight, the strain on Lawrence's face was obvious. All the way over we'd talked, or rather I'd talked. Once I'd had a chance to calm myself, I felt that Peter being at David's was good news. Peter had, after all, asked to see us. And I was reminded of Theresa's words in the café last year: *At sometime, she'll do something that will have him see her for what she is. Hold on to that thought. Be patient. And be ready to pick up the pieces.*

Was it time to pick up the pieces?

David's house was welcomingly warm after the chilly night air and the smell of a late roast and boiling cabbage seeped into the hall from the kitchen. Leaving our coats on the pegs at the foot of the stairs, we followed David into the middle room of the terraced house where Debbie was sitting at the table. She stood up, hugged us and offered us a drink. Lawrence shook his head to yet more liquid and I agreed, adding, 'Maybe later.'

'Do you mind if I finish off in the kitchen? David can fill you in.'

'Of course not,' I said, wondering where Peter was, but afraid to ask. 'You carry on.'

We sat around the white painted table and I tried to read David's expression. I couldn't. And before he said anything, he got up.

'Look, I'm going to have a beer, do you want one, Dad?'

Lawrence shook his head as David poured himself a pale beer into a tumbler from the sideboard and sat back at the table.

'There's no good place to start, so I'm just going to tell you what's happened so far that I know. The rest'll be up to Peter.'

'Where is he?'

'Please, Mum.' David held his hand up. 'Not yet.' He took a gulp from his glass before continuing. 'Peter rang me this morning and asked if he could come over. I was shocked, neither Debs nor I have heard from him for over two years. But I said yes, of course, and he arrived a couple of hours ago. He's in a bit of trouble.'

'Trouble? What?'

'Mum, please, hear me out.'

The smell of David's beer was for some inexplicable reason making me want to retch and I pushed it further away from me. 'Sorry.' I said.

'It appears that Bibby left Pete some time ago. Months ago, in fact, I'm not sure exactly when. It could be a year or more ago. Anyway, less than a week after she left him, Pete had a visit from the police. Bibby had been badly beaten up. Severely beaten up.'

Lawrence shook his head slowly and I took a deep breath. She didn't deserve that. No one deserves that.

'The thing is,' David raised his glass and drank a couple of inches of his beer before adding, 'she blamed Peter.'

Lawrence brought his head up. 'What do you mean, she blamed Peter?'

'Just that. She told the police that Peter had beaten her. That after she left him she was the victim of a vicious unprovoked attack and that Peter was responsible.'

'But surely when the police realised he wasn't responsible…'

'That's just it. They believe he was. He was arrested, charged and is due in court on Tuesday.'

Debbie appeared and put two coffees in front of us and a hand on my shoulder. 'Drink this,' she said. 'You too, Lawrence. You need something.'

She was right. My mouth was so dry I could hardly speak.

'I'll let Pete tell you the rest.' David inclined his head towards the hall door.

I turned to see Peter standing in the doorway. He was smaller in every sense than when I had last seen him and I would not have recognised him but that he was my own son. He came and sat opposite us and Debbie pushed a coffee in front of him too.

'No beer. You need to keep a clear head for the next few days.'

I reached my hand out across the table, but he didn't notice. He licked his lips over and over and I couldn't believe that this shell of a man was our son. He'd lost a couple of stone and his clothes hung on him. His hair was lank and his skin grey. He looked as old as his father.

It was Lawrence who broke the silence. 'What time are you due in court on Tuesday?'

'In the morning. But Dad, I don't want you or Mum there.'

'Of course we'll be there.'

Peter stood up and shouted. 'No!' and immediately sat back down. 'I'm sorry, but I can't have you there. Please. I've made up my mind. David's agreed to be there at my request. And when the verdict's known, if I can't call you, for whatever reason, he will. David will let you know the verdict.'

David nodded and put an arm around Pete's shoulder. It's what I wanted to do. It's all I'd wanted to do since first seeing him stood in the doorway.

Lawrence picked up his mug of coffee, his hands trembling. 'Why wouldn't you be able to call us?'

'Because I might not be in a position to…'

'I don't understand.'

'I might be going to jail.'

'Jail!' Lawrence and I said together.

'Yes. There's the possibility of a custodial sentence.' Peter bowed his head.

'What the hell happened to her?' Lawrence asked.

'I don't know what happened, Dad. I wish I did. But the results of what happened I've seen in glorious Technicolor. The blood. The bruises. The cuts. And I see them most nights. Even sleeping tablets can't keep the images at bay. The police showed me photographs of her injuries. Plenty of them. Her broken nose. Her black eyes. Her cuts, swelling, bruising. She was barely bloody recognisable.'

'But why, Peter? Why would she say you'd done these things?' I said.

'You're asking me why?' He shook his head, before suddenly sitting upright in the chair. 'Oh, I get it. What's this, payback time? What you're really asking is, am I telling the truth? Is this because I doubted you?'

'Not at all.' It was my turn to sound indignant. 'Of course I believe you. I know what she's capable of.'

'Let's stick to the facts,' Lawrence interrupted. 'Someone did beat her and she received those injuries. Who would do something like that? Surely that's your best line of defence.'

'Believe me, Dad, I've tried to come up with the truth in an attempt to save myself. But she's a convincing liar. She has people eating out of her hand.' Peter looked across at me and stretched his hand across the table towards mine. 'I'm sorry. I know that now, Mum.'

I caught his fingers in mine.

'But she told the police a wild and convincing tale and has even managed to conjure up a witness.'

'A witness – how come?' Lawrence said.

'How the hell do I know?' Peter said. 'How can someone witness what never happened?'

'Let me guess,' I said. 'This witness, Peter. I would say it's a man. Tall, blond-haired, about your age.'

'How do you know?'

'Because I saw them together. I saw them together before you were even …married.'

Peter buried his head in his crossed arms. 'Jesus Christ! It gets worse. It just keeps on getting worse and bloody worse.' He looked up at me. 'Why the hell didn't you tell… Ha! Imagine that! I was about to ask you why you didn't tell me. Christ! I've been such a bloody fool.'

On Tuesday, for the first time in his life, Lawrence took a day off work, sick. I hadn't asked him to. I deliberately didn't. I thought that work would be the best place for him, today of all days. But he got up much earlier than usual, around 5am, pulled on an old pair of navy trousers and an even older cable knit jumper and at 8.30 I heard him on the phone saying he wouldn't be at work today. That made two of us. Whatever happened, Lawrence and I had to face it, and it might as well be together. And we knew from what David and Peter had intimated that Bibby had left other trails of debris in her wake where Peter was concerned. But for today, there was the court case.

Lawrence was in the sitting room mending a plug on the table lamp, Vivaldi's Four Seasons booming out of the radiogram.

I would make us a late breakfast. Whether we ate it or not, it didn't matter. It would keep me busy. I was confident that Peter would be acquitted. Bibby might have fooled the police in their desperation to get an arrest, but eventually her lies would catch her out. Besides, I believed in the law. Yet as confident as I was, I simply wanted that final phone call for Peter's sake. He wasn't so confident.

At midday we sat down to back bacon rashers, Walls' pork sausages, tomatoes, mushrooms and egg. I'd laid the table in the kitchen complete with a rack of toast, butter and a pot of tea for two. It was cosier in the winter than the dining room, and warmer.

'This looks good,' Lawrence said, his words not reflected in his eyes, and I watched the pale yellow yolk of his egg seep towards his bacon as he cut into it.

As I poured the tea into Lawrence's cup I realised I felt stronger than I had in a long while. Maybe it was seeing how badly affected Lawrence was by this latest Bibby episode. I felt vindicated. Besides I had already paid the price of Bibby's lies. Lies that had kept me from my youngest son for over two years. But I got no pleasure in being right. No pleasure at all in seeing what Bibby had done, and was still doing, to my family.

Apart from the odd courteous remark over the passing of condiments or fresh cups of tea, we ate in silence. Neither of us switched the wireless on. Maybe we both knew the likelihood of being bombarded with bad news. Stories recounting the deaths of over 900 people, as had happened in a recent mass suicide in South America, or a Liberal MP accused of murder.

No, perhaps it was best we kept horrors to a minimum. We had our own to get through today.

By five o'clock we hadn't heard from Peter or David. Twice I called David's house, but the phone rang and rang. And the longer the not-knowing went on, the less confident I was of the verdict. Lawrence, I thought, would go mad if he didn't stop pacing around the house. And if he didn't, I would.

The sudden bang of the letter box caused me to jump and by the time I reached the hallway, Lawrence was there.

'It's only the evening paper,' he said, dragging it in through the letterbox.

'You go and have a read and I'll get us another drink.' I was running out of things to do and say.

'I can't face more tea, Jetta. And we'd better not have any alcohol in case we have to drive anywhere.'

'Like where?'

'How the hell do I know? I'm just…I'm just… Hell, I don't know what I'm trying to say.'

Lawrence returned to the sitting room and I followed. The fire he had lit earlier in the day was almost out and I added a few lumps of coal from the scuttle on the hearth.

'I'm going around to David's if I haven't heard anything soon,' Lawrence said. 'Then…then wherever I've got to. They've no right to keep us waiting like this.' Lawrence sat down hard in what he considered his chair, leaving the paper folded on his lap.

'They wouldn't do it deliberately, Lawrence. They said they'd call and they will. You know what they say, "No news is good news".'

'Just what we need at this time. Trite bloody little comments!'

'For goodness' sake, Lawrence, what do you want me to say? That I'm as frightened as you? That I can't understand why we haven't heard? That I want to run out of the door instead of sitting here like a trapped animal and keep on running until I get answers?'

Lawrence shook his head. 'I'm sorry. This not knowing is killing me.'

'I know, Lawrence, but we have to keep it together. Look, let's make a pact. If we haven't heard anything by six, you do whatever you feel you have to do. Until then, try and read the paper and I'll try and put some life back into this fire.'

And that's what we were doing when the telephone rang. It was a moment frozen in time. Me putting the brass poker back on its hearth stand, Lawrence turning a page of the evening newspaper. We hadn't decided who would answer the phone, but on hearing it ring I leapt up. Lawrence didn't move, except to lay his newspaper out on the coffee table as if he would resume reading when normal service was returned. The look we exchanged gave me permission to answer.

I lifted the receiver and couldn't speak. I didn't need to.

'Mum?' It was David. I must have made a sound as he continued. 'I'm sorry not to have called earlier, but I've been with Pete. He's in a terrible state. There's no way to wrap this up. He's been found guilty.'

'No! How could they?' My hands were shaking so badly it was difficult to keep my grip on the phone.

'But he won't go to jail,' David continued. 'He hasn't got a custodial sentence. He's been fined and–'

'Thank God. Look, David, I must tell your father. Can you come over now and bring Peter and Debs with you?'

'I don't see why not.'

'Then do it and we'll see you in a bit.'

Without waiting for a reply I hung up and hurried back to the sitting room. Lawrence hadn't moved.

'He hasn't gone to jail, but he's been found guilty.' I looked at the fire; it was making strange hissing noises.

Lawrence nodded and whispered. 'I know.'

Then I realised it was Lawrence. The noise was coming from Lawrence, not the fire.

I knelt beside him, instinctively grabbing his hand. 'Lawrence…Lawrence…what is it? What's the matter?'

His face was ashen, his breathing shallow and irregular. 'I've got such a pain in my chest…it's…it feels as if…as if I've got an elephant sat on it.' And he closed his eyes and groaned.

I didn't wait to hear more. If this was what I thought it was, Lawrence needed to get to hospital, fast. I stumbled into the hallway and dialled 999. Every second seemed like an hour. And all the questions the operator asked – were they really necessary? Eventually I was assured an ambulance was on its way.

Lawrence was exactly as I'd left him, except he nodded when I asked if the pain was worse.

'The ambulance'll be here soon and you'll be fine. Please try not to worry.' I wasn't sure he could hear me, but I had to reassure him. He would be fine, of course he would. He had to be.

I heard the siren before the flashing lights appeared in the driveway. I patted Lawrence's arm. 'They're here now, Lawrence. You're going to be just fine.'

But I don't think he could hear me. Not now. I turned away from him. I would open the front door ready for the ambulance staff to walk straight in. It was then I saw the newspaper where Lawrence had left it, lying open on the coffee table beside his chair.

I put my hand up to my mouth. Oh my God. There on the right hand page was a quarter page photograph of Lawrence receiving his long service award. The caption read: *Lawrence Fellowes receiving his award from Derek Brown, Managing Director of Marshwood Engineering Limited.*

On the facing page, under *Day's Court Reports*, were at least ten column inches devoted to a story which began: *Swindon Man Found Guilty of Vicious Assault on Wife… Peter Lawrence Fellowes, 26, of Newhill Street, Swindon was today found guilty of a particularly vicious and unprovoked attack on his wife. In the attack, which happened in April of this year, Elizabeth Fellowes suffered horrific injuries…*

Chapter Thirteen

Lyme Regis, Dorset, Sunday, July 2006

A burst of activity over near the Cobb caught people's attention and it didn't take long for the ripple of information to make its way to where I was walking along the promenade. The lifeboat had been launched, I heard onlookers say. A dinghy with a young brother and sister on board had drifted too far out to sea and several people had made 999 calls. Apparently.

It was almost midday when I walked into Bibby's Café and, finding it full, was about to leave when I heard someone call.

"'Scuse me!' A lady waved frantically at me from a table near the window. 'We're just leaving,' she said, pushing her overweight companion out of his chair and signalling that I could sit there.

'Thank you,' I said as they squeezed their ample frames between me and a young man sat eating what looked to be a healthy green salad. I would have preferred to sit somewhere less conspicuous but reminded myself that today was the day I was to face my fear.

Once seated, I picked up the menu and browsed. I was facing the window, which allowed me to watch the entrance to the gift shop on my right. The buzz of conversation, mingled with the hiss of the coffee maker, created a soft blanket of sound that I found therapeutic. Hypnotic almost, as I felt my shoulders and jaw relax.

This was to have been my day of rest, but on waking I'd felt refreshed, better than I'd done in weeks and it seemed to be an omen. I would rest tomorrow. I would make Monday my day of rest. Besides, it occurred to me that if Sunday was the shop's busiest day, there would be less chance of Bibby noticing me and more chance for me to observe her unnoticed.

Five or so minutes later, a young waiter asked me if I was ready to order. I was. Tuna salad sandwiches on wholegrain bread and a regular coffee. A youngish couple had stopped outside the café window and although I couldn't make out all they said, it was obvious from their body language and expressions that neither was happy. The only words I did hear were her shouting that she wasn't going any bloody further, at which point he raised his arms skywards, turned about and walked off. I don't know if she followed or continued on her way as I was interrupted by a voice that even after so many years I recognised.

'Brian! Brian!'

It was Bibby. I recognised the voice before her head appeared around the archway. As she called him again, I forced myself to keep looking at her. She smiled at one of the young waiters as he approached her. That sickly sweet smile of old. And my stomach weakened as the waiter who'd taken my order placed my sandwiches and coffee in front of me. I wasn't sure I could stomach this now.

'I need you to help lift one of these boxes,' Bibby said, disappearing back into the gift section with Brian following.

Part of me wanted to stand up there and then, drag her back and confront her before all these people. Let them know what she'd done to me and mine. But I talked myself out of it. I was craftier than that. I would make sure she never did the likes of what she'd done to me and mine to anyone again. Ever.

Minutes later Brian returned and resumed his waiting duties. Picking up one of the tuna sandwiches, I nibbled the edge. Surely confronting fear meant continuing as normal. If I was ever going to get close enough to kill her, I would have to. Using a fingernail to dislodge a seed from between my teeth, I realised my heart rate and breathing were back to normal. I had survived seeing her in the flesh. Hearing her. And this was what I needed to remember and work on if I was ever going to execute my plan. Execute. I smiled at my choice of words.

Slowly devouring my sandwich, I was unaware of the heat of the day, the passers-by or the view. I sat in my private world, cocooned in thought and sound, until a voice interrupted me.

'Is this seat taken?'

A tall gentleman, in his mid to late seventies, I reckoned, stood with his hand resting on the back of the chair opposite. I looked around. Seeing no empty tables available, I said, 'No.'

'Do you mind if I sit here?'

'Of course not,' I pulled my coffee cup closer and continued to eat my sandwich.

All I wanted to do was observe Bibby. But I watched as the tall, lean man removed his cotton jacket and placed it over the back of the chair before sitting down. He was still a handsome man, a Clark Gable lookalike in his younger days, I shouldn't wonder, and he had a kind face. And I knew that at any other time I would have been keen to make conversation.

'Another lovely day,' he said, picking up the menu and folding it back on itself.

'Yes, though rather too hot for me, I'm afraid.'

'I haven't seen you in here before.'

'No.' I took a sip of the now cooled coffee. 'I've only been here a few days, though I have been in once before.'

If I didn't know better I would have thought he was being flirtatious. This was new for me. There had never been anyone else since Lawrence; yet, ironically, for the first time and under other circumstances, I might have played along. I rather liked the look of him. And I felt he did me.

A waiter approached the table as I finished my sandwich. Clark Gable ordered ham and eggs and, looking across at me, said, 'Can I buy you another coffee?'

'No, that's very kind of you but I really must be going.'

As I stood and picked up my handbag, he also rose and offered his right hand. 'It was nice to have met you, albeit briefly. I'm Charles, by the way.'

I shook his hand and backed away, sure my cheeks were reddening. 'Jet-...I'm Jean,' I said quickly before going over to the counter.

My bill paid, I tucked my purse back into my handbag and headed towards the door. And that's when I saw her. She stood tall and straight, in the archway between the café and the gift section. And she looked directly at me. She raised her hand, waved elegantly and smiled, revealing those still perfect white teeth, and walked towards me. My leaden legs stopped, unable to carry me any further, and I closed my eyes. I was going to faint.

I didn't faint. I couldn't have done because now I could hear her saying, *Hello. I didn't expect to see you...* How long I stood there with my eyes closed I don't know, but I knew I couldn't open them until I had mentally prepared myself and my response. I would be cool but not cold, I decided. Polite but not pleasant, surprised but not shocked.

I opened my eyes, expecting to see Bibby stood in front of me. Instead, she was leaning against the counter talking to a young woman. And, as the young woman smiled at her, I realised with the greatest sense of relief that it wasn't me Bibby had noticed after all.

She had passed within inches of me without so much as a raised eyebrow or a tilting of the head. There was no 'Don't I know you?' or 'You look familiar'. No, she had passed by without so much as a second glance.

A grain of excitement rose in me as I pulled the café door open, its bell ringing loudly over my head. It certainly made what I had to do a damn sight easier.

Chapter Fourteen

Hampton Stoke, June 1980

There was no barrier between the garden and what was laughingly referred to as the orchard. A couple of old pear and damson trees were all that was left of any orchard, although Rosebay willow herb, stinging nettles and lemon balm grew in abundance. So did the brightest yellow buttercups I have ever seen. An old bee hive, which I hadn't got around to moving yet, lay rotting on its side in the long stout grass where the garden bordered the corn field. And on the boundary of the field, a row of poplars, which gave the cottage its name, acted as a windbreak.

Turning to face the cottage, I felt the sun's warmth through the thin cotton of my blouse. I loved this garden. This garden was my saviour. I had never wanted to move here. Never wanted to move, full stop. And without this garden to work in, to escape to, I know I wouldn't have given myself the time necessary to make the adjustment.

Back inside the cottage I washed my hands at the Belfast sink, using a nailbrush to remove the black soil from beneath my nails. I could hear my late mother saying of the bits I missed: *A little dirt never hurt anyone.* I leaned over the deep sink awhile, running cold water over my wrists in an attempt to cool myself down. As usual, I'd spent too long in the garden and would have to hurry if I was going to change. The kitchen clock showed it was already past eleven and David had said they'd be here before midday.

I changed into my beige belted shift dress and was making a mental note to put out fresh hand towels when I heard Lawrence call.

'Jetta! Jetta! They're here.'

Before I reached the bottom of the stairs, David was already pushing his way into the hallway with armfuls of equipment.

'Just put everything onto the dining table and we can sort it all out later,' I told him. 'Now, where are those babies?'

'We're here, Grandma,' Debbie said, coming into the hallway cradling Becky in one arm and Andrea in the other.

I kissed Debbie on the cheek. 'Here, let me help.' I took Becky from her. 'You too, Lawrence.'

'It'll be a pleasure,' he said, lifting Andrea out of Debbie's arms and rocking her gently back and forth.

'I'd be careful about that, Dad,' David laughed, on a run through carrying yet more. 'She has a tendency to give her food back when you least expect it.'

'Come on, Lawrence, let's you and me take the twins into the garden and let them finish unpacking the car,' I said.

'Don't let them get in direct sun, Mum,' David said on his way for another load.

'I won't.' I smiled at Debbie as she raised her eyebrows.

'Here.' Debbie manifested two lemon chequered sun-hats and put them on the twins. 'This will stop Daddy fretting.'

Becky and Andrea slept during their tour of the garden, which ended with us sitting on a bench in the shade of the tool shed. The shed which Lawrence had built, alongside the collapsing greenhouse, despite my calls to buy a new one.

'We can't afford to, Jetta, you know that. We've got to tighten our belts.' And as he'd nailed and hammered timbers together in a way that would have any craftsman cringing, I prayed.

'Look at her, Jetta. She's smiling at me.' Lawrence interrupted my thoughts.

'So she is.' I switched Becky onto my other arm, hoping I might get a similar response, but her eyes stayed firmly shut. 'All Becky seems to want to do is sleep.'

Awake or asleep, I couldn't take my eyes off either of them. Their hair, the colour of dark chocolate, peeped out from under their sunhats and each wore a lemon cotton romper suit and white ankle socks. The only difference was that Andrea's romper sported a rabbit motif, Becky's a lamb. And they brought immeasurable joy to all of us.

'Do you know, Lawrence, these two are the luckiest babies in the world. They couldn't have better parents.'

'You're right there,' he said, then laughed before adding, 'Or grandparents.'

'Or uncle,' a loud voice said from behind.

'Peter! You're here already.' He leaned forward and kissed either side of my face. 'You look well.'

He did too. Much better than the last time I'd seen him, although I didn't point that out.

'Good drive?' Lawrence patted Peter's shoulder.

'Not bad. Only a couple of snarl ups. First when I got off the M4 coming past Dryham Park, and then getting through Bath. Apart from that, it was a good drive, though the car's playing up a bit. I thought I could take a look at her on your drive in the morning. It's difficult at home without a driveway and tools.'

'Course,' Lawrence said. 'I thought the last time you were here she was running a bit rich. Anyway, I'm sure David will lend us a hand too.'

Please let David lend a hand, I thought. Lawrence was willing but not mechanically minded.

'Thanks Dad. Now,' Peter turned his attention to the twins 'which one of you wants to come to your Uncle Peter?'

'Here, you take Becky,' I said, handing him my sleeping bundle, 'I'll make a start on lunch.' And as I walked back down the pitted concrete path towards the cottage, I heard the church clock strike midday.

The dining table audibly groaned beneath the paraphernalia that accompanied the twins. There was a sterilising unit, complete with a bottle of Milton's sterilising fluid; tongs, bottles, teats, Ostermilk, blue plastic measuring spoons, a bottle of gripe water, another of Calpol, a tube of Bonjela, two changing mats, two dozen terry towelling nappies, nappy liners, lemon and white nappy pins, a bottle of Napisan, half a dozen disposable nappies, Johnson's baby lotion, Johnson's baby powder, zinc and castor oil cream, cotton wool, popper-under-the-crotch vests and plastic pants. And that's what I could see. As yet this didn't even include the twins' clothes, pram or toys. David had left those in the car until later, he said.

By five and twenty past one we had eaten and the temperature had risen several degrees. The twins were fed, winded and sleeping at opposite ends of a Witney blanket Debbie had laid out on the sitting room floor, each wearing a soft cotton vest and a terry towelling nappy. Disposable nappies, David told me, were expensive and to be kept for emergencies only. Though he didn't elaborate on what constituted an emergency. The babies lay on their stomachs, which was apparently the way it was done now. 'If you let them sleep on their backs you run the risk of them choking on their sick,' David told me. And I wondered how I'd managed to raise two healthy boys in the absence of so much equipment and information.

The men, collectively, had gone to The Ring o' Bells for what Peter referred to as 'a swift pint'. 'Give you women a chance to catch up,' David added, pushing Lawrence out of the door before him. Debbie and I were pleased as we knew the phrase 'swift pint' to be, if not an outright lie, a stretching of the truth, and we liked the idea of being on our own for a while. David was right, we did want to catch up.

Choosing tall glasses of iced orange juice over tea, we sat in the sitting room, its small paned windows wide open and a brass fire-dog holding the door into the hall ajar to stop it from slamming and waking the twins. All I could hear was a blackbird's warning chook, the rattle of ice in our glasses as we sipped our juice, and the buzz of bees as they passed the open windows. Every now and then Andrea or Becky would snuffle and occasionally a car would pass on the lane, which was rare, this being a dead end.

Debbie reached into her plastic drawstring baby bag, pulled out a book and handed it to me. 'This is for you.'

It was a photograph album, its white front cover embossed: *For Our Grandparents.* On the first page was a copy of the birth announcement as it had appeared in Swindon's *Evening Advertiser* three months earlier.

FELLOWES, David and Deborah (nee Vickers) are proud to announce the safe arrival of Andrea Jetta (4lbs 12oz) and Becky Laura (4lbs 13oz), born on April 18th. Thank you to the staff at Princess Margaret Hospital...

Following it was a pictorial record of the twins to date. Photographs of them with David and Debbie, Peter and Lawrence, and me.

'What a delightful keepsake. Thank you.'

After I'd finished cooing at the pictures, I laid it on the coffee table. 'I'll leave it there for Lawrence to look at. I think he'll like that one of him pushing the pram around Coate Water. And that one of the four of you at the hospital. We were only saying earlier that Andrea and Becky couldn't have better parents. You manage everything so well, but it must be hard at times.'

'It is. Much harder than I ever thought it would be. And David…he's worse than I am, fussing, worrying over them. Almost panicking at times. Have I got the milk temperature right? Is the cat net on the pram? Do they need another layer? Honestly, sometimes I could scream, but I know he only wants what's best for them.'

I laughed. 'I think you're right. And believe me, he's not a chip off the old block. Lawrence never changed a nappy, made a bottle or washed a bib. That was always my role. Still, things were altogether different then.'

They were too. Feeding on demand was one thing we never did, but I didn't mention it. I was only too aware of how I could become my own mother.

'It's good of you to have us all here like this for the weekend, Jetta. And to babysit for us tonight.'

'Not at all. We get the joy of having these two to ourselves. Besides, it'll be good for the three of you to have a night out together.' I took a long drink of juice and pressed the cold glass to my cheek. 'How's Pete doing, do you think?'

Debbie hesitated. 'He says he's doing OK. And work-wise, he is. He's been promoted again and he's earning more money. I know he doesn't want to talk to you or Lawrence about it as he's aware of how everything's affected you, what with Lawrence's health, your moving, and your financial situation and all that. Not to mention all the anxiety and hurt over everything else. But he's taken his bankruptcy hard. Bibby really cleaned him out before she left. She'd got him to sign for multiple loans, saying she was due an inheritance, money from a trust fund. You name it, she'd thought of it. Some she promised to pay herself out of her non-existent wages but, of course, never did. She never paid a penny back and finally, when she couldn't get any more, she left. And everything was in his name, so he was responsible.'

Just the mention of her name made my breathing quicken.

I felt it. Would the repercussions of that woman ever leave me and my family alone?

'Besides,' Debbie continued, 'I think Peter blames himself for his dad's heart attack. I mean Lawrence having to give up work and all that and your having to move here. Peter feels responsible.'

I set my glass down on the coffee table. The scent of honeysuckle filled the room, carried in on the warm breeze from the south. I inhaled deeply and sighed. I mustn't let those old feelings return. They weren't healthy, I instinctively knew that. But how could one woman be allowed to cause such misery? Such total disruption of one family's life. My family's life.

'What nonsense. It's Bibby who's responsible. Bibby caused all this. Bibby's the one who ought to be punished. Bibby…my goodness, if I got my hands on that woman!' I stopped. I could hear my voice getting louder. Angrier. I would stop. Now.

'I know how you feel, Jetta. I mean, since having Andrea and Becky I think of how I'd feel if anyone did something like this to them. And, well, it doesn't bear thinking about.'

'No. No, it doesn't.' I drained my glass and rolled it between my hands. 'It was good of you to have Peter stay with you until he got back on his feet a bit.'

'To be honest, Jetta. I think he had a bit of a breakdown. I can understand why. I'm surprised,' she hesitated. 'I…I was surprised you didn't.'

Some days I wasn't sure I hadn't. The tremors. The way a black cloud was always there on waking. The exhausting effort it took to get out of bed and face the day. The constant nausea. But I had to be strong. Strong for Lawrence. Strong for Peter. I was not going to let that woman be the wrecking ball of our lives. After Lawrence's heart attack, he'd been told he had to give up work. Tablets would stabilise his condition, the consultant told us. But he needed to take life much easier, avoid physical and mental strain. He was only 57.

One of the first things Lawrence said to me when he regained consciousness was, 'We're moving. I'm not staying in a town where people will be pointing and saying our son is a criminal. A criminal capable of violent assault on women.'

'But he's not capable.'

Lawrence looked at me, his eyes watery, the oxygen mask making it difficult for me to make out his muffled words. 'We know that, but it's been announced, publicly in that damn rag they call a newspaper.'

I moved closer, being careful not to disturb any of the tubes and wires that led to oxygen, drips and heart monitors. 'But no one will believe it, Lawrence. Everyone knows Peter isn't capable of such a thing.'

'Do they, Jetta? Really? How many evenings have I sat reading accounts of people's charges and their denials, thinking there's no smoke without fire? How many thousands of people will read about Peter tonight and say the same thing? From now on I'll never buy another newspaper. They're purveyors of misery.'

And that's when Lawrence had his second heart attack.

Debbie disappeared into the kitchen with our empty glasses and I put my feet up on the coffee table. The keeper of the twins.

I don't know what any of us had done to deserve Debbie. She was a Godsend. If only Peter could have someone like her in his life. I know he made out he was OK, but it was a front. It didn't matter how much he smiled or how loud he laughed, his eyes gave him away. A mother knows these things. And the way he was with the twins. He'd always said that when he married he would have lots of children. I think that's why he took Bibby's miscarriage so hard. Or what he thought was a miscarriage. Did her capacity for deceit know no bounds? Because of her he now lived in a grotty bedsit, worked more hours than was healthy and, according to Debbie, refused to date.

'It's so quiet here,' Debbie said, returning with more juice.

'I know and I never thought I'd get used to it. But Lawrence seems happier, despite everything.'

'I know, David and Peter...' Debbie stopped.

'David and Peter?' I prompted.

'Well, they were talking the other night and agreed that Lawrence had never been quite so, well, *fatherly* with them as he is now. He rings them up, and now he's gone to the pub with them. Things they said he never did before.'

I walked over to the window and sat on the sill. 'It's true, Debbie. I've noticed it. He seems to have accepted his situation well. It's as if now that he's comfortable with himself, he can be comfortable with them too.'

'And what about you? Are you beginning to like it here?'

I paused. A wasp landed on the edge of my glass and I waved it away, watching it until it found its way out of the window and disappeared behind the lupins.

'I think I am. But it's been difficult at times. Being further away from you, especially now you have the twins. Lawrence not being able to drive because of his medication means I'm responsible for all the driving. Hampton Stoke is a pretty village and we've at least got a pub, a Post Office shop and a bus once a week. Worst of all was giving up my job and the friends I had there. So no, I didn't want to move and as you know, we had many arguments about it. I didn't see why we should let people's opinions make us move. Especially when we're only guessing about their opinions. But Lawrence is a proud man. And to be honest, this was the only thing he's ever insisted on in all our married life. I mean really insisted upon.'

'But this is such a lovely spot, Jetta,' Debbie said. 'I'd love to be out in a tiny village like this.'

'I guess I'm not a country person. I lived in Swindon all my life. I'm used to being on a bus route, having a reference library handy, theatre, choices. But at least I got my way over the house. Lawrence wanted us to have a modern house, but I dug my heels in and told him that if we did live in the country, we would at least live in a cottage.'

That had caused friction between us. And then there was the trouble over money. Lawrence might have been a successful accountant at Marshwood Engineering, but his own finances were not so well handled. The policies and investments intended to give us a worry-free retirement had small print. Small print that effectively meant we would just about get by financially. After selling *The Gables* and paying off the mortgage, we were able to buy the 'ripe-for-modernisation' *Poplar Cottage* without a mortgage. We had already moved when Lawrence was advised of the small print that dramatically reduced our expected income as he'd given up work early. This meant that, to a large extent, Poplar Cottage would remain unmodernised, however ripe it might be.

It was the garden that saved me. Working out there in all weathers, digging, transplanting, pruning, mowing – it gave me the space I needed. It was my sanctuary. I simply resented the fact that our decisions had been forced because of her.

'Look, Grandma!' Debbie stood up. 'Someone's awake.'

Becky's eyes were open and her arms moved as if she wanted to be picked up.

'Shall I pick her up?' I asked. 'She might start wailing and wake Andrea.'

'Of course, although they seem to wake and sleep on cue together anyway.' And with that Andrea opened her eyes.

The change in the weather was dramatic and quite unlike the forecast. I didn't bother hanging the washing out, instead I put up the wooden clothes horse at the end of the kitchen nearest the old Rayburn. I would try and dry the laundry there.

'At least it stayed dry over the weekend with everyone here,' Lawrence said, finishing his elevenses. I think he sensed my frustration at not being able to get on with any of my gardening projects between washes.

'Yes, that's true.' I rearranged two white double sheets over the clothes horse, and the smell of warm detergent drifted around the kitchen. 'What have you got planned for the rest of the morning?'

'I'm going to see what I can do with the greenhouse. I'll measure the broken panes to see if they can be replaced and I thought I'd use some of that leftover wood to build some staging in there for your seedling trays. At least I'll be in the dry as I don't think this rain is going to let up.'

He was right. It had rained almost continually since first light. I had woken to torrents pouring along the guttering, down the drainpipes and noisily filling the drains. Fortunately I had fixed the downpipe leading from the shed roof into the water butt only the week before and now, to my delight, its water level was rising rapidly.

'OK,' I said. 'Ring the glazier too and if he has the glass in stock, we can collect it later.'

Lawrence pulled on his Macintosh and rain-hat and opened the door, revealing an inky black sky. Thunder clapped as I watched him walk up the path and within seconds lightning lit the sky. The storm was almost directly overhead.

Lunch had become a bit of a ritual and today was no exception. Lawrence sat in what was now considered his chair and I sat on the sofa. We shared a plate of sandwiches, followed by tea and then, on doctor's advice, Lawrence would have a nap. Today we had cold beef sandwiches, leftovers from the Sunday lunch. I added sliced fresh tomatoes, home grown, which Lawrence had brought in earlier from the greenhouse, and a sprinkling of salt. Salt was forbidden as far as Lawrence's diet was concerned, but he always insisted on having a pinch on tomatoes as they were 'simply not the same without'.

I put my head around the sitting room door after I'd cleared away the plates and cups. 'I'll leave you to have a nap, and then we'll go and collect the glass.'

Lawrence, I noticed, was staring at photographs he'd taken off the mantelpiece. The walnut frame held a photograph of us on our wedding day. It was strange the things I remember about that day. I remember it was an unseasonably hot day, around 70°F. I remember the generosity of friends, despite continued rationing, although thankfully no one baked us a squirrel pie, as recommended by the Ministry of Food to help cope with food shortages.

And I remember being anxious, almost panicky, at the prospect of my wedding night. I was a virgin and it was only the evening before that I'd found out from my Maid of Honour's mother what I could expect. My own mother would never discuss any part of anatomy above the knees and below the navel. She once pulled me to one side and whispered that I should expect to get the curse once a month, but more than that she wouldn't say. The prospect of being cursed so regularly filled me with dread, but luckily for me a friend enlightened me.

'You look beautiful there, Jetta.' Lawrence tapped the picture.

'Thank you.' I wanted to say thank you again, over and over. I couldn't remember Lawrence ever telling me I was beautiful. Certainly not since we'd been married. It was unlike him. This was unlike him.

I looked at the black and white photograph, noting for the first time a slight crease across the top right corner. I wasn't beautiful. I could never have been described as beautiful. Attractive, possibly, but I didn't kid myself, I had never been beautiful. Because I was good with a needle and thread, the floor-length white wedding dress flattered me. And the veil was becoming. Lawrence, then 23, had already taken part in a world war and looked fine in his Royal Air Force uniform. The war hadn't long been over, I was 20 and had no idea what life was about. Not really. And later that night I discovered that Lawrence didn't have much idea about some things either. He too was a virgin.

The other photograph was of Lawrence, me and the boys when David was three and Peter was one. It was in a deep, polished leather frame. David wore a short royal blue coat, which I'd knitted, and Peter was in a white romper suit with a panel of red cross-stitch on the bodice. They got their dark hair and colouring from Lawrence, that was easy to see from the photograph. And David and Peter each held an arm of Googlins, the knitted bear my mother made them from the wool left over from David's coat, swinging it to and fro between them.

'I was so proud the day that was taken,' Lawrence said. 'Proud of you. Proud of David. Proud of Peter.' He took hold of my hand and squeezed, gently. 'And I'm still proud. But I never let you know, do I?'

I shrugged and smiled.

'You did a good job raising those boys, Jetta.'

'*We* did a good job.'

'No,' he said, shaking his head. 'Now you're being generous. But I've been doing a lot of thinking lately. I've had time to…and well…I'm trying to make it up to you all. And I will do.'

Encircling his shoulders with my arms, I kissed the top of his head. I don't know when I'd last done that. He smelt of sawdust and Brylcreem and his hair needed washing.

'There's nothing to make up,' I said, and meant it.

He leaned his head back and placed his lips gently on mine. And he kissed me. And the kiss spoke of love, memories and the joy of now. Before he could see the tear that threatened to spill onto my cheek, I patted his shoulders and told him to have his rest. I would go and wash up and wake him with a cup of tea in an hour.

And that's what I did. Except an hour later I couldn't wake him. Even screaming didn't help.

Lawrence was dead.

Chapter Fifteen

Lyme Regis, Dorset, Monday July 2006

On days such as this, I resent dying. Yet I know I am fortunate to have already taken more than my biblical three score years and ten. It isn't so much that I'm dying, I suppose everyone is, right from the moment they're born. It's the realisation of all that I haven't done, or appreciated, or will now never do. It's a bugger. It really is.

Below, in the garden, hotel guests breakfast outdoors. It's not yet nine o'clock, but already the breeze drifting in through the open window carries the heat of the sun. I feel strange suddenly. As if I am part of the scene. Being witnessed rather than the witness. I feel the blades of grass from the lawn tickle my legs and the smell of the ocean wisps into my nostrils. I am the curve of The Cobb. The red fishing boat bobbing in the harbour. The glint of the sun against the old stone wall. For a moment, I am it all.

I try and hang on to the feeling, it's rather delicious. Yet the more I try, the more it fades. I look again across to the scarves of coastline, sea and sky. Once more I am the observer. Surely no one would want to part themselves from this beauty, this tranquillity. Yet, as the sound of seagulls screeching breaks my spell, I acknowledge that life isn't always this perfect. Sometimes it gets fractured. Smashed. And hell encroaches too. It must do, otherwise I wouldn't even be here.

Today was to be my day of rest. Although yesterday, after my near encounter with Bibby, I had sped back up the hill to the hotel in record time, I'd hardly noticed the climb or the distance. It reminded me of something I'd read somewhere about how shocks can give people bursts of strength and energy, which accounted for them performing heroic acts in the face of adversity. People who couldn't usually lift a heavy shopping bag could lift a car off someone trapped beneath. Or they carried people twice their own weight out of burning buildings. Maybe the shock of seeing Bibby had given me such a burst. But if it had, the energy spent had left me weaker than ever today. I decided this was an omen for me to rest, at least physically. There was nothing to stop me thinking. Besides, after yesterday's brief encounter, a seed of something was nagging away at the back of my mind. Something which, if I could only bring it to the fore, I felt certain would help my plans.

Noticing it was past nine now, I picked up my handbag and left the room, placing a 'Do Not Disturb' sign over the handle. Not that I had the energy for much this morning. Scrambled eggs and coffee would be plenty for breakfast, then I would ring Marilyn.

It was mid-afternoon by the time I tried Marilyn's number. Her home number rang and rang and I felt guilty. I'd initially intended calling her on Saturday, but got engrossed in a *Midsomer Murder* on one of the hotel's numerous TV channels. The irony of which wasn't lost on me as I watched DCI Barnaby and Sgt Troy trying to solve yet another murder. And last evening, ringing Marilyn had simply gone right out of my head, something which appeared to be happening more and more frequently.

Marilyn did, however, answer her mobile.

'It's Jetta. How are you?'

'More to the point, how are you?'

'Getting more forgetful with every day, but apart from that...'

'Where are you?'

'I'm sat in a hotel room with the most splendid view of the sea and coastline,' I said, suddenly wishing I hadn't given so much detail.

'Where?'

'On the south coast still.'

'You're being deliberately evasive, Jetta. What does it matter if I know where you are? I'm not going to come and drag you home.'

I knew she was right. But I couldn't let there be any ties between me and here. Just in case. So I closed my eyes and, hating myself for it, said, 'Torquay.'

'Torquay! Jetta, I simply can't imagine you going to Torquay! Do you have friends there?'

'No...no, it's just that I haven't been here for years so I thought I'd spend a day and a night here.'

'Where to next?'

'Wherever the mood takes me. But enough of my travels. Tell me how you and yours are. How the cats are doing? And whatever other news you can think of.'

'I'm good, though I spent too long in the sun over the weekend. Tony and I were gardening and now we're both a bright shade of pink. And it looks most unflattering on me. The cats miss you, I'm sure, although your absence hasn't affected their appetites. Their bowls are always licked gleamingly clean. And the news is that you are all over the village.'

'Me? What do you mean?'

'Well, Jetta, you didn't seriously think your incident with Peggy would go unannounced?'

'Oh, my goodness. I'd forgotten all about it. Truly I had.'

'Well, fortunately for you, so has she,'

'What do you mean? You just said that—'

'I know,' Marilyn laughed. 'I was teasing. It seems I really am the only person she's told. She paid me a visit and asked if we might keep the incident between ourselves. She didn't think it would do you any good if it got out...'

'Do me any good!'

'I know, I know, Jetta. But you know what she's like, she has to save face. You and I both know that she would be mortified if anyone knew she'd incurred that reaction from you. And everyone would be pleased, secretly or not, I can assure you. They would think the worse of her, not you, and I suspect Geoffrey explained that to her.'

'Do you think so?'

'I'm convinced so. Perhaps he'd had enough of her that day too and when she told him what you'd said, he told her a few home truths. Maybe, if he was mad enough, he told her that everyone was dying to say it to her but that most were far too polite.'

'Do you believe that?'

'Yes, I do. Let's be honest, Jetta, Peggy isn't a likeable woman. She's self-centred, which is putting it mildly, opinionated and a gossip. They're hardly qualities that endear her to folk. Honestly, Jetta, if you'd done what you did publicly you would have received a standing ovation.'

I laughed at the thought.

'Any idea when you're coming back yet?'

'Not really. Not just yet. I'll definitely be away until the end of this week though.'

'OK,' Marilyn said. 'But don't worry about a thing. Your cats and cottage are fine.'

'Thanks, Marilyn. You're a good friend.'

'Aren't I just?' she said. 'Oh, and something else I meant to tell you. Bill from the Ring o' Bells is on crutches. He fell down the trap door apparently, broke his leg and is suing the brewery for negligence because...'

But I wasn't listening. The seed that had been irritating me since seeing Bibby the day before had germinated.

'That's it! Marilyn, you've done it,' I interrupted.

'Done what? What's happening? What are you on about?'

'Sorry, Marilyn, ignore me. It's the answer to something that's been puzzling me all morning.'

'Do you ever let your mind rest?'

I laughed. 'Not if I can help it! Anyway, I'll call you again later in the week. And thanks. Thanks for everything.'

After I'd finished the call to Marilyn I leaned back in the chair and smiled. That was it. Bibby walked with a limp, a pronounced limp. Of course, I'd first seen her at the rheumatic hospital in Bath and this, I was sure, was the link I needed to gain access to her apartment. I simply needed to work out how. I remained at the desk with my spiral pad and pen in front of me but couldn't seem to pull any thoughts from the tangle in my head. I knew I'd promised myself a day off, but I needed a walk.

I sat on the wooden bench at Bell Cliff, short of breath, having walked almost the length of Broad Street. I could easily tire of long hot days. In the car park below, a group of backpackers paused hopefully outside *The Cobb Gate Fish Bar*. It was closed. One of them pointed to *The Pilot Boat Inn* across the road, beyond which a square church tower nudged the skyline. They needn't worry, I thought, my gaze drifting to the coastline; from my limited experience of the town there wasn't a shortage of places to eat and drink.

'Hello again.'

I looked up to see the gentleman from Bibby's café.

'Hello, Charles, isn't it?' I rapidly pushed all thoughts of Clark Gable from my mind.

'Well remembered, Jean.'

'Ditto,' I said, rising from the bench and, putting my hand to my hair, fingering a few strands around my ears. I didn't want to get involved in conversation. 'But I was about to get going,' I lied. 'Sorry I can't stop.'

I made my way to a nearby tea room, pausing to read the specials chalked on the blackboard by the door. Not that I needed prompting. As I went down the stone steps into the tea rooms, I knew I would have a cream tea.

'Are you meeting anyone?'

I turned. Charles was standing behind me. 'No,' I said, quickly realising my mistake.

'In which case, would you mind if I joined you? It's just that I assume you're on your own, as am I, and I get the feeling I'd enjoy your company.'

'As long as you realise I'm not in the habit of taking tea with strangers.' Even I wanted to laugh at my pompous response.

'Of course,' he said, extending his arm for me to continue down the steps before him. 'Of course.' And I had a feeling that inwardly he was laughing at me.

The Bell Cliff Tea Rooms were busy and, after seating ourselves at a table near the central panelled wall, we ordered a cream tea for two. Charles talked with ease and, apart from a few comments, I sat in relative silence until our order arrived. I watched Charles split his scones neatly before carefully spooning in thick cream and jam, all of which was produced locally, according to the menu.

'Would you like me to pour your tea too?' I asked as he took a bite of scone.

He nodded, putting his hand to his mouth to save a dribble of red jam dropping to his napkin.

I was a messy eater and immediately I began to tuck in, crumbs of scone dropped to my plate, along with a blob of jam and cream. I quickly checked to see if Charles had noticed but he seemed oblivious to my table manners.

'Delicious,' he said, preparing his second piece of scone after taking a sip of tea.

I nodded in agreement, watching his long nimble fingers. Not a hint of an arthritic joint. In fact he looked remarkably lithe. He had a fine upright posture and, much like myself, he carried no extra weight either. People often said I was too thin, but it was usually overweight people who made the comment.

Charles' white hair was thick and well cut, I thought, and his shaved neck hair told me he was a man who looked after himself. For the first time since Lawrence died, I found myself thinking that it might be nice to have a companion. A male friend. And I wondered what the family or Marilyn would say if they could see me sat at a table for two with a strange man.

'Are you on holiday?' Charles asked, wiping his mouth on his napkin before screwing it up and throwing it onto his empty plate.

'Wouldn't really call it a holiday. More a few days away. What about you?' I asked in an attempt to divert his attention from me.

'I live here.' I don't know why his answer surprised me, but it did, and before I had a chance to reply he added, 'And I don't make a habit of joining women for cream teas, if that's what you're thinking.'

I laughed. 'It wouldn't be my business if you did,' I said, though strangely I felt flattered at his reply.

But what was I doing sat here enjoying the company of a man I didn't know, when I had promised myself I would keep a low profile? I was my own worst enemy. I always did talk too much. Too freely. It was one of the highlighted differences between Lawrence and me. I would make conversation with anybody and everybody, whereas he was always polite and no more. I would put a stop to this before I gave away too much about myself.

I took a five pound note from my purse. 'I've just remembered I've got to get going.' I laid the note on the table and stood up, 'And here's something for my share of the tea.'

'Please,' Charles stood up. 'I tagged along with you, remember, paying is the least I can do.'

'No, really, I wouldn't dream of it. Thank you for your company.' And I swiftly left the tea room without giving Charles a chance to say another word.

The late afternoon sun was still hot and the walk back to the hotel took it out of me. But instead of going to my room to rest, I got into my car and drove back down through the town. Within minutes I was parked in the lay-by near Cliffside Apartments. I had decided to keep watch over Bibby for a second evening to see if she followed the same pattern.

She did. A taxi pulled up, a white taxi the same as before, at 6.30, only minutes earlier than it had on Friday. The driver held open the rear passenger door and Bibby emerged clutching a handbag and a Co-op carrier. I watched as he walked with her towards the apartments' entrance. She placed her hand on his arm and he threw his head back and laughed. She had him under her spell. She might be older now, as were the men she charmed, but it was obvious that charm them still she did.

After the taxi pulled away I drove to the rear of the apartments and watched her balcony. And sure enough, within less than ten minutes, she appeared with what could only be a bottle of wine in one hand and a glass in the other. Placing them on the table beside her, she came to the balcony's edge and even from where I stood, I noticed her limp. She was unsteady on her feet. And, watching her lean on the balcony and gaze out to sea, I imagined how easy it would be for someone as unsteady as her to topple. To topple over the balcony onto the hard jagged landscape below. It wouldn't take much. Especially with a little help from a 'friend'.

Chapter Sixteen

Lyme Regis, Dorset, Tuesday, July 2006

It was after lunch and I lay propped against a pile of soft pillows on the bed in my room. I was tired, but not as tired as I had expected, considering I hadn't slept for a minute the night before. On the horizon I noticed rain clouds, darkening by the minute, threatening to burst and I, for one, wouldn't be sorry. Thunder had rumbled long and low throughout the night and once or twice I thought I'd seen flashes of lightning, yet still no rain. It could only be a matter of time.

Picking up my new mobile from the coverlet beside me, I clasped it in both hands, fearful of what I was about to do. This had to work. Had to. If it didn't, I would have to start all over again with another plan, another plot, another scheme, though I had no idea what. I had already spent the night, fuelled by mugs of dark coffee, coming up with this one.

I would ring Bibby now whilst she was at work. She would be busier and have less time or inclination to ask too many questions. The down side was that she might not want to talk at all. As I keyed in the number, 01297 44…my hands trembled. I looked at my thin, large-veined hands. I had a touch of arthritis in my left index finger and right thumb, though not enough to worry me. These hands had cooked meals, rocked babies and planted bulbs. They had written letters, driven miles and worked thanklessly for

80 years. Yet never once had I envisaged that they would murder. Not until that moment. The moment when Bibby stood…

It's no good, Jetta, I chided myself, *just do it. Stop thinking and dial.* But that didn't stop me shaking as I pressed the final four digits.

When the number rang I wanted to stop the call, switch the phone off, do anything other than what I was about to do. Yet if I didn't do it now, when would I?

The phone wasn't answered immediately and part of me thanked some invisible deity. Maybe an answering machine would take the call or it would be left unanswered if they were busy. But before I had a chance to speculate further, a voice came on the line. *Her* voice.

'Bibby's Café and Gifts. Good afternoon.'

My mouth was instantly dry and I wished I'd thought to put a glass of water within reach.

'I'd like to speak with Elizabeth Fellowes. Bibby Fellowes, if that's possible please,' I said, after what seemed an age.

'Speaking.' She sounded almost pleasant.

'Ah…Mrs Fellowes, you won't know me, my name is Jean Francis and I'm helping the patients' group at The Royal National Hospital for Rheumatic Diseases.'

'Oh, yes.'

'Several patients have had their names chosen at random to see if they're willing to help with a survey I'm conducting on behalf of the patients' group. You're one of those names,' I said, stopping to run my too dry tongue around my too dry lips. 'And I'm contacting you to ask if it's convenient for me to call to see you so you can help us with our survey.'

'Well, I work and it's not convenient…'

'I'm happy to come to your home, Mrs Fellowes, and it won't take more than half an hour. And it really would be an enormous help to patients now and in the future.'

There was a pause I didn't fill. Couldn't fill. My mouth had ceased working. My tongue was unable to help form words.

'I don't get home until around seven most evenings, and I don't suppose you can come during the evening...'

'That's not a problem to me,' I said, sensing her barriers drop slightly. 'And as it's to be an evening appointment, I'll even bring a bottle of wine. It's not exactly part of the rules, so we won't put that on the form, but I really would appreciate your help with this. You're one of the few younger patients, you see, so your views would be an enormous help.' I stopped, aware always that I could say too much.

As she spoke, a crack of thunder boomed overhead and drowned out her answer.

'Sorry, I didn't catch that.'

'Yes. I said yes, but only if you can make it Wednesday, as in tomorrow night. It really is the only evening I can do this week. I'm sorry if that's not any use to you.'

'Oh, but it is.' I felt my shoulders relax. 'Now, what do you prefer – red or white, or rosé?'

'There's really no need, Mrs....er...'

'Francis.'

'Yes, sorry, Mrs Francis.'

'I insist,' I said. 'It's the least I can do.'

'Well, since you insist, I prefer a dry white.'

'And what time would be best for me to call?'

'Let's say 7.30. Do you know where to come?'

'The hospital gave me your address, so I'm sure I'll find it. I look forward to seeing you tomorrow evening at 7.30.' And with that I hung up before either of us could change a thing.

The rain came as I congratulated myself on my performance. Spits at first that slid slowly down the window panes until, amidst much cracking of thunder, the heavens opened. I forced myself off the bed and across to the window. The breeze was almost chilly, and reluctantly I closed the window. Everything had gone like clockwork. I knew I had to get into her flat, invited, during the evening, with wine if the first part of my plan was to work. And that's exactly what I'd achieved. The rest I hadn't finalised yet but I had almost 24 hours in which to do so. And with that thought in mind, I sat at the desk with my pad in front of me and listened to the rain pounding on the window.

The next part wasn't going to be a fraction as easy. But nothing was ever achieved by procrastination, I'd learned that. If only I'd learned that earlier, much earlier in life. But I wasn't going to go down that route. I remembered Omar Khayyam's words:

The moving finger writes and having writ
Moves on, nor all thy piety nor wit
Shall lure it back to cancel even half a line
Nor all thy tears wash away a word of it.

So I picked up my pen and began to write. A list in blue ink which started:

Wine (white, dry)
Identity tag
Clipboard

And, as I continued to write, the plan began to form in my mind. The plan which, if successful, meant that by tomorrow night, Bibby Fellowes would be no more. She would be dead. Murdered. And as far as the police were concerned, it would be by person or persons unknown.

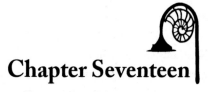

Chapter Seventeen

Lyme Regis, Dorset, Wednesday, July 2006

The best time to visit reception, I decided, was during breakfast when the hotel staff were busy. By eight, I had showered, pampered myself with the hotel's complimentary magnolia body lotion, and was about to dress. Sat on the edge of the bed in my cream petticoat, I realised I was running out of clean clothes. Either I would have to visit the charity shop in the hope of finding something suitable, or find a launderette.

I rolled a pair of tan tights up my legs, wishing I was the sort of woman who could go tightless. But I wasn't. It wasn't proper. The sight of my pale 80 year old legs without tights wasn't a sight I wished to share. And as I pulled on a straight green linen skirt, I realised how ingrained my habits and beliefs were. I smiled at myself. In the scheme of what I was about to do, going tightless outdoors wasn't worth a mention. Murder was.

With a dab of face powder on my nose, cheeks and forehead, pale blue shadow on my eyes, and a stroke of orange on my lips, I was ready to face the world. Picking up my handbag and cotton shopping bag, I left the room and went along the wide corridor to the landing. From here, if I leaned far enough over the balustrade, I could see into the reception area below, certainly enough to see if it was manned or not. It was. Matthew stood with his back to the small office, which lay behind the desk, looking through a sheaf of papers. I'd return later.

At 8.30 I took my chance. The reception was empty and the dining room was almost full, and it seemed that with a couple of staff off sick, it was all hands on deck. Maybe even Matthew had been called upon to wait tables as I couldn't see him anywhere – although I could hear guests requesting eggs turned, scrambled and poached; hot buttered toast with smoked kippers and pots of breakfast tea or freshly ground coffee.

At reception I casually leaned an elbow on the counter and, after checking there was no one in sight, peered over at the desk behind. It was remarkably clear except for a neat pile of brochures, room keys on hooks, a mug of pens and a guest book. Everything else I guessed must be kept in the office. Checking the coast was still clear, I ducked behind the counter and knocked on the office door. Getting no response, I tried the handle. Unlocked. An open invitation if ever there was one.

I slipped in and shut the door behind me. Three desks almost filled the floor space, a computer stood on one, and on the far wall was a staff rota covered in black, red and green marker pen. Cups half full of cold dark coffee sat on desks alongside empty Twix wrappers and there were piles of paper everywhere. The place was a tip and how anyone knew where anything was, I couldn't guess.

Luckily, that wasn't my concern. I was looking for something else and it didn't take many minutes to find one lying in a letter tray on top of a grey two-drawer filing cabinet. The staff security badge had a card with a picture already in it and, unlike Matthew's, it was on a chain to hang around the neck. It would do perfectly.

'Mrs Francis. What are you doing here?'

I turned to see Matthew coming through the doorway. Quick thinking was needed, but I couldn't think.

'What are you doing?' he repeated, seeming more puzzled than angry.

'I…I was looking for you,' I said. 'And when I couldn't raise you on the desk I thought perhaps you were in here working. Still, now you're here, perhaps you can help me.'

'Certainly. What did you want?'

'I wanted to know something.'

After a long pause, during which Matthew could only stare at me, he said, 'Know what?'

'Dare say I shouldn't be in here, should I?' I said, playing for time.

'It is usually out of bounds to guests.'

'There you are,' I said, moving slowly towards the door and smiling. 'Let's not break any hotel rules.' And as soon as Matthew turned to leave, I snatched the identity tag from the tray, dropped it into my shopping bag and followed meekly behind.

'Can you remember what it was you wanted to see me about?' he said from his position back behind reception.

'Yes,' I said, pleased at my sudden quickness of thought. 'Is there a launderette in the town?'

'I think we can do better than that, Mrs Francis,' he said, taking a leaflet from the desk and handing it to me. 'We have a laundry service here at the hotel and this tells you all you need to know.'

I took it, dropped it into my shopping bag and thanked him before heading towards the dining room for breakfast. So far so good could surely become my mantra.

The Post Office in Broad Street stocked clipboards in an assort-ment of colours and I selected black. It seemed fitting. I bought an A4 pad there too before going to the nearby Co-op, where I bought two bottles of Australian Chardonnay and, as an after-thought, a packet of chicken salad sandwiches for lunch.

By the time I crossed the street to the charity shop it was drizzling and I bought a rain hat which I was certain matched my raincoat. Walking slowly back towards the hotel, I mentally ticked the items off my list one by one. But before I reached the milliners I spotted a familiar figure across the road. It was Charles, standing outside *The Mad Hatter* restaurant. I immediately bowed my head in the hope he wouldn't see me. It worked. It wasn't that I didn't like him; I did. And under any other circumstances I would have crossed the road to talk to him. But circumstances dictated I get back to the hotel unscathed and unseen. My plan was to gather my props this morning and rest this afternoon and, so far, my plan was shaping up well. Rest was essential, because whatever happened this evening I would need energy and lots of it. And I had to be prepared for any eventuality. Well, as much as I ever could be.

Walking up to the hotel entrance, I realised it was a place I'd become comfortable with in less than a week. The herbaceous borders glistened under a mantle of raindrops and a blackbird hopped across the lawn flapping is wings and tail madly, giving a warning chook as a ginger cat edged its way between a butterfly bush and a white flowered rambler I couldn't identify. It was strange the things that moved me. The sight of a yellow beak jabbing the lawn in search of a worm. A flower losing its final petal to the breeze. And as I went up the wide steps into the hotel hallway, I recalled how as a child I'd stood in front of the class nervously reciting the words of William Henley:

> *The nightingale has a lyre of gold,*
> *The lark's a clarion call,*
> *And the blackbird plays but a boxwood flute,*
> *But I love him best of all.*

Funny the things I remembered, and when.

'Did you enjoy your walk, Mrs Francis?' Matthew smiled at me from behind the reception.

135

'Yes. Much better now it isn't so hot.' I removed my rain hat and placed the heavy shopping bag on the red carpet.

'Would you like me to carry that up for you?'

Before I could reply, he came from behind the desk and lifted the bag, causing the wine bottles to clink loudly.

'They're presents,' I said, following him up the stairs.

'You don't have to answer to me, Mrs Francis,' he said, turning to wink at me. 'You are on holiday, after all.'

Usually I would have argued, but I was too busy running out of energy. By the time Matthew left my room, my breathing was shallow and every muscle, bone and organ ached. And I had learned that when I felt this way there was only one answer: painkillers and rest.

Terrified of oversleeping, I sat on the edge of the bed and rang reception.

'Yes, Mrs Francis.'

'Matthew, I forgot to say I'd like an alarm call for three o'clock.'

'Certainly. I'll make sure you get a call then.'

I expected to be awake before then, but I must be sensible and make back-up plans. There was still much to organise and there was no room for error. Placing a few pillows behind me and one under my drawn up knees, I curled into a comfortable position. The window was still closed and now, with the rain stopped and the sun emerging, the room would eventually become too hot. But for now I wasn't going to move. It required too much effort.

It's funny the things I noticed when I stopped. When I stopped doing and started being. I noticed details that had previously gone unnoticed, such as the upholstery on the chair. It depicted a colourful elephant, an Indian elephant. I could see that now; now that I'd taken the time to stop, to slow down. And I was at that welcome stage where sleep was almost upon me. The painkillers were taking effect and my limbs felt loose and light.

And that was the last I remembered until the phone rang and Matthew told me it was three o'clock.

I was half-asleep as I replaced the handset. I'd been in the midst of a dream I couldn't remember and my head felt full of cotton wool. Forcing myself upright, I realised that in four hours I would be making my way to Cliffside Apartments. And the enormity of what I was about to do hit me.

I ran the cold water and splashed it on my face and on the inside of my wrists. I was getting anxious. I knew the signs. A slight tremor, increased heart rate, light-headedness. Soon, I would be sat face to face with the woman who had come into my family's life and wrecked it. Bit by bit, by bit.

I reached for the bathroom light pull and caught sight of an old lady in the mirror. That was one thing – surely Bibby would never recognise me. How could she? I almost didn't recognise myself.

I tried to pull back the wrapper on the chicken salad sandwiches but couldn't, so resorted to using my teeth, which worked. Packaging these days was impossible – child-proof, tamper-proof, theft-proof – it didn't matter that the average purchaser couldn't access the goods as long as it met with some European Packaging Directive. Not so long ago, I'd written letters about it to the local newspapers.

Biting into the sandwich was difficult. I wasn't hungry. I felt sick at the prospect of food, yet felt I must eat something. I refilled the kettle and turned it on before opening the window and sitting at the desk. I really ought to sit still and eat. I'd get indigestion walking and eating, though it seemed to be the done thing nowadays. Everywhere I looked people were pacing the streets chomping.

The kettle boiled before I'd finished the sandwiches, but I made myself stay still until five minutes after I'd taken the last bite. Then I made a cup of Earl Grey, took it back to the desk and began my lists. There was the list of things to do before I left, and the list of things I needed to take with me. And, as I sat there with the distant sound of screeching gulls and laughter trickling through the open window, my tension eased and I felt a sense of calm wash over me.

As if murder was the most natural thing in the world.

Chapter Eighteen

Lyme Regis, Dorset, Early Wednesday Evening, July 2006
The traffic lights at the bottom of Broad Street turned red as I approached and I drew the car to a gentle halt. It was almost 7.15. I'd noticed a queue outside the fish and chip shop near the clock tower and the smell of frying drifted in the open car window. I wasn't hungry. On the opposite side of the road a teenage girl fed a dark-haired young man chips as they walked in the direction of the Tourist Information Centre. His hands were otherwise engaged. One holding up his baggy jeans, the other tucked into the back of her trousers. How times had changed.

Half an hour earlier I had sat in the hotel bar with a gin and tonic for Dutch courage, even though I'd taken several painkillers before leaving my room. The leaflet accompanying the medication said they were not to be taken with alcohol. It said much else too, most of which was to list their side-effects. I gave up reading after 'spasm of the bile ducts and inflammation of the liver or pancreas'. I was unconcerned; for the moment they helped the pain. I didn't kid myself I would be around for any long-term damage they might do.

Strangely enough, in the few minutes it took for the lights to turn green and for me to drive out of the town centre, I felt more collected. More in control. Maybe the gin and pills were taking effect. The town was full of holidaymakers and I slowed as a muscular young man in shorts, carrying a young boy on his shoulders, criss-crossed the road absent-mindedly near the car park. A lady, presumably his wife, shouted after him, 'Watch where you're going, you silly bugger!' and gave me an apologetic look as I drove past.

Once in Cliffside Road, I pulled into the lay-by and tucked the nearside of my car up against the hedge. Hopefully it was barely noticeable from the apartment block. Better than leaving it in the car park where prying eyes might remember the number plate. I got out of the car, locked it, checked my cardigan pockets and walked towards the apartments clutching my handbag and a Co-op carrier bag. Co-op carriers were commonplace in Lyme.

I had all I needed. And I felt certain my ploy was strong enough not to arouse suspicion. After all, it seemed plausible that someone from the hospital where Bibby was a patient would contact her. Who else would know she was a patient? It wasn't as if it was a local hospital that everyone might attend. This was a specialist rheumatic hospital, in Bath too, a couple of hours' drive away. And it wouldn't seem out of place that someone of my age would be a patient or a member of its Patients' Group. No, all in all, I thought this part of my plan stood up well to scrutiny. All I had to do was follow through on the rest.

As I crossed the road towards the apartments, I felt in control, if slightly light-headed. The building appeared to be moving towards me as opposed to me moving towards it. Where the uneven road turned into the apartments' entrance, the tarmac was cracked and I walked steadily, so as not to trip, yet not too fast. It was important I remained as anonymous as possible in case seen. Luckily there wasn't a soul about. I supposed the only people that came this far down a dead end were coming to the apartments and, with some of them empty, the traffic, pedestrian or otherwise, would be limited.

A footpath led to the front of the building and ended at a wide recessed entranceway. Set into the right hand wall I noticed a square speaker alongside rows of chrome-coloured round buttons. I set my carrier down on the step in front of the double half-glazed doors and looked closer. All the buttons had names beside them, yet many were faded and almost illegible. I worked my way down the names to find the one I wanted at the bottom. *Number 16. Fellowes. E.* Despite being anxious, frightened possibly, I felt strangely excited. An odd combination of fear and anticipation. A combination that wasn't, after all, unpleasant.

Previously I'd decided I wasn't going to be overly concerned about leaving fingerprints. I couldn't imagine my ever being a suspect and my fingerprints had never been taken so were definitely not on any computerised records the police held. However, I wouldn't be silly and take unnecessary risks either. I pressed the round button next to her name with the knuckle of my index finger and waited. Nothing. No answer. I waited a minute or so and pressed again. Nothing. I couldn't believe that I'd gone to all this planning for her not to be here. I'd thought of everything, except this.

I rang again, pressing the button harder and for longer this time.

'Yes?' a woman's voice said immediately.

'I'm from The Mineral Hospital Patients' Group. We spoke yesterday. I said I'd…'

'Of course. Push the entrance door when the buzzer sounds, take the lift to the fourth floor and I'm number 16.'

The buzzer sounded and I plucked my carrier bag from the step and pushed the door open. Inside the foyer was cool, a welcome change from the muggy evening, and behind me the door shut automatically. I was surprised at how well appointed the entrance was. A reproduction Pembroke table sat neatly between a pair of Regency style chairs and several decorative seascapes brightened the walls. As I crossed to the lift I noticed a well tended rubber plant in a gleaming brass planter. Someone obviously made the effort to keep everything tidy.

I kept my head bowed permanently in case there were security cameras. It wouldn't look that odd for a woman of 80 with arthritis. Once inside the lift I put my carrier down and watched as the shiny steel doors slid closed. This was it. No going back. I closed my eyes. 'Come on, Jetta, old girl. You can do it,' I said aloud, reaching out and pressing the button for the fourth floor with my knuckle.

When the lift came to a standstill the doors parted slowly, revealing a carpet-tiled hallway. A sign on the wall opposite indicated Apartment 16 was to the left. Stepping out of the lift, I followed the sign and towards the end of the hall on the right I came to her door. It was ajar.

Taking several deep breaths, I reminded myself that all I had to do was act. Act a part. Be Jean Francis, steadfast member of the Patients' Group for the evening. That's all it would take. An act. And with that I pushed the door open, put my head around and called into the dimly lit hallway.

'Hello? Hello, anyone home?'

Bibby stepped into the hall from an open doorway and limped towards me, her right hand outstretched. 'Hello, Mrs Francis, isn't it?'

'Yes…yes, that's right.' I shook her hand, willing myself not to recoil. 'Fancy you remembering.'

'I'm good with names. Not so good with faces though.'

That's good for me, I thought as she pushed the front door closed. Unless…no, she couldn't be bluffing. She couldn't possibly remember me. Nonetheless, it would pay me to remember who I was dealing with.

'Let's go in the sitting room.'

I followed her through the open door and was reminded of the first time I'd seen her. She had stood 6 feet tall in platform boots and she was almost as slim now as she'd been then. The memory of her then, how she had been, caused a pressure to build within me, yet I knew I must remain cool. For the moment I was Jean Francis.

The sitting room was not what I'd expected. Set on the corner of the building, it was at least 30 square feet with picture windows around two sides. French doors led out onto the balcony, which also wrapped around both sides. And it was the view that took my attention.

'My goodness!' Holding on to the carrier, I crossed to the window. 'What a view!'

No rooftops. No treetops. No cliffs. Just an uninterrupted view of Lyme Bay with nothing other than bobbing buoys and sailing vessels between here and the horizon. If I'd wondered before about why she chose to stay in an apartment that would eventually slip down the cliff, I now had the answer.

She opened the French doors. 'It is very beautiful. Would you like to look from out here?'

I stepped out onto the balcony after her and couldn't help smiling. Later this evening, under cover of darkness, she could come out here. I would suggest it. But she would be very different from the way she was now. She would feel groggy, fuzzy-headed, drunk perhaps. In truth she would be drugged, medicated, poisoned. She'd lean lazily on the rail in an attempt to keep herself upright. The rail at the side of the apartment that didn't overlook the car park. The rail well away from the chance of a prying eye. I'd make sure of that.

And when she least expected it I would grasp her slender ankles and in one swift movement, I would upend her. I could do that. I knew I could. And I would tip her body over the rail and watch as it dropped and finally thudded against the rocks almost 50 feet below. Her head would strike the rocks and break open. Wide open. Her body would smack the stones immediately after. In pieces. As had Peter's life when she'd finished with him. And her blood would spatter far and wide from the force of the impact, as the repercussions of her actions had upon my family. And she would be dead. Dead. Unable to use her sick warped charm on Peter or anyone like him ever again. My only misgiving was that it would be quick. Too quick. Too painless. Unlike the poison she'd drip-fed into my family. Unlike the way she'd killed Lawrence.

'I never tire of the view,' Bibby was saying as she walked back into the sitting room. 'Never. Now, where would you be most comfortable, Jean?'

'Where will you sit?'

'I usually sit on this chair.' Bibby patted the back of an armchair facing the coffee table. 'It's a bit higher than the rest and with my hip, but if you would–'

'No, that's fine. I'll sit there.' I pointed to the large comfy sofa on the opposite side of the table. 'I can spread my papers around a bit. But first things first.' I reached into the carrier and took out the Chardonnay. 'I hope you like this.'

Bibby reluctantly took hold of the bottle. 'You needn't have done. Yet I have to say, it's most welcome. And it's nice to have someone to share a glass with. So, if you'll join me, I'll get a couple of glasses.'

'I'd love to.'

Clutching the wine bottle, she went through a door into what was presumably the kitchen. I would have to get rid of my wine somewhere. I couldn't possibly drink any more alcohol. I needed to keep a clear head.

I looked around me. The room was pleasantly furnished. Large comfy sofas, an upright piano, full bookcases, Indian rugs and an eclectic mix of paintings and *objets d'art*. A large wide television was perched on a stand at the other end of the room and nearer to me a mahogany side table was topped with a pair of Victorian vases and a photograph in an ornate silver frame. The room was tidy yet not obsessively so. It was obviously a lived-in apartment. Lived in by someone with a life.

Though not for much longer.

Bibby returned with two glasses and put them and the opened wine on the coffee table. Seizing my chance whilst she was occupied pouring the wine, I began my rehearsed introduction.

'Better get the formalities over with whilst you're doing that,' I said, and from my cardigan pocket I pulled out the identification card I'd taken from the hotel and waved it in her general direction. 'This shows you I am who I say I am. Jean Francis. I'm on the main committee of The Patients' Group of The Royal National Hospital for Rheumatic Diseases. Or The Min or Mineral Hospital, as you may prefer to call it.'

Bibby raised her head and glanced at my identification tag as I stowed it back in my pocket.

'Yes, I see.' Clearly she hadn't.

'The Patients' Group are conducting a survey to see how patients view their experiences as outpatients.'

'Doesn't the hospital conduct such surveys?'

'I'm sure they do. But we feel that as lay people and users of the service ourselves, people are more candid with us about their experiences, especially any less than favourable comments. We then share any concerns with the hospital staff in the hope that our ideas and comments will be implemented. People feel it's safer for a group to voice concerns or bad experiences, if any, because they worry that as an individual they might be considered a troublemaker or, worse, have their treatment compromised. This isn't going to happen, of course, but nonetheless if people fear it would they'll never be honest. This way, we as a group voice the concerns so individuals remain anonymous.'

'That sounds perfectly feasible.' Bibby placed the bottle on the table between us and held her glass up. 'Cheers.'

'Cheers.' I lifted my glass and took the tiniest of sips before placing it back on the table.

Bibby leaned back in her chair and looked at me over the top of her glass. 'So, how can I help?'

'We've compiled a questionnaire and after choosing patients at random, we interview them one by one, as I am with you this evening. Your answers are kept confidential, so you'll have to do no more than what you're doing with me now. But you can rest assured your help will ensure a better service not only for yourself and current patients, but for future patients.

'First I ask you a series of set questions before asking about your particular experiences.' I took the pad and pen from my bag as Bibby nodded in agreement. I was finding it difficult to concentrate. I needed to get her to set her glass down and leave the room. 'Firstly, just a few basic questions.' I frowned and put my palm to my forehead. 'Oh dear, how silly of me, I've forgotten to take my tablets. Do you think I could trouble you for a glass of water before we go any further?'

'Of course.' Bibby eased herself from the chair, set her almost full glass down on the table and went to the kitchen.

I had no time to lose. As soon as her back was turned I withdrew one of the several twists of greaseproof paper from my pocket, together with two tiny breath mints. I opened the twist and leaned forward, ready to shake the decapsulated sleeping powder into her wine.

'Do you want water or would you prefer fruit juice?'

I looked up to see Bibby stood in the doorway. Oh my goodness. Had she seen me? No, what was there to see? Nothing yet.

'I'll have squash, if that's OK. I prefer it,' I said, knowing it would take longer to prepare.

'I've only got blackcurrant.'

'My favourite.'

'Ice?'

'No. Actually, yes. Yes, I will.' I smiled as I watched her turn and go back into the kitchen.

Wasting no time, I tipped the powder into her wine and watched as it lay across the top of the wine in a white coil. Needing to act quickly, and in the absence of anything else, I used my finger to stir. Slowly the powder dissolved and Bibby reappeared as I threw the empty greaseproof twist into the bottom of the carrier. Picking up the two white mints from the coffee table, I took them with the squash, pulling a face each time.

Opposite me Bibby raised her glass to her lips, took a large gulp of wine and paused. I prayed. Prayed she wouldn't detect a different taste. Prayed she would drink a lot. Prayed she would drink quickly. That would make it all a lot easier.

'Plenty more where that came from,' I said, pointing to the carrier bag. 'I've another bottle here.'

'Um…tastes a bit…don't know how you'd describe it really,' she said, before tasting more.

I picked up my glass and sipped. 'Yes, there is rather a prominent taste, but I don't think it's unpleasant. Trouble is, I'm not too good when it comes to choosing wines. I'm sorry if it's not…'

'Oh dear! How insensitive of me. Please don't think I'm suggesting there's anything wrong with your choice. Take no notice of me. A wine buff I'm not.'

Using every advantage I could, I immediately suggested I top up her wine, which she readily accepted.

'The following questions are a formality,' I said, picking up my pad and pen. 'What is your date of birth?'

September 30th, 1958.'

My mental arithmetic told me she was seventeen when Peter had first brought her to our house. So young. So young, Yet so evil.

'And your place of birth?'

'Canada.'

'Really? How interesting.' I remembered how she had told Lawrence she was from New Zealand. Peter had queried it because she'd told him Canada. Which was it? 'Whereabouts in Canada?' I said. 'Purely as a matter of interest.'

'Nova Scotia.' Her face hardened and she took a large slug of wine before sitting back in the chair, clutching the glass in both hands.

'And your full name?'

'Elizabeth Jane Fellowes, though everyone knows me as Bibby.'

Fellowes. She had no right to use that name and I wanted to scream so. But I remained silent as she rolled the glass against her lips and tilted her head back, allowing her soft hair to fall away from her face. A vision of Pete after he'd been convicted came into my consciousness and a savage, primordial anger welled in me. I had an urge to stand over her, grab her hair, yank her head back and pull her hair out in handfuls. I wanted to smash her in the way she'd smashed him. Instead I watched her swallow the pale poison, knowing that every swallow brought her end closer.

'Marital status?'

'Married.'

It was what I dreaded and I realised the saying 'my blood ran cold' was true. I shivered as my warm blood turned to ice water. She was married. Still had the name Fellowes. It could only mean one thing. I clutched my slightly trembling hands around my tumbler, drained it of blackcurrant and watched as Bibby slowly drained her glass of wine.

'Would you mind if I had another glass of blackcurrant?' I held up the empty glass. 'I seem to have rather a thirst this evening.'

'Of course.'

As Bibby went into the kitchen I immediately took another paper twist from my cardigan pocket. After emptying its contents into her glass, I threw the empty twist in the carrier and poured wine into the glass, stirring constantly with my index finger.

'Does your husband work away?' I asked as she came back into the room carrying the replenished glass.

'No. We're not together any more.' She put the tumbler in front of me and limped across to the window. Less steadily than before, if I wasn't imagining things. Turning her back to the window she added, 'He was a good husband, but it wasn't to be. Now? Well, look at me. Approaching 50 with a false elbow and a couple of arthritic hips, so I'm hardly the season's catch, am I?'

Was it my imagination or was her voice beginning to slur? *A good husband but it wasn't to be.* How could she stand there and make such trite comments? Such glib remarks after all she'd done. Done to Peter. After all she'd done to *us*. It took every ounce of willpower not to hurl abuse at her. Wasn't to be? What did she expect after she'd faked a pregnancy, a miscarriage and cancer? And did she really expect it 'to be' when she'd falsely accused her husband of beating her to within inches of her life, and when he was finally found guilty and sentenced? Did she expect it to be when she had driven a stake through the fabric of his familial relationships, pitting son against mother and drawing every family member into her web of deceit? And when Lawrence's heart gave out under the strain and he could stand the humiliation no more and was forced to move, did she think it was to be then? Within a year of moving Lawrence was dead. And *she* had killed him as certainly as if she had plunged a knife into his heart.

But I hadn't come this far with my plans to spoil them now. I willed myself to be calm, to keep to my plan. I took another deep breath.

And that's when the doorbell sounded.

'I'm not expecting anyone,' Bibby said, going into the hallway. 'Excuse me a moment.'

Now I was not calm. This was not in my plan. *Don't panic, Jetta*, I told myself over and over, *be calm. Think. Think.*

The muffled sound of a woman's voice came from the hallway and I heard Bibby say, 'Come on in and I'll see what I can do.'

This was it. I couldn't take any chances. I stood up, snatched Bibby's glass from the table and shattered it against the side of the coffee table. The fragments fell onto the carpet, the contents causing a wide dark stain. I couldn't waste any time.

'I'm so sorry,' I said immediately she came into the room, closely followed by a woman of a similar age. 'I've knocked your glass over and–'

'Don't worry, I'll soon deal with that. I'll get a cloth and clear that up and then I'll introduce you to my neighbour.'

But I didn't sit back down. I kept my head bowed, picked up my handbag and carrier and headed towards the hallway.

'I'm so sorry. I've realised I should be somewhere else right now. I'll call you again.'

It was at that moment I noticed the photograph. It stood in a silver frame on the mahogany side table. And even from this distance I could see it was him. My breath caught in my throat, but I couldn't stop. I kept moving.

'Mrs Francis.' Bibby followed me into the hallway. 'There's no need for you to go.'

But I dashed through the front door uttering apologies before she had a chance to stop me. I had to get out of there. Get away. I hadn't reckoned on this. My plan was failing. Had failed. But I couldn't, wouldn't, stop here. Not now. Especially not now. Not now I'd seen the photograph.

It wasn't a great photo, but it was him alright. It was definitely him.

Chapter Ninteen

Lyme Regis, Dorset, Thursday Morning, July 2006

Despite my best efforts I didn't sleep a wink. Ironically, I had considered taking one of the sleeping tablets, but decided against it. I needed a clear head more than ever.

All I could see was the photograph. I don't know where or when it was taken but it was him. And why would she still have a photo of Peter, especially displayed so prominently? My fear was that Bibby and Peter had never actually divorced. He'd never mentioned a divorce and at the time refused to speak of Bibby or anything about his life when asked. And back then, he'd been the sort of disorganised man who would let such a thing slide. But his recent business successes were becoming the subject of much publicity and if she discovered this, I had no doubt she would do her best to help relieve him of his funds. Leopards didn't change their spots.

No, it was now more important than ever that I accomplish my mission.

Today would be a day of rest. A day of getting over the shock of the past 24 hours and a day of gentle thought on the way forward. To this end, after breakfast, I left the hotel on foot, but instead of dropping down into the town, I turned left out of the hotel entrance and began the steady climb uphill. As it was a gloriously hot day I felt it would be better to get the climb in first, allowing me the luxury of a downhill descent on my return.

I crossed the road and walked steadily up Pound Street. It was only ten o'clock, yet there wasn't a parking space to be had. As I crossed over the junction at Pound Road, I paused briefly to let an elderly gentleman on an electric scooter pass. Ha! Who was I calling elderly? Most likely he was younger than me. I noticed a tea room in the Holmbush car park opposite. Maybe on my way back I would rest there and treat myself to a cup of tea or an icecream. I would probably need something by then.

Further up the hill the pavement petered out and I walked against the oncoming traffic, not that there was much. An unusual cottage on the opposite side of the road drew my attention, with its ornate carvings and octagonal thatched roof. On my way back I would take a closer look, but for now my mission was to reach the top of the road out of Lyme.

As I reached Clappentail Lane I heard a voice calling, 'Jean! Jean!' and turned to see Charles waving at me from back down the hill.

'Jean! Jean, wait!' he shouted, waving frantically.

Too late to pretend I hadn't seen him, I waved back and waited for him to catch me up.

'I've been calling you for ages,' he managed to say between pants as he approached.

'I didn't hear you,' I said, thinking how well he looked in his pale blue cotton open-necked shirt.

'You passed my place back there.' He pointed down the hill. 'I was sat out enjoying a cup of coffee when I saw you pass. Why don't you come and join me?'

'I couldn't. I've got to…' But I couldn't finish the sentence. What excuse could I come up with? It was obvious I had time on my hands. I hesitated. Got to what? What could I say?

'You needn't stay long. And even if I do say it myself, I make excellent coffee.'

After a slight pause, I said, 'Lead the way. That's an offer I can't refuse.'

His place turned out to be the ground floor apartment of a spacious detached Edwardian house set back from the road. Curving around the front and side of his apartment was a paved semi-walled area in which stood a green iron garden table and mismatched chairs surrounded by pots of shrubs, climbers, herbs and flowers.

'You sit there,' Charles pointed to a cushioned chair, 'and make yourself comfortable while I make a fresh pot of coffee.'

A half-empty mug of coffee stood on the table alongside an opened packet of digestives and from where I sat I could glimpse the bay through a belt of distant trees. It was pleasant. No, it was more than pleasant, it was almost perfect. Lavender tumbled out of a tall terracotta pot beside me and the still morning air was punctuated by the hum of bees and birdsong. The welcome aroma of freshly roasted coffee reached my nostrils and I leaned back and closed my eyes. I could get used to this. Someone to bring me a coffee, someone to share moments with. A man. God forbid I should ever feel my life was empty without a man, but male company was different from the interaction I had with my other friends. And sometimes I missed it. It might also be nice to have someone to say goodnight to. Or good morning, for that matter, but I didn't allow my thoughts to drift too far in that direction. It could never be. I was here for something far more important and nothing would detract me from that.

The exterior brick walls of the house provided a perfect backdrop for the clematis and other healthy ramblers that clung eagerly to their trellis supports. Charles surely had green fingers. Maybe he talked to them as his royal namesake did. I'd ask him; that way at least I could keep the conversation from getting on to matters too personal.

'Here we are.' Charles emerged from the half-glazed door bearing a tray on which stood a cafetiere, a jug of milk, a bowl of brown sugar cubes and two grey and blue pottery mugs. 'I'm afraid I've run out of cakes. But I can offer you a digestive,' he said, placing the tray on the table. 'God, what a heathen I am! I haven't even brought out plates.' He picked up the opened biscuits and held them out to me. 'That's what comes of living alone.'

I accepted a biscuit and took a bite, holding my hand beneath my mouth to catch the crumbs. 'No sense in making lots of washing up.'

'A woman after my own heart,' he said, sitting opposite me. 'Now, how do you like your coffee?'

'As it comes with a dash of milk and lots of sugar.' I watched his long thin fingers push the plunger into the cafetiere. 'This is a delightful spot,' I added. 'And your plants all seem so healthy – what's your secret?'

'Like most things, they thrive on love and attention. And I've got enough time on my hands to give them plenty of both.'

For some reason I found myself at a loss for words. It wasn't the response I'd expected and I quietly accepted the coffee and added several lumps of sugar.

For a while we sat in silence, each sipping our coffee and dunking the odd biscuit. It didn't feel awkward; on the contrary, it felt comfortable. Relaxed. The right place to be.

'Have you lived here long?' I asked when my mug was almost drained.

'Two years. Yes, two years it must be now.' His voice had a calming quality to it; no forced jovialness; no speaking for speaking's sake. He was, I believed, quite simply a nice man.

'What made you come here?'

'It's a long story.'

'One you want to share?' I heard myself ask.

'I'm not sure. I've never shared it before.'

'Please don't think I'm prying. It's just…'

'No. I don't think that for a moment, Jean. The short version is that I moved here to be near my daughter. The reasons for doing so are what makes the version longer.'

'It's not that unusual when you get to our age; a desire to be near your children is understandable. Many do it.'

'Yes, but you see I didn't know my daughter before I moved here. I moved here to be near her. To discover more about her. To make amends, if you like, before it was too late.'

'I see,' I said, taking the last sip of coffee from my mug and placing it on the table. 'And did you?'

Charles raised his eyebrows and looked at me. He held up the coffee pot as if to ask if I wanted more coffee and I nodded.

'Yes, I did,' he said, and as he poured the rest of the coffee into our mugs, added, 'and this has turned into one of the most satisfying periods of my life.' He sat back in his chair after pouring milk into the coffee. 'No, I've no regrets about coming here. So, what made you choose to come here?'

Despite feeling strangely drawn to Charles, I couldn't possibly enlighten him as to my reason for visiting Lyme Regis. Instead I replied with a question of my own. 'Do you mind telling me why you didn't know your daughter before coming here?'

'Not really. But it's a long story, as I say. And afterwards you might feel somewhat differently about me.'

'Why should I?'

'Not sure. Maybe because I haven't always been the man you see before you.'

'And do you think I've always been this quiet grey-haired old lady with time on her hands?'

He laughed.

'Well then.'

'OK. You win.' He set his mug back on the table after taking a large gulp and leaned back in his chair, folding his hands in his lap. 'Many years ago I was married and we had a child, a daughter.

I worked long hours to support my wife and daughter and life at home was difficult, to say the least. It didn't seem to matter how many hours I put in, or how much money I earned, there was never enough. My wife suffered from severe mood swings and when I tried talking to her about it she was argumentative, often abusive and sometimes violent towards me.

'When my daughter was four I went home one evening to an empty house. My wife had left, taking our daughter and leaving a note: *Don't bother trying to find us, it's over.* That was all it said. Of course, I made enquiries and following up on rumours and other bits of information I gathered, I eventually found her. She was living in a seedy run-down apartment with a younger man. When I called and demanded to see our daughter, my wife was amenable and suggested I came back at the weekend so I could spend a whole day with our daughter. I agreed, but when I returned that weekend, they'd moved and I never saw my wife again. As bad a wife as I knew she was, I didn't have any reason to suspect she was a bad mother.

'It was only years later I discovered the truth. My daughter had been exposed to a series of different men, or "fathers". Most were on drugs, as indeed I found out my ex-wife was, which explained the mood swings and lack of money in our early married life.

'As my daughter grew up she became more and more devious, more adept at getting money for her mother. Her mother always needed just one last input of cash to make her life right, and our daughter felt it was her responsibility to help her get it. Because this time it would be alright. This time it would be different. This time her mother would give up her habit. Worse still, the sort of men her mother lived with became more and more violent. Often threatening to beat my ex-wife unless our daughter came up with the goods. Whatever the goods happened to be that week – money, property, drugs.'

Charles paused and reached for another sip of coffee. I didn't know what to say. It seemed grossly unfair that this gentle man should have such to bear, but then I remembered why I was here. Life wasn't always fair.

Watching Charles as he placed his mug back on the tray, I leaned across and, without thinking, touched the back of his hand. He looked at me and smiled. A smile that only reached one corner of his mouth.

'Do you know what the worst thing is?' he added, continuing before I could answer: 'It's what all this did to my daughter. Not surprisingly, she couldn't trust men after all that happened. The men in her life were users, not to be trusted, unreliable, violent if things didn't go their way. She learned from an early age to be manipulative and secretive. And me, her own father, had abandoned her to all that.'

'You didn't abandon her, your wife took her.'

'A four-year-old doesn't know that.'

'But you did look for her and found her, it wasn't your fault your wife took her away again.'

'No. But I could have kept looking.'

'I'm sure you did all you could.'

'If I'd done all I could I would have found her. I should never have given up. But life got in the way. I had to work and I found out they'd left the country and after that my efforts drew a blank. Selfishly I married again, but it didn't last. I don't suppose I'd got over my first experience.'

'But you're here now and you have a good relationship with your daughter?'

'Yes, yes, I do. And the best bit of news after all those wasted years was to discover I have a grandson. He's at university now in Plymouth. So, yes, I'm an extremely lucky man to have been given a second chance with a daughter who's so forgiving and generous.'

157

He looked up.

'Enough of this, Jean,' he added. 'How about we change the subject and talk about you.'

'Another time, maybe.' I stood up and brushed the digestive crumbs from my skirt. 'But for now there really are things I must get on and do.'

'Surely not?' Charles stood and seemed genuinely despondent at my leaving.

'Afraid so.'

'OK, but tell you what, how about we do this again tomorrow?'

I edged away from the table. 'I'm not sure what I'm doing,' I said, aware of how much of an excuse it sounded.

'Have I put you off with my potted history?'

'Far from it.' I paused before adding, 'Why don't you come down to my hotel for morning coffee. I'll meet you in reception at 10.30.'

'Which hotel?'

'The Admiral's House Hotel in Pound Street.'

'I know it,' Charles said, a smile spreading across his face and the life returning to his eyes. 'I'll be there tomorrow morning, 10.30 sharp.'

What on earth possessed me? I asked myself as I retraced my steps down Pound Street. What was I thinking of, inviting Charles to the hotel for coffee? I must be mad. However drawn I felt towards him, I must remember why I was here. But listening to Charles had neatly allowed me to avoid thinking about my own list of things to do. Most importantly, how I was to get back into Bibby's apartment.

And on that note I made up my mind that once back in the hotel, I would make the phone call. The phone call to her. To Bibby Fellowes, to arrange yet another appointment for murder.

Chapter Twenty

Lyme Regis, Dorset, Thursday afternoon, July 2006

Sitting in the garden of the hotel, I retrieved the mobile I'd bought in Honiton from my handbag and placed it on the table in front of me. There were a few guests sat out enjoying the afternoon sun although most would be in the town now, or on the beach, or touring the surrounding area, according to the conversations I'd overheard at breakfast. That suited me. Out here in the shade of the large canvas umbrella on a lawn that sloped gently away towards the sea, I could almost have been in my own bubble.

I'd done a lot of thinking about Charles and his conversation with me that morning. And I couldn't help but think that if things were different, we might have struck up a long-lasting friendship. Maybe more. But it wasn't to be. I had lied to him. Lied about who I was. Lied about why I was here. He didn't even know my real name. And it didn't seem fair. He deserved better. I should never have invited him for coffee in the morning. Letting him know where I was staying was a mistake. I was supposed to be keeping myself to myself, blending in with the background, being Mrs Grey. Instead, here I was inviting a man to have coffee with me. I could kick myself for my stupidity. I didn't even have his phone number to ring so I could put him off. Though I did know where he lived, and could drop a note through his door later – if I could summon the stamina for the hill again.

The screech of a seagull brought me back to the present and the job in hand, and I picked up the mobile and entered Bibby's number into the black keys. I waited. The phone rang a long time and I was about to try again when a man's voice said, 'Bibby's Café and Gifts.'

'Is Bibby there?'

'She's busy with a customer at the moment. Can I help?'

'No. I need to speak with her. Please tell her Jean Francis called and I'll call her back.'

'OK. Hang on,' the voice said, 'I think she's finished. What did you say your name was again?'

'Mrs Francis. Mrs Jean Francis.'

After a slight pause, during which I heard muffled voices, a now familiar voice said, 'Hello again, Mrs Francis. I'm glad you called. I was rather worried about you after the way you dashed off last night. Is everything alright? Are you OK?'

'Yes, I'm so sorry about that. I forgot completely about an important appointment I had. Please forgive me. It must have seemed so rude to you, and after you agreeing to be so helpful too.'

'Not at all. It just seemed rather sudden, that's all. I hoped there was nothing wrong.'

'Not at all. Not at all. But I would like to make another appointment to see you so we can complete the Patients' Group survey.'

'I don't mind, but it's as I told you – Wednesday was my only free evening this week. So we're going to have to make it an evening next week.'

Inwardly I sighed. I'd already been here a week. The longer I stayed the more difficult it would be to remain anonymous. Besides, I didn't want the family or Marilyn beginning to pry into my whereabouts.

'The trouble is, I'm not really around next week. I understand it's probably not very convenient, but could we possibly make it over the weekend?'

'Weekends in the summer are very busy for me, I have a little shop, you see.'

'I'm so sorry to press you, but it would be so useful to have the input of someone younger such as yourself.'

There followed a silence which I dared not break. I knew I could say too much and instinctively felt it was a time to stay quiet.

'Well, maybe Saturday evening. I'll have had a busy day, so I don't know quite how much use I'll be to you. But if you really can't be around next week then…'

'Thank you. Thank you so much,' I effused. 'We'll do it on the same lines as before, with me bringing wine.'

'There's really no need.'

'No, I insist. It's the least I can do after you giving up your valuable spare time. I appreciate your help and I know future patients of the hospital will too.'

'Well, in that case, let's say 7.30 again on Saturday. I'll see you then, Jean.'

After the call I relaxed back in the chair and allowed the warm breeze to caress my face. A pair of gulls squabbled on the rooftop behind me and a man and woman on the table further down the lawn looked and laughed. The sort of holiday laugh that indicates freedom from work. Freedom from home, domesticity and other responsibilities and duties. The sort of laugh that would probably disappear on the Monday morning they returned to work. With the advantage of age, I could see how futile striving was when you got to realise you were striving for the wrong things. But then I remembered my mother and how she'd always said you can't put an old head on young shoulders.

Hearing a familiar ring tone, I reached in my handbag for my old mobile. 'Marilyn calling' came up on the screen. I pressed the green button to take the call.

'Jetta? It's Marilyn.'

'Lovely to hear from you. How's life in Hampton Stoke?'

'Not the same without you here. When are you back?'

'The early part of next week, possibly Monday or Tuesday.'

'Thank goodness for that. Where are you now?'

'Right now, Marilyn, I'm sat on a sloping lawn in the shade of an umbrella looking out to sea. And it's heaven.'

'Sounds it. I can see the attraction. I just wish I was there with you. Tony's been so miserable this week. He's got lots of problems at work and insists on bringing them home at night. I could throttle him. And I don't have you to escape to now for a sherry and a chat.'

'You soon will have, Marilyn,' I said.

And after we talked and I'd said goodbye, I realised she wouldn't have me for too much longer. All the more reason to make the most of what time I had left. And to that end, Saturday night would be the focus of my attention now.

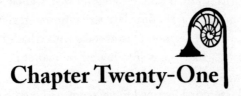

Chapter Twenty-One

Lyme Regis, Dorset, Friday morning, July 2006

It was a summer that would never end, or so it seemed as I woke to yet another sunny morning. I lay for a few minutes with my eyes closed until I heard the clatter of a house-keeping trolley in the corridor outside my room. Whatever time was it? Looking at the clock on the bedside table, I saw it was gone nine. I'd overslept. Pushing back the covers I placed my feet flat on the floor and immediately felt giddy. I had got up too quickly. Giving myself a few moments to regain my balance, I cursed. This morning of all mornings I'd slept later than I wanted. My intention had been to breakfast early, pay a visit to the shops in Broad Street and return in time for my coffee appointment with Charles. Now the shopping would have to wait.

Pulling on the bra, skirt and blouse I'd worn the day before, I fished a clean pair of tights from the chest of drawers and rolled them up my lean legs before padding into the bathroom for an early morning wee. Unusually, I hadn't got up in the night and my bladder felt as if it would burst. Ablutions complete, I hurried down to the dining room and was surprised to find it almost full. The 'No Vacancies' sign outside the hotel wasn't a lie, every room and suite was occupied.

Choosing to sit alone at an empty table for two, I felt awkward. Normally I would have chosen company, someone such as the woman who was sitting on her own and smiled welcomingly as I passed her table.

'Lovely morning again,' she said.

'Yes, isn't it just,' I said, walking on past. I knew she wanted me to join her but I didn't dare strike up more conversations. I'd already made an enormous mistake with Charles, I was sure of it. No, best I kept myself to myself, no matter how difficult I found it.

Breakfast over, I returned to my room, wishing I hadn't bolted the fried bread and eggs so greedily. Indigestion threatened and I'd run out of Gaviscon. That was one of the items on my shopping list. I seemed to get a lot of heartburn lately. Whether it was the medication I'd been given or the stress of what I was about to do, I didn't know. All I did know was that the pink aniseed liquid helped.

I studied the contents of my wardrobe, wondering why I was making such a fuss about what to wear. I knew why, of course, and chastised myself. It was because I was meeting Charles. But after that I would commit murder and never see him again, so why? I wished I was one of those women who could pull on a pair of trousers and a blouse and look elegant without trying. But I wasn't. Settling on a sky blue blouse and navy skirt, I avoided looking at myself in the full-length mirror. Instead I threaded a brown leather belt through the skirt's belt loops and slipped my feet into a pair of low-heeled brown shoes. I wasn't happy with how I looked, but this had to be it if I was to meet Charles on time.

Before descending the stairs, I leaned over the balustrade to see if he was waiting. He was. Sat on a sofa near the hallstand scanning *The Independent*, one of the daily papers left in reception. Stupidly, my heart rate quickened and I felt a blush come to my cheeks. This was ridiculous. I wasn't some young thing about to go on a date, I reminded myself, and immediately felt a wave of sadness. This would be the last time I would see Charles.

Putting my handbag over my arm, I took a deep breath and walked slowly down the stairs.

'Morning, Mrs Francis.'

Intent on Charles, I hadn't seen Matthew behind the reception desk.

'Morning, Matthew. How are you?'

'I'm fine, Mrs Francis, and you have a visitor,' Matthew said, inclining his head towards Charles and smiling.

'Yes, yes, I was expecting Mr...' I stopped. I didn't even know his last name.

'Jean!' Charles stood and thrust the newspaper down onto the seat behind him. 'I was a bit early.'

'No matter. Now, would you rather have coffee in the conservatory or in the garden? Your choice.'

'It seems a shame to stay indoors on such a beautiful morning. What say we take our coffee in the garden?'

'You leave that to me, Mrs Francis,' Matthew said. 'I'll sort that out for you. Is that two regular coffees?'

I nodded. Charles agreed.

'Do you want anything with that – selection of biscuits or cakes?' Matthew added.

I looked at Charles. 'Biscuits?'

'Yes,' he said, looking at Matthew. 'Biscuits will be just fine.'

Leading the way through the conservatory and out into the garden, I chose a table situated in the middle of the lawn and sat on a chair facing the sea. Charles sat opposite me, half turned towards the view.

'This really is a spectacular location,' he said, an appreciative look on his face. 'You chose well when you chose this hotel, Jean. Have you stayed here before?'

'No. Never. And I was fortunate to get in at such late notice this time of year. They had a last-minute cancellation.'

'You hadn't booked the holiday in advance?'

'No. It was a last-minute decision that brought me here. A desire to get away. Spend some time on my own.'

'Do you live alone?'

'Yes.' And, wishing to change the subject, I added, 'Look at that view Charles, isn't it priceless?'

Through the canopy of a copper beech, the ancient Cobb was visible as it unfurled into the sea. Fishing boats huddled together in the harbour and in the middle distance a pleasure cruiser cut across our line of vision. The sun's rays hit the taffeta bay and somewhere deep within I experienced a lurch of panic. This was too perfect. It couldn't last. Couldn't possibly last.

Charles interrupted my thoughts. 'Looks as if our coffee's about to arrive.'

I turned as a waiter approached carrying a tray. Behind him the hotel stood in the sun as it had done for a century or more, its pink-washed walls covered in wisteria. From here I could see my bedroom window and was sorry that it would only be so for another few days at the most. I missed Marilyn, my cats and the family, but I would miss here too. Circumstances dictated, however, that once I left I would never return.

Both Charles and I unashamedly dunked our biscuits into our coffee once the waiter had left and I noticed Charles favoured the digestives. Strange. They'd been Lawrence's favourite too.

'Well, I have to say life hasn't turned out so bad after all,' he said. 'Sat here in this setting with such ideal company.'

'You flatter me. Besides, you don't even know me.'

'I know enough to know that you're someone I'd like to spend more time with.'

'But you know nothing.'

'It's not always about what's said,' Charles said. 'It's often about what's not said. Besides, I'm a great believer in gut instinct.'

'I thought it was only women who followed intuition. Men usually pooh-pooh such things.'

'Maybe I'm not your regular man.'

And I thought how right he was.

'I've discovered that it doesn't pay to let things go unsaid,' he added. 'I spent too many years thinking about the right thing to do when I should have done the right thing. If I'd done the right thing I would have had a daughter for a much greater part of my life. And, as importantly, a grandson.'

'Yes, grandchildren are rather special.'

'Have you got any?'

'Two girls. Becky and Andrea. Twins.'

'Do you see much of them?'

'Not as much I'd like, but they lead busy lives of their own.'

'You said you live alone…'

'Yes, my husband died. Twenty-six years ago, in fact when the twins were just a few months old.'

'I'm sorry.'

'Yes, so am I. I still miss him.'

'Was it…?'

'Heart. He had a heart attack. And you,' I said, looking up at him. 'You never married again after your second?'

'No. I'm afraid I've lived a rather reclusive life where women are concerned. I allowed my previous experiences to colour my view for too long. But that's all changed now. I've learned that I can't allow the past to dictate my future.'

I looked across the table at Charles. There was a brightness to his eyes and I had the sense he really had let go of his past.

My thoughts were interrupted by a miserable looking middle-aged couple emerging from the hotel followed by a noisy boy holding a kite. It was obvious the boy would rather be on the beach kite-flying than out here in the hotel garden and I won-dered if the couple were his parents or grandparents. It was hard to tell these days, with people having children later in life and with many grandparents looking and dressing almost as young as their offspring. Charles said good morning as they passed and asked the young boy if he could see his kite.

'What a smasher,' Charles said as the boy proudly unfolded the kite. It was a myriad of bright primary colours with tails that swept the ground for yards behind him. 'I bet that goes beyond the clouds.'

'I got it for my birthday,' the boy said.

'How lucky,' Charles said, 'and how old are you?'

'Six and three days.'

I smiled at his preciseness.

'Stop pestering people,' the lady shouted back, 'you know what we've told you about that.'

'He's no trouble,' Charles began to say, but the lady decided he was and returned to drag him off by the arm.

'Poor little beggar,' Charles said. 'Don't reckon he's going to have much of a holiday with that pair, do you?'

'No, I don't. But it was nice of you to try and engage him.'

But that seemed typical of the little I knew of Charles. As I'd thought before, he was a nice man.

When we finished our coffee I suggested to Charles we take a walk. That way I would be in control of when I returned to the hotel – alone.

By the time we left the hotel through the front reception, grey rain clouds had gathered overhead, making a mockery of that morning's weather forecast, which was for sun all day with temperatures in the mid 70s. Good job I'd collected a cardigan from my room on the way out. We decided to walk to the Cobb and turned left out of the hotel entrance, walking slowly uphill. Charles walked on my right, next to the road, and I carried my cardigan over my left arm and my handbag in my right hand to ensure he couldn't take hold of my hand. Not that I was certain he would or even wanted to, it was simply a precaution on my part.

We passed Stile Lane and reached the corner of Cobb Road, where we turned left. Charles told me that John Fowles, the author, lived in a house there. He wasn't somebody I'd read, but I didn't say so.

From here, thankfully, it was all downhill to the Cobb. I'd worry about the walk back later. For now I wanted to enjoy Charles' company and, for an hour or two at least, put everything else to the back of my mind. After all, this would be the last time I would be in his company and I wanted to make the most of it.

Chapter Twenty-Two

Lyme Regis, Dorset, Friday afternoon, July 2006

There was only one empty table outside *The Cobb Arms* as we passed. An overweight yellow Labrador tied to one of the table legs was amusing onlookers there as he caught crisps thrown to him by a young girl wearing a pink bikini and a vibrant beach towel around her shoulders. The dog's owners didn't seem to notice. They were too engrossed in the pile of chips and fresh fish that lay before them. And as they tucked in heartily I couldn't help thinking that, judging by the size of them, they probably wouldn't worry too much about the dog getting fat on titbits anyway. What was that expression about dogs being like their owners?

Across the road, people queued for icecreams and rock, and children bought buckets and spades in the time-honoured tradition of the Great British seaside holiday. The darkening rain clouds were not going to stop anyone from having a good time. I remembered the first time Lawrence and I had taken the boys to the seaside. We rented a chalet at Westward Ho! complete with gas lighting, and despite the temperature being in the high seventies, Lawrence refused to wear sandals or shorts. He spent the whole week in long trousers, socks and shoes, even on the beach. But the boys loved it. David spent most of his time building enormous sandcastles with water-filled moats and Peter fished for crabs in the rock pools with a line and a hook.

'Penny for them.'

I smiled at Charles. 'I was remembering the first seaside holiday we took our boys on. Children love the seaside.'

'Not just children,' Charles said. 'I never tire of the coast, summer or winter. Since being here I get to appreciate all the seasons. In the winter I can walk on Monmouth beach most mornings and not meet a soul. And when the summer comes…well, I love being here among the tourists, or grockles, as they're often called. The place comes alive with people enjoying themselves and I feel privileged to live somewhere people are so keen to visit. People come here all year round, yet in the winter it does tail off and then I get to see another, quieter side of Lyme. And so it goes.'

As we walked past the lifeboat shop the halyards of the boats moored nearby clanked against their masts. The breeze became fresher and I was sure I felt a spot of rain. We walked to the end of the Cobb where a young woman stood with her back to the sea, arms outstretched, laughing as her boyfriend took pictures of her.

Charles pointed at her. 'Do you remember Meryl Streep standing there in that famous scene from *The French Lieutenant's Woman*? You know, the one where she's wearing a black hooded cloak. I can't tell you how many people I've seen pose for pictures there.'

'I haven't seen the film or read the book,' I said. 'Shame on me.'

'I hadn't either until I moved here. Then my daughter bought me the DVD. It's interesting looking for the bits of Lyme. It starts with Jeremy Irons in *The Three Cups*, that wonderful old hotel in Broad Street. Been empty for years, apparently. Sad to see it let go. Still, you'll have to come over to me and watch the film sometime, I'm sure you'd enjoy it.'

'I'm sure I would,' I said, safe in the knowledge it would never happen.

171

By the time we got back to The Lifeboat Shop my stomach was grumbling. The blackening sky appeared threatening and the drop in temperature had people pulling on cardigans and jackets.

'I don't know about you,' I said as we passed a middle-aged couple eating hot dogs, 'but I fancy a bag of chips.'

'In that case, I know just the place.'

Charles led me behind *The Cobb Inn* and down Marine Parade. We gazed in shop windows, including a boutique beside a fishing tackle shop. I smiled at the name over the clothes shop, *Persuasion*, presumably named after the novel Jane Austen was said to have penned in the town. Eventually Charles stopped outside a fish and chip shop where the queue reached the door.

'Do you want anything else – fish, fishcake, sausage?' Charles asked.

'No. Chips'll be great, but I do like lots of salt and vinegar.'

'Why don't you carry on, save waiting here? There's a long seat further up on the left hand side, set into the wall. Sit there and I'll bring the chips along.'

I didn't need persuading. Not only were my feet beginning to ache from the walk, the rest of me was too. And I didn't have any painkillers with me. Before lowering myself gently onto the blue wooden bench I pulled on my cardigan, pleased I'd thought to bring it with me. If I wasn't mistaken, we'd have rain and lots of it before the afternoon was out.

It felt strange sat there staring out to sea, waiting for Charles to bring the chips. What would my family say if they could see me? They'd never believe it. Their mum at the seaside in the company of a man. I could hardly believe it myself. What was I doing here? How had it happened? How had my life brought me to this point? Just as well we don't know our destiny. I never would have guessed this in a million years. Me? Mild-mannered Jetta Fellowes, a murderess? Or was that murderer? Technically at the moment I wasn't, of course, but I soon would be. That was the one certainty in my future.

'Anyone sitting here?'

'Charles! I didn't see you coming,' I said, taking the wrapped parcel he offered me.

'You looked deep in thought.'

As I opened the wrapper the sight and smell of the fresh vinegar-soaked chips made my mouth water. I had no idea I was so ravenous. It must be the fresh sea air, I thought, as Charles handed me a wooden fork.

We sat and ate and chatted and watched the changing scenery. People came and went, some sat beside us briefly to rest before moving on to the next attraction. Children with icecreams, day-trippers with dogs on leads, some dragging their owners along the sea-front, and couples strolling arm in arm. There was much to watch. A lady on a scooter with a Siamese cat in a basket, and a man in a wheelchair being pushed by a lady who looked as if she could do with a turn in the chair.

'Would you like an icecream?' Charles asked as he squashed our empty wrappers into the overfull waste bin nearby.

I hesitated. 'What I'd really like is a cup of tea. There's nothing like a cup of tea after chips.'

'Tea it is then. Where shall we go?'

'Is there anywhere we can get a take-away tea?'

'There's a kiosk along Marine Parade.'

'Lead the way, I could murder a cup.' And realising what I'd said, I laughed out loud.

'What's so funny?'

'Nothing,' I said, fastening the buttons of my cardigan against the rising breeze and smoothing my skirt as I stood up. 'Nothing. Really.'

We got our tea from a kiosk towards the clock tower end of Marine Parade. Standing under its red awning, we noticed a group of white plastic chairs alongside the railings overlooking the sea and swiftly sat in two as soon as they became vacant. The rest were occupied by a group of seniors who, keen to chat, told us they were on a day-trip from Shaftesbury.

'You on holiday?' asked a woman with thinning hair and stilettos.

I spoke at the same time as Charles. He said no and I said yes, which caused her to raise her eyebrows.

'I'm on holiday, Charles lives here,' I said, immediately irritated with myself that I felt it necessary to explain.

'Oh, did you know each other before you came?' she asked, to the obvious annoyance of her friends.

It struck me that she was the sort of woman who lost friends easily and before either of us replied, another of the group, a man with a walking stick and faded trilby, stood up and suggested it was time they got going. 'We're going on a fishing trip,' he told us, and they left in the direction of the harbour.

'That was a lucky escape,' I said.

Charles nodded and smiled as he put his feet up on the lower railing and tilted his head back. I watched the breeze lift his hair. He had good thick hair for his age, well cut too and not a stray hair on his neck as so many older men had. He took care of himself, in an unaffected way, which appealed to me. And that was the trouble. So much about Charles appealed to me.

'This is a lovely cup of tea,' I said. 'Or is it just because I've had chips? Tea always tastes great after chips.'

'It certainly does, but I better watch out that my daughter doesn't see me.'

'Why's that? Would she mind you having tea with a lady?'

'Not at all. I think she'd quite enjoy my having a lady friend. No, it's just that she runs a café herself and would wonder why I didn't take you in there.'

'Really. Whereabouts?'

'We passed it back there,' Charles indicated back the way we'd walked. 'I would have taken you there, but you said you wanted a take-away tea and they only do sit-in orders. But you've been there.'

'Have I?'

'Yes, it's where I first joined you, if you remember?'

I looked back the way we'd walked. The only place we'd passed where I'd been before was...

My mouth was suddenly dry. 'You don't mean...Bibby's Café?' I almost couldn't say the words.

'That's right.' He took his feet off the railing and took another sip of his tea. 'She's made a great success of the business, even expanded it to include gifts. She's worked hard, blooming hard. And it's paid off, although she's not been in the best of health.'

I had a feeling Charles was still talking, but I couldn't hear the words. My mind was working overtime as I tried to take in the implication of what he'd said.

'Do you mean that Bibby...Bibby is your daughter?'

'Yes, that's right, and very proud of her I am too. I'd love you to meet her.'

I knew Charles was talking but his words floated unheard into the ether. This couldn't be. I couldn't believe it. Of all people – Bibby. That conniving, hateful bitch was Charles' daughter.

The nausea started at the same time as the palpitations and the sea merged with the pebble beach, which merged with the esplanade and the people walking along it. I was about to faint. I knew it.

Chapter Twenty-Three

Lyme Regis, Dorset, Friday afternoon, July 2006

I didn't faint. Somehow I managed to stand. Retracing my steps along Marine Parade at something approaching a running pace, I cut through Langmoor Gardens, certain there was a short-cut back up to the hotel that way. I climbed the steep incline with ease, adrenalin fuelling every step. Although aware of people around me, their faces and voices were a blur as my mind whirled with the implication of Charles' words. I can't remember going into the hotel or climbing the stairs. The next thing I knew I was in my room.

I crossed to the window, pushed it wide open and the cool air hit my face. Stripping off my cardigan, I threw it onto the chair by the desk and went into the bathroom. With the cold tap on almost full, I held my wrists under its rapid flow to cool myself. Perspiration trickled between my breasts and across my forehead. Squeezing my flannel under the cold running water, I held it across my forehead in an attempt to cool myself further.

Sitting on the bed, I kicked my shoes off, swung my legs onto the coverlet and lay back against the pile of pillows. My head pounded and I couldn't stop the constant volley of thoughts.

How could she be his daughter? How could someone such as Charles father someone such as Bibby? I was fond of Charles. More than fond. I thought back to what he had said to me earlier that morning: '…I know enough to know that you're someone I'd like to spend more time with.' If only he knew the real me. Not the me that was Jean Francis, holidaymaker. The me that was Jetta Fellowes. The Jetta Fellowes that was here to murder his precious bitch of a daughter.

Sitting upright on the side of the bed, I took several deep breaths and tried to relax my muscles. Reaching across to the bed-side table, I took two painkillers from the drawer and went into the bathroom for a glass of water. I was swallowing the second pill when the trembling in my hands started. It was so violent I dropped the glass into the porcelain sink and watched in slow motion as it shattered into large jagged pieces.

I don't know how I got from the bathroom back to the bed, but I had only been lying there a couple of minutes when there were several rapid knocks at the door. I didn't answer. Couldn't answer. I didn't want to see anyone about anything. Another knock came, followed by a familiar voice.

'Jean? Jean?'

I lay perfectly still, except for the tremor in my hands. He was the last person I needed to see.

'Jean, are you alright? It's me, Charles. Please answer the door.'

I neither moved nor answered. He would go away soon enough.

'Jean, I know you're in there and I'm not going until I know you're alright.'

He would. All I had to do was wait.

'Jean, I'm worried about you – I know you're in there. The young man on reception said he saw you.'

He was bluffing.

'If you don't answer the door I'll assume it's because you're too ill and I'll get the manager to use his pass key.'

I remained silent.

'Right, I'm calling the manager.'

I opened the door in time to see him reach the end of the corridor.

'Charles,' I called gently.

Back in the room I sat on the chair by the desk and Charles came in, his face pale as he closed the door behind him.

'Jean.' He perched on the edge of the bed. 'Whatever's the matter? Are you ill? Tell me.'

I looked at him but didn't speak. What could I tell him?

He leaned forward and took hold of my hand. 'Jean, you're trembling. Look, why don't you let me call a doctor? You're obviously not well.'

Feeling his warm hand grasp mine, I knew I should snatch my hand back and tell him to leave. But there was something comforting about having him close. Having someone hold my hand again after all these years. And as much as I wanted him to leave, to go away and get out of my life forever, I wanted him to stay.

'Would you mind if I didn't say anything, Charles?'

What could I say? That I was here to murder his daughter? That if my initial plans had come to fruition she would already be dead? That he sat clutching the hand that would eventually bring his daughter to her death?

No, it would be better all round if I didn't speak.

Eventually Charles let go of my hand and dialled room service. He asked for a large brandy to be brought to my room. When it came, Charles held it to my lips and insisted I sip it gently whilst he made us both a strong coffee. He didn't ask questions and I didn't feel the need to speak so we sat and drank in silence.

The rains eventually came around six, the same time as a tray of food Charles had ordered from room service. Pewter clouds darkened the sky and the occasional flash of lightning brightened the room as the storm passed directly overhead. Thunder crashed and the curtains flapped noisily as the wind increased, yet I insisted the window stayed open. I needed the cool air in my lungs. Besides, I found the sound of the rain beating against the window panes and gushing along the guttering into the old iron downpipes soothing.

I wasn't hungry, yet found myself picking at the scrambled eggs Charles put before me. I wanted him to leave. I didn't want him here. How could I possibly want him here, knowing who he was? The father of *her*? *She* who had caused me and my family such damage? Yet I didn't want him to leave. Once he left I knew I really would never see him again. And I knew it wasn't his fault that *she* had acted as she did. He wasn't responsible for her vile, callous behaviour. There was a part of me too that was frightened to be alone. Once Charles went I'd be left with my thoughts and I couldn't face them – not yet.

When Charles went into the bathroom, I sat on the edge of the bed. I felt weak, exhausted, yet I was frightened of sleep. Once I awoke I would have to make decisions. Put plans into action and every fibre of my body was pleading for calm and rest. Respite. The pain was severe now and, unconcerned whether it was more than four hours since I'd had the last painkillers, I took two from my bedside drawer and took them with my cold coffee dregs. I wasn't sure it was such a good idea, having had the brandy earlier, but I had to do something if I was to get myself out of this mess. I brought my feet up and lay back on the bed. *Just for a minute or two*, I thought, *until the pain eases.*

When I woke, the storm had passed and the desk lamp was on, casting a warm glow over the room. Someone, Charles presumably, had pulled the window almost shut and drawn the curtains halfway across. I was snug. He'd covered me with the bottom half of the eiderdown, tucking it around me. How thoughtful he was. Turning slightly, I saw Charles lying fully clothed on the bed beside me, at a respectable distance, asleep.

I was surprised but not shocked and I lay there watching him, his breathing slow and even. His chest rose and fell rhythmically and his nostrils flared slightly as he breathed out. In this light, any wrinkles or blemishes on his skin were so indistinct he could have passed for almost half his age. I saw he'd removed his shoes and his feet, crossed at the ankles, looked small for a man of his size.

For now, all thoughts of Bibby and her impending death left me. I was left only with a desire to reach out and touch the man next to me. I couldn't remember the last time I'd felt this way. More than 20 years ago, at least. I wanted to trace the outline of his face with my fingers. I wanted to feel the rise and fall of his chest against mine. I wanted to have him hold me so hard that my breath could only come in pants. I wanted…

It was pointless continuing, whatever I wanted, it could never be. Yet I could not turn away. From here I could see that it was after 11. I should wake him. Tell him to go. I reached out to shake him, but couldn't. Never again would we lie together. Never again would I be this close. And I didn't want the moment to end.

Eventually, I eased myself off the bed and went into the bathroom, where I cleaned my teeth and freshened up. Charles had cleared up the broken glass. Returning to the bedroom with a fresh tumbler of water, I took a few sips and set it on the bedside table. Before turning off the desk lamp I switched on my bedside light and turned it to its dimmest setting. The storm was long since over and I left the window open to let in the cool night air. With the room barely light I lay back on the bed. Charles, still asleep, had turned to face me. I covered him with the eiderdown and, keeping fully clothed, slid under its soft cover to join him. I turned to face him and tried to imagine what would have happened if I had been Jean Francis. Jean Francis, holidaymaker and not Jetta Fellowes, murderer. I told myself to forget that train of thought and to live in the moment. And in this moment I was lying here next to an honourable man. A good man. A man I'd only known for a few hours in total.

Gently, I laid my arm across him and closed my eyes. I felt his warm sweet breath on my face and I wanted to open my eyes. To study him. To enjoy him. But I was scared. Scared he would be looking at me. Scared I wouldn't be content to simply lie there.

But I did lie there, eyes closed, and after what seemed like hours, I drifted into sleep. And I slept a deep, dreamless sleep next to a man who, if things had been different, I would have chosen to spend the rest of my life with.

Chapter Twenty-Four

Lyme Regis, Dorset, Saturday morning, July 2006

It was light when I woke. The lamp still glowed dimly on the bedside table and the sun's rays filled the room. The clock showed it was 7.35. And I remembered Charles. Not wanting him to know I was awake, I remained still, facing away from him; I had much to consider. His arm was curled around my waist, his chest pressed into my back and his legs followed the contours of mine, but he didn't stir. Maybe he was awake, playing the same game, waiting to see who made the first move and what the move would be. The strange thing was that everything seemed much clearer this morning. There was only one move I could make. I had to be strong, not let my heart rule. And to this end I closed my eyes momentarily and allowed myself the brief indulgence of what could have been.

At eight, I gently lifted Charles' arm from around my waist, slipped out from beneath the cover and sat on the edge of the bed, keeping my back to him.

'Morning.'

I tensed at the sound of his voice. 'Morning,' I said, without looking at him. He wasn't part of my plan.

Aware that Charles was watching me, I selected a fresh set of clothes from the wardrobe, but I refused to make eye contact. I didn't trust myself.

'Is there something wrong, Jean?' he asked, sitting on the edge of the bed and stretching his arms over his head.

'No…yes… Yes, there is actually. You staying the night wasn't a good idea.'

'I was worried about you. You weren't well.'

'Well as you can see, I'm well now. And I'd appreciate it if you left.'

'Jean–'

'Preferably without drawing attention to yourself.'

'Is that it? You're worried about what people will think?'

'I'm not particularly proud of the fact that I had a man I barely know spend the night in my room.'

'This is ridiculous, Jean. You–'

'I'm asking you politely, Charles. I'm going into the bathroom now to change and when I come out I'd appreciate it if you were gone.'

'But Jean.' He stood up.

'Please, Charles. Don't make this difficult.'

'When will I see you?'

'You won't.'

'Why? What's happened? Have I done something to offend you?'

'Nothing's happened and you've done nothing.' Clutching my clothes, I opened the bathroom door. 'Please, Charles, don't make me ask you again. If you really are considerate of my feelings, you'll leave right now.'

Shutting the bathroom door behind me, I pushed the bolt to the engaged position and leaned back against the door. I put a hand to my mouth and closed my eyes. I hardly dared breathe. Several minutes later I heard the bedroom door shut. Dropping my clothes to the floor, I went into the bedroom. Charles had gone. There wasn't a trace of him in the room. It was if he'd never been there. I dropped onto the bed and crossed my arms over my chest. Already I missed him. I wanted to run after him and beg him to come back. But I couldn't. I was here for something far more important and I couldn't let anything or anyone prevent that.

Holding up the cover we'd slept under, I buried my face deep into the fabric, desperate to catch a smell of him. Suddenly, I felt engulfed by loneliness and wanted to weep for all that might have been. But I couldn't. I was so numb, I couldn't shed a single tear.

It was with enormous effort that I overrode every instinct to return to bed. Instead I showered, dressed and ate breakfast in the dining room. Life must go on. Well for some, anyway.

Stepping out into the bright sunlight lifted my mood almost immediately. There wasn't a cloud to be seen as I left the hotel. The previous night's rain had left the garden looking refreshed and in a shaded area I stopped to breathe in the musty aroma of the still damp earth. Across the lawn, in full sun, I spotted a wren in a pot of gazanias and watched, captivated, as the tiny bird poked the fresh earth around the bright yellow flowers. I missed my garden. It would be getting too overgrown now. The lawns would need cutting and with the combination of sun and rain we'd been having, the borders were probably knee-deep in weeds. No use worrying, I reminded myself, when I considered its importance in the great scheme of things. No, I would deal with that when the time came. It would, after all, be a welcome relief.

Broad Street was busy. A long line of slow-moving vehicles snaked down the street towards the traffic lights and parking was, as always, at a premium. The pavements were teeming with locals and holidaymakers, some dawdling and browsing in the shop windows whilst others chased around more focused. The Co-op was packed and several times as I squeezed up and down the aisles, locking baskets with other shoppers, I was tempted to abandon the shopping and come back later. But I didn't. Who was to say it would get any better? Joining the queue at the checkout, I swapped my basket from arm to arm as I waited. It held a bottle of Australian Chardonnay, a packet of cheese ploughman's sandwiches, chewy mints and my handbag. Not a lot to show for over half an hour in the store.

When my turn came, the cashier remained cheerful and waited patiently while I counted out the correct money. My purse didn't hold much change.

Standing outside Hilary Highet's, with my carrier at my feet and my handbag over my arm, I considered what to do next. A walk down to the sea front was what I favoured, but I didn't want to bump into Charles. In which case, I decided, it made sense to spend as little time in town as possible so I picked up the carrier and made my way back to the hotel. This could well be the last night I spend here, I reminded myself as I entered reception. But I had a lot to do between now and then.

Not least, commit a murder.

Chapter Twenty-Five

Lyme Regis, Dorset, Saturday evening, July 2006

I followed the same pattern as before, even using the same Co-op carrier bag, and having a gin and tonic before I set off. The wine was the same too, but I'd only bought one as I had a bottle left from my previous visit.

The digital clock on the dashboard showed it was 7.20 when I drew the car to a halt in the lay-by at Cliffside Road. I felt more in control than on my previous visit. This time I knew what to expect, more or less, once inside. And I wouldn't need to prove my identity. No, on this occasion it would all go like clockwork. I knew it. And far from feeling fearful, I almost felt a sense of euphoria.

When I reached the entrance to the apartments, I placed the carrier on the step and pressed the button next to her name, using my knuckle once again so as not to leave fingerprints. She answered almost immediately.

'Is that you, Mrs Francis?'

'Yes. Yes, it is, but call me Jean – please.'

'OK, Jean, come on up. I'll open the apartment door, just walk in and close it behind you.'

I entered the now familiar foyer and, keeping my head bowed, took the lift to the fourth floor, where its doors parted and I once again found myself in the carpeted hallway. Turning left I walked to the end of the hall and saw her apartment door ajar. I didn't bother knocking. Walk straight in, she'd told me. So I did and felt emboldened with every step.

'I'm here,' I called, walking into the sitting room.

'Be right with you,' she shouted from the kitchen. 'Make yourself comfortable.'

Sitting on the sofa in the spacious bright room, once again the view across the bay drew my attention. It was one I would certainly never tire of. The French doors, wide open, allowed the cool early evening air to fill the room. It was the perfect temperature for me.

'Good, you've made yourself comfortable,' she said, coming into the room. I noticed her limp was more pronounced this evening. 'Now, before we start, can I get you anything? Wine? Tea? Coffee?'

I took one of the bottles of Chardonnay from my carrier and offered it to her. 'Please. I'd love a glass of wine, and I insist you join me.'

She took the wine from me and smiled. 'This really wasn't necessary. Besides, it's my turn. You brought the wine last time.'

'It's the least I can do after you giving up yet another evening.'

Bibby walked across to the kitchen. 'I just hope I'll be of some use to you. It's been a long tiring day, if I'm honest, and my brain's more fuddled than usual.'

'I needn't bother with the formalities this time, if you don't mind,' I said as we sat with our full glasses of wine on the coffee table in front of us. 'You know who I am and why I'm here. And I've got your basic details such as your date and place of birth, so we can get straight down to your experiences of the hospital, its staff and treatment.'

I watched as she took a sip of wine from her glass. She looked tired and there were dark circles under her eyes. Maybe this would be easier than I thought.

'The first question I need to ask is… Oh dear, silly me. You're going to think I'm the one with the fuddled brain. I did this before when I came –I've forgotten to take my pills again. That's what I get for rushing out at the last minute. Could I trouble you for…?'

'A glass of blackcurrant juice with ice, if I remember rightly,' she said, standing up and going to the kitchen. 'I won't be a minute.'

As soon as her back was turned I followed the pattern of my previous visit. Undoing the twist of greaseproof paper, I emptied its powder contents into her wine, stirring quickly with my index finger before dropping the paper into my pocket. I removed two tiny breath mints from my bag, placed them on the table and by the time she returned I had relaxed back on the sofa as if I hadn't moved.

'Hope that's strong enough,' she said, handing me the full tumbler.

'Perfect.' I washed down the two mints one after the other, pulling the requisite pained expression.

She leaned back in her chair, put her feet up on a leather footstool and took a sip of wine. I watched her closely. She didn't appear to notice anything wrong with the taste.

'Do you play?' I pointed to the upright piano on the near wall.

'Not really. I wanted to learn, but haven't got around to taking lessons. I can play a tune by ear, but that's only using a finger or two, so it doesn't count. My father brought the piano for me last year as an incentive to learn. I will do. Probably when I'm less busy with the business.'

'Your father – does he live locally?'

'He does now.'

'Now? Has he recently moved here?'

'Yes, not too long ago. I'm delighted. I'm biased of course, but he's a wonderful man.'

'That's good to hear.' Her opinion of Charles was something we would agree on. 'That's not the general impression given of many men these days!'

'That's true. I've certainly known some bastards in my time.' She took a slug of wine and I wondered if she considered Peter to be one of those bastards. 'Still,' she added, 'you're not here to talk about that. Let's get down to business.'

I took a sheaf of papers and a pen from my bag. 'So…who first referred you to the Mineral Hospital and when, roughly?' I asked, making the script up to suit as I went along.

'It was my GP. About 20 years ago.'

'Your local doctor here?'

'No. I was living in Wiltshire when I first had arthritic problems. My doctor in Swindon referred me.'

Swindon. My home town. The place where I was born. And the place where, in all likelihood, I would still be living, with Lawrence, if she hadn't wrecked our lives.

'And did anyone else in your family have similar problems?'

'I don't have any siblings, and neither of my parents had problems I was aware of.'

I continued in the same vein, asking her about her health and treatment, making each question up as I went along and recording her answers on the sheets in front of me. As she talked, she drank and I made a mental note of all the ends I would need to tie up once I'd killed her. There would be fingerprints to erase, surfaces to wipe, glasses to dispose of and papers to remove. All evidence of my every having been in the flat would be gone. Gone for good, as would *she*.

I'd been there almost an hour when I asked, 'Do you know if your mother has osteoporosis?'

'My mother's dead. She died more than 20 years ago.'

'I'm sorry. She couldn't have been very old. Was it an accident?'

'Depends how you view it.' She leaned forward and placed her glass on the table. I immediately topped it up. 'You've hardly touched your wine,' she said.

I took a tiny sip from my glass. 'I don't mean to pry, but what did you mean about your mother's death being an accident, depending on how you viewed it?'

'She died from an overdose.'

'Took her own life?'

'Accidentally. She…she was a drug addict.'

She lifted her now full glass to her lips and held it there momentarily before drinking. We were on the second bottle. She could certainly hold her wine.

'That must have been a difficult time for you.'

'It was. I'd done everything I could to help her, or so I thought. I didn't realise then that the only person who could help her was herself. Still, it was a long time ago. I was a lot younger. More naïve.' If I wasn't mistaken, her voice was starting to slur. The powder was taking effect. 'Still, you're not here to listen to all this. We'd better continue or else you'll be here all night.'

'I've got all the time in the world. If it helps to talk.'

'I don't know why I'm mentioning this.' She leaned forward, almost staring at me, her eyes slightly glazed. 'Do I know…no, I can't do…but you look familiar. For a moment I thought you…'

'Lots of people say that. But it's not surprising, is it? Another grey-haired old lady like so many others.' Suddenly, I put my hand up to my right eye. 'Oh! I seem to have got something in my eye…it's watering badly. Can I trouble you for a tissue?'

She stood up, rather unsteadily I thought, and put her glass on the table. 'I'm sure I've got some in the bedroom.'

As soon as she disappeared into the hallway I took another greaseproof twist from my pocket and emptied the contents into her glass. I was still trying to get the powder to dissolve when I heard her coming back down the hallway. Keeping my back to the door I continued to stir the wine with my finger, desperately willing the white powder to disappear.

'Here you are.' She placed a square box of tissues on the coffee table.

I straightened up, keeping my hand over my eye. There were a couple of tiny white flecks floating on the surface of her wine, but hopefully none that she would notice.

'I saw something land in your wine but I think it's gone now. That's the trouble this time of year. So many bugs about.' Removing a tissue, I held it to my eye and rubbed. 'That's better,' I said, after a minute or two. 'Now, where were we? You were telling me about your mother.'

'I don't know why.'

I smiled. 'I can empathise. It would be rare to live as long as I have without experiencing some of life's problems.'

'I didn't know she was an addict, of course. I now realise she was even before I came along. And after I was born she got worse.'

'Your father?'

'As far as I was concerned he'd abandoned us when I was about three or four. I had vague memories of a man reading me bedtime stories. We lived in an apartment near a lake outside Halifax and I remember one time him taking me skating on the lake when it froze in the winter.'

'Halifax?'

'Nova Scotia. We lived in Canada then. Some nights, long after he'd left, I would lie in bed imagining I could still feel his firm hold on my gloved hand as we slid across the ice. And the way he called me Bibby – never Elizabeth, as my mother insisted. No, I was always his little Bibby.'

Little Bibby. A vision of Charles skating across a frozen lake clutching the hand of his young daughter came to mind. I saw him tucking her up in bed, reading her stories until she slept.

That sounded like the Charles I'd met. The Charles I had started to know. The Charles that… I stopped. It was a chain of thought that wasn't helpful.

'Of course, I know now that my father hadn't abandoned me at all. My mother left him, taking me to live with her and a series of men. Dealers. Junkies. No-hopers. She had enormous mood swings, some violent, and the men she lived with were violent too, occasionally towards me, often to my mother. And I believed it was up to me to get her out of the situation.' She paused briefly to drink more wine. 'Like most kids, I was desperate for love and approval, irrespective of how she was with me. And I spent my whole life, up until she died, trying to make her and everything alright.'

'These men you mention, are they the…the bastards you referred to?'

'Oh, I know it's easy to generalise and, believe me, I've met some men, one in particular, who turned that whole theory on its head. But you had to see things from my position. The men we knew wanted more and more money to feed their habit, as did my mother. I worked from a real early age, but I never earned enough. They always needed more. 'Everything will be alright this time, Elizabeth,' she'd say. But it was always going to be alright this time. Until the next time. She always needed just one more injection of cash, if you'll forgive the pun.'

Beads of perspiration began to form on my face and body and I fanned myself with the sheaf of papers. 'The man you mentioned who turned your…your bastard theory on its head…'

'Him.' She didn't look at me. Instead she gazed at the colourful Indian rug at her feet, her words less distinct now. 'I married him.'

Despite the perspiration on my body, I shivered. Surely this was Peter. My son. The man she… *Don't go there, Jetta*, I told myself. *Keep focused. Not long now. You might need another powder.*

'And?'

'My getting married didn't stop my mother needing me or, more accurately, needing money. She put more pressure on me to provide it. I was living a double life. It was a nightmare. I was young and stupid and didn't know a good thing when I had it. I'm not proud of how I handled my life then. I became a consummate liar. And the one time I refused to help her, one of her so-called men friends taught me a lesson. Their words, not mine.'

'How?'

She swallowed hard before she spoke. 'He beat me. Severely. Even that I could have coped with, but he threatened to do far worse to my mother if I didn't do as he asked.'

I closed my eyes briefly, trying to rid my mind of an image I'd seen years ago. 'Which was?'

'Money. It was always about getting money. Everything came back to that. And they didn't care who got hurt in the process.'

An image of Peter after the court case came into my mind. She'd done that. She'd inflicted that pain and suffering on him. On the man who'd only ever had her best interests at heart. A wave of heat flooded my body. I needed air.

'Would you mind if we took our drinks out onto the balcony?' I said. 'I feel terribly hot and it's such a pleasant evening.'

'Not at all.' She stood and picked up her glass, leading the way out onto the balcony. 'It's a good idea.'

I followed and she indicated for me to sit on a chair facing the view. She sat alongside me, putting one of her legs up on a low table in front of her. Yawning, she stretched her arms over her head. 'Excuse me.' She put a hand to her mouth. 'I feel particularly tired this evening. I apologise.'

'Not at all. I've got almost all I need from you.' I glanced down at my papers. 'I can enjoy my wine now.'

Out of the corner of my eye, I studied the woman beside me. Where was the young woman she had been? Before I'd come here I thought I knew. She was still there, the same conniving, vindictive bitch who'd ruined so much of my family's life. I knew the husband she'd referred to was Peter. He was the good man.

And then I thought of her early life with her mother. What must she have witnessed? And that beating? Surely it was the beating she'd accused Peter of. What would I have done at that age if someone had beaten me and threatened to do that and more to someone I loved if I didn't comply? Oh, for Christ's sake Jetta, I asked myself, why are you putting yourself in her shoes? Did she once put herself in Peter's? Or yours?

'I hope I haven't bored you with all my ramblings this evening. I don't know what came over me. You're so easy to talk to. And, I suppose, apart from my father, I've never really admitted to anyone how bad life was then.'

'It's often easier with a stranger. Someone such as myself who isn't involved.' She drained her glass and I poured her a refill. 'There's plenty more where that came from.'

She yawned. 'I couldn't really,' she slurred. 'I feel quite heady.'

I stood, clutched my glass, walked around to the side of the balcony and peered over the ornate railings to the enormous rocks far below. It wouldn't be me who would kill her ultimately. It would be those rocks that provided the final murderous blow. All I needed to do was to lure her here and then…

My mind was a jumble of thoughts and images. Charles lying next to me; Bibby as a young girl; Peter shrunken, beaten; Charles skating hand in hand with a young girl and that same young girl trying desperately to put her mother's life back together again. She was all the King's horses and all the King's men. I felt confused. It was the wine. After all, I'd hardly eaten. A packet of ploughman's sandwiches was all I'd had since breakfast and that was hours ago. I knew I should have eaten something before I left. But I couldn't. I'd felt slightly nauseous, despite the gin and tonic I'd had to help settle any nerves.

'I hope I haven't troubled you,' she slurred, coming and standing alongside me. She leaned her elbows on the rail, her forearms extended over the balcony, wine glass cupped in both hands.

'Not at all. I'm simply enjoying the glorious views.'

She was making it easy. It would be so easy now. All I had to do was to take her off-balance and tip her over the edge. My heart rate quickened and my breathing came faster, shallower. A vein in my head pounded painfully and the feelings of nausea returned with a vengeance. This was it. The moment I'd planned for. It was actually less than a fortnight since I'd made the decision, although it seemed much longer. What was I waiting for? All paths had led me here. Seeing her in the Mineral Hospital the day after I'd been told I had inoperable cancer. My finding her so easily. That man, Nomad, with the big hair and bright eyes, telling me that my search would bear fruit. Yes, it had all led to this moment.

Somewhere, against the background of thoughts, I was aware of a noise. It came from behind me. But before I even had a chance to turn, a voice boomed out. 'Hello, Mother.'

Bibby jumped, her glass slipping through her fingers to drop and crash on the rocks below. We both turned at the same time to see him stood there. It couldn't be, I told myself. It just couldn't. But it was. It was him.

And Bibby said, 'Hello, Peter.'

Chapter Twenty-Six

Lyme Regis, Dorset, Saturday evening, July 2006

Unable to move, I watched them from the corner of the balcony. It was as if the clocks had turned back in time.

'Peter! What a lovely surprise, I wasn't expecting you until tomorrow.'

He put his arms around her shoulders as she reached up and kissed his cheek. She was tall, but he was taller.

'You OK?' He stood back. 'You look rough.'

'Thank you for that vote of confidence!' She stretched up and ruffled his thick black hair. 'Actually, I believe I've had too much to drink.'

In that moment it all became clear. He had the same thick black hair. The same broad-mouthed smile. The same build. This time, it was me who dropped the glass. It hit the floor and shattered, and a dark stain seeped across the concrete. And that's when Peter noticed me. The visitor.

Bibby turned. 'Oh, Jean. Don't worry. Peter, get the dustpan and brush, would you?'

As she took my arm and led me back inside, I don't know which of us was the most unsteady. I sat back on the sofa, aware that Peter was clearing up the glass outside. Peter. Peter. Peter. It had to be, but the dates didn't add up. Charles had said his grandson was at university in Plymouth. That would have made him in his late teens or early twenties. But who was I kidding? There was no mistaking him. He was the image of my Peter at that age. I looked at the silver-framed photograph that stood on the side table. It was Peter, of course. But not the man I'd thought. It was a young man named Peter. And he was named after his father. He was my son's son. Which made him my grandson.

Bibby interrupted my thoughts. 'I've put some coffee on. I think I've had too much wine. We could probably both do with a strong hit of caffeine.'

I nodded, unable to speak as I watched Peter walk through the sitting room carrying a dustpan of broken glass.

The coffee was what I needed. It was strong and black, Bibby's the same. Peter declined coffee, opting for fruit juice instead.

'This is Jean. Jean Francis,' Bibby said to him.

He extended a long arm towards me and I shook it. 'Pleased to meet you,' he said, and I resisted the urge to hang on to his hand. 'Seems I gave you both a shock, if the breakages are anything to go by!' He smiled to reveal large, even white teeth, and pushed a stray twist of hair back from his face.

'Jean's conducting a survey on behalf of the Mineral hospital,' Bibby added. 'But I'm afraid I sidetracked her somewhat.'

I shook my head. 'Not at all.'

We stayed that way as Bibby and I finished our coffees. I know we talked, but I can't remember what about. Watching Peter was of more interest. He busied himself emptying his backpack, taking bits to his room, sending texts from his mobile, draining his glass of juice and refilling our coffee cups when empty.

Dusk arrived and went. The lamps, now lit, highlighted the comfort of the room. It was homely, even I couldn't deny that. I noticed how Bibby had brightened since Peter's arrival. He did seem to bring a good feeling with him, the sort of liveliness only youth can generate. So, this was Peter's home too. My grandson.

And I didn't want to leave. Because I knew when I did it would be the last time I would see him.

'Would you like Peter to run you back to your hotel?' Bibby asked when I said I ought to be going.

Yes, I would love my grandson to take me back to my hotel, I thought. But it was ridiculous to even consider it. What was I thinking? I needed to get out of here before the situation got even more complicated.

'No, that's fine. It's a kind offer, but I've got my car.'

'I really don't mind,' Peter said. 'Whereabouts are you staying?'

I wanted to lie but couldn't. 'The Admiral's House Hotel.'

'I can run you up there in your car if you like and I can walk back, it's not far. Then you'll have your car there ready for the morning.'

'I wouldn't dream of it. I'm sure you've got lots more important things to do here. I'll leave you both in peace.'

Despite their protests, I insisted I was well enough, and sober enough, to drive. Gathering up my papers and bags, I thanked Bibby for her help.

'Not at all. It should be me thanking you for listening.'

'It was nice to meet you, Jean,' Peter added.

'Likewise,' I said, taking a long last look at him. At his faded jeans and bare feet. His black T-shirt and tanned arms. And his smile. I would never forget his smile. I wanted to hold him. To hug him. To feel his arms around me. And to know how it felt to be hugged by my grandson. But that would never happen. Not now. It couldn't. And I left before my overwhelming sense of regret exploded. Or imploded. I said goodbye knowing this was the last time I would see my grandson.

I'm not sure what time I arrived back at the hotel, but as I was about to climb the stairs, a voice called from reception.

'Mrs Francis?'

I turned. The man on reception was not someone I'd seen before. 'Yes…?'

'There's a note here for you. It was dropped in earlier.'

I thanked him and took it to my room, confused. Who knew I was here besides Bibby, and now Peter? Piling my bags on the bed, I sat down and looked at the small white envelope.

JEAN FRANCIS
c/o THE ADMIRAL'S HOUSE HOTEL

Of course. The printed handwriting was unfamiliar but I knew instinctively it was from Charles. He was the only other person who knew I was here. Well, whatever he had to say, I wasn't interested. I threw it unopened into the empty wastepaper basket beside the desk. I had too much else to occupy my thoughts.

I undressed for bed and knew I wouldn't sleep. Reaching into my cardigan pocket, I removed a twist of grease-proof paper and emptied its contents into a small glass of water. And as I drank the liquid before turning out the bed-side light, the irony of what I'd just done wasn't lost on me.

Chapter Twenty-Seven

Lyme Regis, Dorset, Sunday morning, July 2006

As soon as I opened my eyes, the events of the past 24 hours were there. Disturbingly, the new-found knowledge loomed over me and I was at a loss as to what to do next. Time and space were what I needed to collect my thoughts and consider my next course of action. Peter had a son. The statement, however much I tried to prevent it, was a constant thought.

Splashing my face with cold water in the bathroom did nothing to clear my thumping head and as I finished getting dressed, I knew I couldn't face breakfast. The only thing I was sure of was that I would spend the day away from Lyme Regis. It didn't matter where. I would go anywhere, as long as it was away from here, and Charles. The unopened letter in the wastepaper basket reminded me that he was not going to give up easily. He was a regrettable mistake on my part. And now there was the knowledge that we shared a grandson. I closed my eyes. What a ghastly, God-awful mess.

I took the A3052 out of Lyme Regis. It would take me further west towards Seaton and Sidmouth. Both sounded a possibility, but as yet my destination was undecided. The road meandered along the coast and, ignoring a sign to Seaton, I drove over a tram crossing and into Colyford. Seeing a row of old disused petrol pumps on the left, I checked my fuel gauge. It showed almost empty. I must find a garage, and soon.

Climbing the hill out of the village, I found a petrol station sited on another left turn into Seaton. After queuing on the crowded forecourt, I filled the car. I didn't want to run out of petrol on these unfamiliar country roads.

Continuing on the A3052, I passed Hangman's Corner and not long after saw a sign that read 'Beer 2 Miles'. The name appealed to me. It seemed as good a place as any to consider the future.

Parking was difficult. A Sunday in July probably wasn't the best time to find this unspoilt seaside village quiet and sleeping. Driving cautiously through the busy village centre, I noticed a small stream following the sloping street and guessed it ran on into the sea. The shops and galleries on both sides of the road looked interesting and would, I thought, provide a welcome distraction if only for a while. Provided I could find a parking space.

Finding the car park behind the shops full, I continued around a narrow right hand bend at The Anchor Inn. Here the road climbed steeply. On the right, a row of flint-faced fishermen's cottages stood facing the coastline as they probably had for a century or more, whilst on the left the pub garden and allotments enjoyed the same view. Behind the low stone wall of one of the cottages, a 'For Sale' board leaned awkwardly in the small front garden, and I wondered what the asking price was. A figure guaranteed to be beyond the wildest dreams of its original occupants, I guessed.

I imagined myself living there. Strolling to the newsagents every morning for my daily paper, making a bamboo wigwam for my runner beans on the allotment, buying freshly caught local fish, and…

I stopped. They were nice thoughts, but not worth pursuing.

As I reached the top of Common Hill, the road petered out. The only route was into a grassy cliff-top car park and driving in there, my mood immediately lightened. Many cars were already parked haphazardly on the wide open headland, but with so much space it was easy for me to park without being close to other vehicles. Facing my car towards the sea, I lowered the windows and turned the engine off. I couldn't remember when I'd last noticed so much sky. The view was stunning and I simply wanted to sit awhile and take it in. Breathing deeply, I filled my lungs with the fresh coastal air, confident I could taste the sea on my tongue. It was easy to understand why people went to the seaside to recuperate and convalesce.

Far to the right, pastel caravans clung to the headland and ahead of me the blue of the sea merged with the blue of the sky, interrupted only by a wisp of cloud and the occasional bob of a boat. Around the bay to the left, I saw what I guessed to be Seaton in the distance, hugging the picturesque shoreline. Maybe I'd call there on my way back. The open grassy space in front of me sloped away to a distant narrow pathway, behind which lay a mature hedge almost obscuring a couple of houses. One was a generous size if its roof and chimneys were anything to go by.

For a long while I sat and watched. Cars came and went. A couple, around my age I guessed, sat in deckchairs beside their old green Fiesta, topping up their mugs from a thermos she retrieved from a chequered holdall. They didn't talk much. He read *The Sunday Mirror* and she sat, pen in hand, completing what I took to be a crossword. Fleetingly I felt a stir of envy, but dismissed it quickly. I was getting good at that.

Not far from them, a large silver estate car disgorged two adults, three children and two dogs. It took them almost half an hour, I noticed, to catch the dogs, tether them on leads, strap the baby in its pushchair, and unpack the car. The eldest child, a boy, insisted on riding a scooter and scooted down the uneven path towards the exit, despite cries from his mother to stop. Exasperated, she sat on the edge of the car's open boot, her young face showing the strain of raising a family. I didn't envy her. It was easier to raise a family when I was younger, despite all we didn't have. Or maybe because of all we didn't have.

Families. That's what I was here to think about. What to do next. Should I return home and forget the events of the past two weeks? Impossible. There was too much outstanding. Yet I couldn't decide on my next course of action. I couldn't think objectively. My thoughts were dominated by my youngest son, my grandson and Charles.

Walking back down Common Hill to The Anchor Inn, I turned right and followed a wide steep incline down to the beach. A neat line of deckchairs faced the sea, their occupants watching the activity around The Pearl and Lively Lady, both fresh in from sea trips. Fishing nets, winches, crab pots and thick ropes snaked across the pebbles and at the landing stage on the fore shore, I could make out signs offering afternoon fishing trips. It seemed that the boats that went out sea fishing that morning would tout for customers to go mackerel fishing that afternoon. July was a busy time.

The sheer white cliffs surrounding the small cove made it a veritable suntrap on such a sunny day and surely offered shelter from the storms that attacked the coastline. The row of painted wooden beach huts sited up off the beach on a boardwalk against the cliff reminded me of a painting Peter did as a child. It stayed on the kitchen wall of The Gables for years. Matchstick figures of a mother, father and two children standing outside a primary red beach hut. Peter always loved the seaside.

I removed my cardigan and carried it over my arm, unable to tie its arms around my waist as I'd seen others do. It just wasn't me. Tables outside a café on the beach filled quickly and the faint smell of cooking reminded me I hadn't eaten. I still wasn't hungry and I began the walk back up to the main street. A coffee somewhere quiet would do me.

The going up was tough and I stopped and leaned back against the thick stone wall to catch my breath. A couple of fishermen passed carrying a box of crabs and the young boy I'd seen in the car park raced past, closely followed by his father carrying the scooter.

I smiled. His wife, dogs and two other children were nowhere to be seen. The man reminded me of Peter at that age and I hoped he realised how fortunate he was. However much hard work his children were, he was there with them. Enjoying them, being frustrated by them. Loving them. Peter had never known he was a father. And I thought of all he had missed. His son's first steps, first teeth and first day at school. Christmases. Birthdays. And it wasn't only the joys of parenthood, it was the sorrows too. All were valuable and all were lost, never to be regained.

In the main street I found an inviting café a short walk past The Marine House Gallery. Through the gallery window I'd seen many interesting items and would pay a visit there after my coffee. For now I needed a rest. It was lunchtime, seats in the café filled quickly and it was impossible to sit at a table on my own. Seeing a couple of women sat at a window table, I asked if I could join them.

'Certainly,' the elder of the two said, lifting her green leather handbag off the spare chair. The younger one, who I took to be in her 40s, smiled and said it would be good to have company. I soon learned they were mother and daughter on a weekend break at a guest house in Exmouth.

'We're getting away from the trials and tribulations of family life,' the mother said, ignoring the look her daughter gave her.

'I know all about that,' I said, picking up the plastic-covered menu and scanning the list of beverages.

The mother smiled knowingly and pointed at the menu. 'The roast is supposed to be good. Reasonable too, if you fancy it.'

'I'm only having a coffee. I'm not that hungry.'

'Sadly, you can't do that.' The daughter indicated the line that read: *At weekends in the summer, between 1-2pm, due to the high demand from customers for our lunches, drinks can only be served with meals. Thank you for your understanding.*

I checked my watch. It was a quarter past one. 'Oh well, I'd better try something,' I said, unable to face the prospect of finding another place to sit and drink. My body ached.

The waitress took our order of three roast chicken dinners. My companions ordered a pot of tea for two and I said I'd wait until after I'd eaten. I always found a drink before meals suppressed my appetite.

'Are you on holiday?' the mother asked, whose name I now knew to be Doreen.

'Yes.'

'Where are you from?'

'Bath.'

'You lived near Bath for a while, didn't you, Sarah?' Doreen turned to her daughter.

'Yes. Limpley Stoke. Delightful little village. Whereabouts are you?'

'Hampton Stoke.'

'What a small world,' Sarah added. 'I don't know it well, but I've eaten at the pub there once or twice. The Ring o' Bells, isn't it?'

I nodded.

'Have you lived there long?'

'Over 26 years now.'

'With your family?' Doreen asked.

'No, I live alone.'

'Oh, it's just that when I mentioned family you…'

'My husband died in 1980.'

'Just after you moved there?' Sarah calculated correctly.

'Not too long after.'

'Do you have any other family nearby?'

'I have family in Swindon, which isn't too far. Two sons and two granddaughters and,' I heard myself adding, 'a grandson in Lyme Regis.'

'We adore Lyme Regis,' Doreen said. 'We often go there in the summer, the whole family for Lifeboat Week, but this year… well, things are rather more difficult.'

Seeing the look that passed between mother and daughter, I didn't pry. I was shocked I had told two strangers about Peter. Yet as I heard myself speak, I felt proud. Proud of the tall, handsome young man that was the image of his father. Yes, I did have a grandson. Nothing could change that. And without waiting for my lunch or ordering a drink, I told Doreen and Sarah that I must be going.

'I've remembered something important,' I said, rising from the table and thanking them both for their company. 'Please apologise to the waitress for me.'

Dashing from the café, I knew the two women would comment on my strange behaviour. It didn't matter. Something far more important had come up. I passed by the gallery, no time for that now, I had things to do.

Arriving back at the headland car park, I realised I hadn't stopped on the upward climb. The aches and pains I'd felt earlier were gone. Or if they were there, I simply didn't notice them. Funny how the mind can override the body when it has a purpose.

I took one last look across the bay to where the sea met the horizon, pulled the sun visor down, turned the key in the ignition and followed the signs out of Beer. I wouldn't stop at Seaton. Not now. I had a phone call to make.

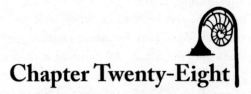

Chapter Twenty-Eight

Lyme Regis, Dorset, Sunday afternoon, July 2006

It was clear what I must do. Of course it would be complicated and lives would be disturbed. But that was life. That's how you know you are alive. Being alive means having challenges to meet and decisions to make, however unpleasant. The women I'd met in the café earlier had family problems, that much was obvious. Everyone does, I realised, when you scratched the surface of their lives. Few of us get off scot-free. Yes, I was alive. And without a crystal ball I had no idea for how much longer, which was all the more reason to act now.

By the time I got back to the hotel I was hungry. I would eat before I did anything. It would also give me time to plan what to say. Afternoon tea was served between 2.30 and 5.00pm, and it was 2.35. Perfect. Choosing to eat in the plush sitting room, I ordered finger sandwiches of granary bread filled with Lyme crab and lemon, a freshly baked scone with locally produced strawberry jam and clotted cream, and a pot of Darjeeling for one. There was no-one else in the sitting room. Most people opted to take tea in the conservatory or the garden on such a sunny day. But the sitting room was cool and made a welcome change from the heat of the afternoon sun. Relaxing on the large comfy sofa, I put my feet on a footstool and closed my eyes to consider recent events. Life, it seemed, was always full of surprises.

'Mrs Francis... Oh, I'm sorry, did I wake you?'

I opened my eyes to see a waitress stood in front of me.

'No. I was thinking, that's all.'

She placed the tray on the low coffee table and my mouth actually watered. 'Would you like me to pour for you?'

'No, that's fine. Thank you.' All I wanted to do was eat.

As soon as she left I picked up a crab sandwich and took an enormous bite. The combination of crab and lemon was delicious and I made short work of the six fingers. I wondered if I'd ordered enough in one scone, but by the time I'd finished eating, I was sated. Wiping my mouth with the white linen napkin, I poured tea into the bone china cup and sat back. I was on my second cup when Matthew came in.

'How are you, Mrs Francis?'

'I'm well, thank you. The sandwiches were delicious.'

'Good. The afternoon teas are popular.' He paused, then added, 'A gentleman came in earlier asking for you.'

'Gentleman?'

'Yes, said his name was Charles. Charles Sherman.'

'What did you tell him?'

'I suggested you were out as you didn't answer the telephone when I rang your room.'

'I was. Did he leave a message?'

'Only that he'd call back on his way home from town.'

'How long ago was that?'

'Over an hour. I asked if I could give you a message, but he said no. Just to tell you that he would call back.'

I hesitated. 'I don't want to see him, Matthew. When he returns, please tell him I'm not back.' I was embarrassed at asking him to lie for me. From the way Matthew stood and moved, I sensed he had more to say. I was right.

'I get the feeling, Mrs Francis, that he might keep coming

back until he does find you in, if you get my meaning.' Matthew was a perceptive young man.

'Sadly, I think you're right. In which case, if he comes back again after today, please tell him I've checked out.'

'If that's what you want…'

'Yes, Matthew. That's exactly what I want.'

Upon reaching the door, Matthew turned. 'Won't he recognise your car if it's outside?'

I thought for a moment. 'No, it's OK. He doesn't know what I drive.'

Finishing my tea, I gathered up my cardigan and handbag, but as I was leaving the sitting room I caught sight of Charles coming up the front steps. Immediately I stepped back into the room, leaving the door ajar. I watched him as he pressed the bell on reception and checked his watch as the grandfather clock struck the half hour. It was 3.30. He stood tall and upright, his beige slacks neatly pressed and he'd rolled the long sleeves of his pale blue shirt above his elbows. With his back to me I couldn't see his face, but in my mind I saw every detail.

'Hello again.' Matthew appeared from the office beyond the desk.

'Has Jean…I mean has Mrs Francis returned yet?' Charles' voice was level, yet I detected a note of anxiety.

'I'm sorry, she hasn't. But I'm happy to give her a message when she does.'

'There's no message. In fact I'd rather you didn't mention at all that I called. I'd rather keep it a surprise.'

'Certainly,' Matthew said. 'I understand.'

Charles was concerned about me, I knew that, and watching him leave I resisted the urge to call after him. It would be impossible to have anything to do with him. I had to be realistic. Besides, he was here asking for a woman who didn't exist. A woman who had conned him. A woman who, if her plans hadn't been aborted would have… No, I couldn't even think about that now. He was a good man; better than I deserved. But that didn't stop me missing him.

When I was certain Charles had gone, I thanked Matthew for his help.

'All in a day's work, Mrs Francis,' he said, and winked at me as I turned to go up the stairs.

Back in my room I leaned against the door as it closed. The room was warm, too warm. Crossing to the desk, I picked up the town street map and studied the smaller map on the rear. The one that showed the towns and villages within a 20 mile radius of Lyme Regis. After a couple of minutes, I decided on Honiton; it seemed as good a place as any. Most importantly, it wasn't Lyme Regis.

I opened the window and voices from the garden flooded the room, but no breeze. The air was still, stifling. Sitting near to the window, I stared down at the mobile in my hand. All I had to do now was dial the number.

I took a deep breath, dropped my shoulders and pressed the keys. I closed my eyes. With every unanswered ring, I considered ending the call. If I continued, it would start a chain of events that would change people's lives forever. I knew that. But I let it ring anyway, and prayed I was doing the right thing.

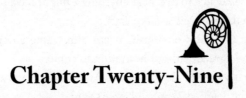

Chapter Twenty-Nine

Honiton, Devon, Monday morning, July 2006

For a Monday morning, Honiton seemed busy and finding a parking space was difficult, despite it being only 9.05. I'd left the hotel early, feeling under siege there in case Charles decided to pay an early morning visit. I couldn't risk coming face to face with him. Unable to find a parking space in the High Street, I took a left into a narrow street between a travel agent's and Lloyds bank. Cars parked on yellow lines made progress difficult but eventually I found a parking space in a car park opposite the library.

Now I had to find a place for us to meet. There were plenty to choose from and after checking several coffee shops, bakeries and cafés, I settled on the Boston Tea Party. If we sat at one of the tables in the garden, we could talk without being overheard. Before going to the counter to order, I rang his mobile.

'Where are you?'

'I'm just passing through a place called Monkton,' he shouted. 'I should be there in no time.'

I explained whereabouts the cafe was situated in the High Street and told him I'd be at a table in the garden. He approved as it was already, in his words, a bloody warm day.

Sitting at an old wooden table alongside a straggly overgrown buddleia, I buttered my croissant and bit into its flaky coating. I was hungry. In my rush to avoid Charles, I'd left the hotel without eating breakfast. A group of women with young toddlers occupied several tables nearby and sat chatting and laughing as their children crawled and ran around on the grass. They were far enough away not to overhear anything I might have to say when he arrived. But what *would* I say?

Even though it obviously meant him taking a day off work, Peter had agreed without hesitation to come.

'What's wrong?' he had asked. And, before I had a chance to answer, he'd added, 'You're ill, aren't you?'

'No,' I lied, promising myself that would be the only lie I would tell him. There were, for now at least, more important things to deal with.

'So what's so urgent that you're asking me to make a three-hour drive to come and see you on a week day? And why there? What's going on?'

'Don't ask questions now. Please just come and I'll tell you everything. You know I wouldn't ask unless it was important.'

And so he was coming. He would be here within half an hour. And I needed to think of what I would say and how.

I finished the croissant, picked the stray flakes of pastry from my plate between thumb and forefinger and put them into my mouth. Setting my empty tall latte glass down onto the rickety table, I picked up the napkin and wiped my mouth. I was still hungry.

When Peter emerged from the door of the café into the sunlight, my breathing quickened. I noticed one of the young mothers look at him as he passed her table. He was probably twice her age yet he was still an attractive man. Today, in jeans and cotton shirt, he cut a good figure and his once dark hair, although mostly grey now, gave him a distinguished look. He carried a jacket over his arm which he threw on the back of the chair opposite before embracing me and kissing both my cheeks.

'It's so good to see you,' I said. It was. His mere presence lightened me, even today, despite what I was about to do.

'You too, Mum. Although I don't understand what's going on. Why you wanted to see me so urgently. And why here? What's going on?'

'Time enough for all that in a minute,' I said. 'Let's order and then we can talk.'

Suddenly my hunger left me. Seeing him opposite me, eagerly awaiting whatever news I had to impart, I felt out of my depth. How could I explain to him how and why I came to be here? No, I hadn't thought this through, there would be too many gaps in the information. Gaps which, if filled honestly, would undoubtedly mean the end of our relationship.

Half an hour later, after he finished his breakfast of bubble and squeak and scrambled eggs, I watched Peter stir his coffee. He took it without milk and I was beginning to wish I'd done the same. The small talk was over. We'd done the weather and work and family updates. Now I could see Peter was settling in for the real reason I'd asked him to come here. And he wasn't prepared to wait any longer.

I was in a bubble. A bubble in which only Peter and I existed. A bubble in which I heard myself talk as I fingered the edge of the wooden table, unable to meet his gaze.

'About ten days ago I booked into a hotel…thought I'd have a bit of a break, a change of scenery.'

'Here in Honiton?'

'No. Lyme Regis. The Admiral's House Hotel. It's pleasant enough,'

'But why the secrecy?' he interrupted. 'Why didn't you tell us?'

Us? Had he mentioned my call to David? 'Do David or Debs know I asked you to meet me here today?'

'No, I haven't spoken to either of them. I spent most of the evening organising people to take my place today. You didn't exactly give me much notice.' He sipped his coffee.

I watched him wipe the corners of his mouth simultaneously with thumb and forefinger before I continued. 'I couldn't. I…well, never mind. You're here now.'

'Yes, and getting uneasier by the minute, Mum. I wish you'd cut to the chase.'

'Well, on my travels around Lyme Regis I came across someone. Someone we both know. Someone who in the past caused us…well you, mainly you…heartache, trauma…'

'Bibby!' he said loudly, smacking both his palms down noisily on the table. 'I might have guessed.'

'Yes.' I looked at him. 'How could you possibly have guessed that?'

'I've known for ages, years, that she was living in Lyme Regis. I don't live in a bloody vacuum, you know.'

'But if you knew, why didn't you say? Why didn't you tell me? What…?'

'Why didn't I say? I didn't say because you would have raked up the past. The past that's best left dead and buried. We all knew she was in this part of the world.'

'We?'

'Me, David, Debs.'

'But none of you ever said.'

'We couldn't. We could never tell you because you've never let her go. You've never left her in the past where she belongs. We could never have talked to you about her. None of us. We couldn't do it. She's a taboo subject. We've all moved on. I've moved on, Mum, in case you hadn't noticed. And I'm sure Bibby has too.'

Anger flared in me. I wanted to shake him physically, emotionally. 'Oh yes, she's moved on alright. I'll tell you how far she's moved on, shall I?'

'No you won't, Mum. Because I'm not going to sit here and let you. I can't believe I came here today for this. It's about time you let her go. In case you hadn't noticed, I'm happy. I've got a great business, great friends and, most of the time, a great family.'

'Happy! How can you say you're happy? You never remarried and I know how much you would have loved children. Don't bother denying it. Look how happy you were when you thought she was having your baby, and how devastated you were when you found out she wasn't. You can't deny that.'

'I wouldn't even try. But I was young, much younger. And the reason I never remarried was because I never met anyone I wanted to marry.'

'Because you lost faith in yourself, in women, in marriage.'

'Maybe I did for a while, but I've–'

'And what about your father?'

'What about him?'

'If it hadn't been for her he would still be with us.'

'How can you say that? He had a heart attack.'

'Brought on by all the stress and strain she put on you and the family. He couldn't hold his head up in his own town anymore. We were forced to move.'

'Mum, he was a prime candidate for a heart attack, you know he was. He was a worrier. He smoked. He took exercise under duress. It could have happened at anytime. Besides, he was happy to move to the country. That was his dream. You said yourself he'd never been easier to live with. We all noticed the difference in him. It was you that didn't want to move.'

'How can you defend her…?'

'I'm not defending her.' He stood up, snatched his jacket off the back of the chair and leaned towards me. 'For years, Mum, she's been festering in you. A cancerous growth that you've continually fed and watered. And that's why we could never mention her.'

His mention of the cancer stilled me. Silenced me.

'And I'll tell you something else whilst we're on the subject. I have met someone else. Someone I am going to marry. Someone

I was going to invite you to meet next weekend. But after this, Mum, I've got second thoughts, I truly have.'

And he left without saying another word.

I don't think I sat there long after Peter left. From the looks on people's faces nearby, it was obvious they'd overheard some, if not most, of our exchange. It was time to leave.

Back inside the car, I turned the ignition on and lowered the windows. I don't know what I'd expected from my meeting with Peter, but this wasn't it. Everything whirled across my mind as I took the Axminster road out of Honiton. I couldn't believe that he and David and Debs had known about Bibby and never told me. And now Peter was telling me he'd met someone he intended to marry. How could I throw the sword that was his son into the heart of that relationship? This might be his only chance of happiness. Because, despite what he might say, I knew how much he'd wanted a traditional family life. Or did I? As I passed the turreted Copper Castle on the road out of Honiton, I despaired. Maybe I didn't know anything any more. Oh my Goodness, what a mess. What a God-awful, unholy mess.

Some miles later, after stopping for petrol at a Texaco station, I pulled into a lay-by on the road that bypassed Axminster and parked in front of a white van. Putting the driver's window down, I was immediately assaulted with the noise of traffic thundering past. But rather that than sit in the car without fresh air in this heat. I knew my boys would laugh at me and remind me that I had air conditioning. But I was against sitting in the car with its engine running just so I could keep cool when I could open a window. Especially with fuel fast approaching a pound a litre.

In my rear view mirror I saw the driver of the van behind, a man, reading a newspaper and drinking from a can. Taking my mobile from my handbag, I sat for a while and debated whether to make the call. If only something or someone would give me a sign. That was one of the things about being on one's own, having to make all decisions unaided. Always being the final arbiter. Then I reminded myself that there was a time in the past when I'd craved that, probably as many people did. But at times such as these it would be nice to have someone to bounce the ideas and consequences around with.

Glancing up, I noticed the van driver holding a mobile phone to his ear and I took that as my sign. Rightly or wrongly, I would make the call.

He answered after several rings. 'Yes?'

'Peter. It's Mum. Are you driving?'

'No. Why?'

'I need to speak to you.'

'Haven't we discussed this?'

'Look, Peter, this isn't easy what I've got to say but I do need to see you.'

'I haven't time for all this.'

'You must make time. This is too important. I need to see you.' I paused briefly. I wanted to speak calmly. 'Peter, you're a father.'

'What do you mean, I'm a father? What on earth are you talking about?'

'You, Peter, you're a father. You have a child. You and Bibby have a son.' There I'd said it. It was right. I instinctively knew it was right. He had a son. And now he knew. 'Say something, Peter! Talk to me.'

But it was no use. The line was dead.

Chapter Thirty

Lyme Regis, Dorset, Monday Afternoon, July 2006

Turning right off the A35 at Hunter's Lodge, I took the road that led through Yawl and Uplyme and within 10 minutes was back in Lyme Regis. As I drove down Pound Street, I made up my mind that once back at the hotel, I would pack immediately and check out. I wouldn't stay. Not now, there was no point.

Leaving my car alongside the curved gravel walkway at the side of the hotel, I nodded in greeting to the gardener as she tended the borders near the hotel entrance. Rapidly mounting the steps, I went through the open double doors into the cool hallway.

'Ah, Mrs Francis.' Matthew looked up from behind reception. 'You are popular today. You've had two visits, both from Mr Sherman.'

'Did you tell him I'd checked out?'

'No. It was before I came on duty. There was a note here on reception saying he called. Twice.'

'And now you have another visitor, Mrs Francis,' a familiar voice said behind me.

I turned. Standing up from the sofa and placing a neatly folded copy of *The Independent* back on the hallstand stood Peter.

'How did you…?'

'You told me where you were staying. It wasn't difficult.'

'But…' I couldn't find the words. Everything was running away from me. And I gripped the counter as the room swayed before me.

I don't know how long it took for Peter and Matthew to help me to my room, but it took longer to assure them I didn't need a doctor.

'I have tablets,' I told them. And I did. 'In my handbag. A strip of 10. Just give me two.'

Matthew fetched me a glass of water and I took the pills and insisted he left. 'I'm fine now, honestly. My son's here.'

'Promise you'll ring down if you change your mind about a doctor.'

I nodded.

'Don't worry,' Peter added. 'I'll make sure she does as she's told.'

Matthew smiled. 'From what I know of your mother in the short time she's been here, that could be difficult.' And he closed the door behind him.

Peter switched the kettle on as I lay back against the pillows. I stretched out, my body relishing the bed's cool support. I needed rest. The hum of the boiling kettle filled the room. And when I next opened my eyes an hour later, there was a cold cup of tea on the cabinet beside me and Peter was sat at the desk staring out to sea, talking softly into his mobile.

'I don't know yet. I haven't got any details. It's difficult to say, but I'll call you again later…of course I will…you too. Bye.' And with that he sighed and laid his phone on the desk in front of him.

I watched as he put his hand to his mouth, rubbing the side of his index finger back and forth across his lips. He was worried. And why wouldn't he be? He'd just found out he was a father. He had been a father for 28 years without so much as a clue. How would anyone react to such news?

The phone on the bedside table rang and Peter jumped. I swung my legs off the bed and picked up the receiver. It was Matthew.

'Just to let you know, Mrs Francis, that Mr Sherman has been in again.'

'Did you tell him I'd checked out?'

'I said that you vacated your room this morning. It implies the same. Besides, you did. He asked if there was any message and I said not.'

Inwardly, I gave a sigh of relief. 'Thank you.'

'How are you feeling now?'

'Much better. I simply needed to rest.'

Placing the receiver on the handset, I lay back against the pillows. Peter turned to face me, his expression gave nothing away.

'I think there's a lot you're not telling me. Who did you want to be told you'd checked out?'

'Peter,' I sat forward and pushed several pillows behind my back to prop myself upright. 'There's so much to tell you I don't even know where to start.'

'With my son might be a good idea. That's if…'

'If you're going to question whether you have a son, save your breath. I've never seen a father and son more alike.'

'You've seen him!' Peter stood up.

'Yes, purely by chance. At first I thought my mind was playing tricks. I thought he was you.'

Peter crumpled back into the chair, rubbing the palm of his hand across the back of his neck. 'I can't take this in. None of it makes sense. What on earth made you come here in the first place? Why? And who is this Sherman character?'

Ha! Who was this Sherman character? How could I tell him? That Charles was a man who, if things were different, very different, I would willingly spend the rest of my life with, however short that life might be. But now my priority was my son. My son and his son.

'I'll tell you all about Charles – Mr Sherman, but not now. But I will tell you why I came here,' I said, knowing I needed to be economical with the truth.

'A couple of weeks ago I went for a routine appointment at the Mineral Hospital in Bath and saw Bibby there. She didn't see me, but I was fascinated; I felt it was fate that I should see her there. I discovered she lived in Lyme Regis and decided to see for myself how she was living and with whom. I didn't think it would be difficult, after all this isn't a huge town. And…and I don't know, call it what you will, maybe it was a matter of morbid curiosity on my part, but I was intrigued.'

'But why use a false name?'

'I don't know. Perhaps I thought that using my real name might cause someone to be curious in a small town. After all, she's still calling herself Fellowes.'

Peter nodded thoughtfully.

'She wasn't difficult to locate. There's a café and gift shop on the esplanade bearing her name and she works in there regularly.'

'Really?'

'Yes, it's a thriving business seemingly.'

'You've been in there? You've met her?'

'Yes I have met her, but not in there exactly – I went in for coffee and snacks and saw her there, but she didn't recognise me.'

'It's been almost 30 years.'

'I know. But seeing her made me even more curious. Where did she live? How did she live? So…' I paused.

'So?'

'So I went to her apartment.'

'Just like that! You turned up on her doorstep after all this time. I don't believe you could do such a thing!' Peter stood up and went into the bathroom, returning with a glass of water. 'Oh God, please don't tell me you–'

'No, no. It wasn't like that. I…I made an appointment to see her.'

'An appointment?'

'Yes. I told her I was…conducting a survey…'

'A survey…oh my God, Mother, this gets worse! You mean you went there under false pretences?'

'Yes, if you want to put it like that.' I stood up, walked over to the kettle, checked it was filled with water and pushed the on switch. 'I pretended I was doing a patient survey for the Mineral Hospital. She was pleased to help, I didn't have to force my way in or anything like that.'

'And?'

'And I did get into her home. Twice in fact. The first time I saw a photograph and I thought it was of you. But on my second visit…Peter, her son…your son…came home unexpectedly and I realised the photograph was of him. That's when I knew for sure that you have a son. And I have a grandson. He's the right age, he has your hair, your colouring, your build and…and he's a lovely boy. And I couldn't have gone on in this life keeping it from you. You have a right to know.'

Peter looked ghastly and, despite the warm air filling the room, I saw him shiver slightly. I pointed to the tea as I went to make a cup but he shook his head.

'I'm going for a walk. I need to clear my head.'

'I'll come with you,' I said, abandoning the tea-making and grabbing my handbag and cardigan off the bed. 'We can walk together.'

He didn't answer. He simply lifted his jacket off the back of the chair, and walked across to the door and I followed. We made our way downstairs in silence. That was the trouble with knowing something. Once you knew it, you couldn't unknow it.

Matthew was busy on reception booking in a middle-aged couple, the woman loudly listing her dietary requirements. She was gluten and dairy intolerant, apparently, and it seemed there was more but fortunately I was out of earshot by then. Was it *de rigueur* among the so-called middle classes these days to have some form of food intolerance?

I remembered an Indian gentleman who used to come to the surgery in Swindon saying there was no such thing as bad natural foods. He said if we were out of balance, certain foods would aggravate or pacify conditions until we changed our lifestyle. But it seemed that people would do anything these days rather than change lifestyles. They would take medicines, drugs or alcohol to alleviate stress rather than rid themselves of the real problem. They would take pills to lose weight rather than eat less or exercise more. No, it seemed to me that we were living in a world where people refused to take responsibility for their lives. Better to blame it on Tony Blair. Whatever happened to the Great British spirit?

As we emerged from the hotel into the bright day, I suggested we take a walk down to The Cobb. 'I'll be OK going down, but I might need a taxi back up.'

Before Peter had a chance to answer, I heard someone call. And it was a voice I recognised only too well.

The sight of Charles as he came from the side of the hotel caused me to stop in my tracks. He appeared older, greyer, unshaven, and his clothes looked dishevelled as if he'd slept in them. Yet looking at his bloodshot eyes, I doubted he'd slept at all. I closed my eyes momentarily. What had I done? What had I started? What a mess. What a ghastly mess. And it was all down to me. I wanted to turn the clock back. Start again. Save the heartache for everyone. Because that's what it would be – heartache. I couldn't kid myself. Not one of us would emerge from this unscathed or unchanged.

But I also knew it was too late. What I had started someone else would finish. And I had no idea where the finishing line was or how any one of us would get there.

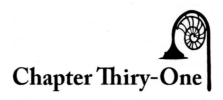

Chapter Thiry-One

Lyme Regis, Dorset, Late Monday Afternoon, July 2006

Charles touched my arm. 'Jean, I've been worried. I've tried to see you several times.'

Peter turned and I saw the puzzled expressions on both their faces.

'Why's this man calling you Jean?' Peter asked in a low voice.

I hesitated. 'It's a long story. One that I'll tell you later. Not now.'

'Why have you been avoiding me?' Charles said. 'Why haven't you answered—?'

Peter stepped towards Charles and visibly stiffened. 'Is this man bothering you, Mum?'

'Not at all.' I grabbed hold of Peter's arm. 'Please. I'll explain everything, but this is neither the time nor place.'

Peter looked unconvinced. 'If you're sure.'

'Is everything alright, Mrs Francis?' I looked up to see Matthew standing in the hotel doorway. 'Anything I can do?'

And standing there in the heat of the afternoon, I wished there was. How easy to hand the whole mess over to someone. Someone young, fit, resourceful. Someone emotionally detached.

'No…no, everything's fine, Matthew, just fine.' I watched him go back into the hotel and turned my attention to Charles. This wasn't the time for introductions and niceties. 'If you don't mind, Charles, my son and I have a bit of catching up to do.'

'But...'

'I'll see you later.'

'When later?'

'When we've have had a chance to talk. I'll come up to your place and see you there.'

'You will?'

Seeing the pained expression of disbelief on his face, I smiled weakly and nodded. I nodded because I had to make him walk away. To leave. To go. I couldn't tell him the truth. How could I? That I'd come to Lyme to kill his daughter. No, I couldn't tell him anything. I simply stood there, upright, hopefully looking outwardly composed, and watched as he scrunched along the gravel path towards the road that would take him out of my life. Forever.

After he disappeared from sight, I turned to Peter, 'Why don't you go for that walk on your own? I'm popping back to my room.'

'Any reason?' he drew his hand across his mouth, wiping the perspiration from his upper lip.

'Yes, I'm off to pack.'

'Pack?'

'Yes. I've decided to move to another hotel. You and me. By the time you get back I'll be ready to leave.'

'But...'

I shook my head. 'Please, Peter. Don't question me. I promise you, I'll explain everything. But I need to be in the right place to do it. And that's not here.'

Once packed, I lay on the king-size bed and thought back to the day I'd arrived. It was much the same as now. I'd lain here propped against the plump cool cotton pillows, the room still warm from the rays of the midday sun and a gentle breeze fluttering in through the open window. How could I possibly have known what was to come?

The thought of what I had hoped to achieve shamed me. The thought of the pain, distress and suffering I would have caused so many, including Charles and my grandson, shamed me more. I would have robbed a man of his daughter and my grandson of his mother. But there was more to it than that. There was Bibby. I had to be honest with myself. She wasn't the woman I had thought her to be. That Bibby was a figment of my imagination. A mother's imagination. She wasn't someone who'd deliberately set out to ruin my son's life. Listening to Charles had taught me that. She was a messed up, screwed up young girl who had married my son. She was a girl who'd learned from an early age the lessons of survival from a mother dependent on drugs and the men that supplied them.

With a sense of shame, I remembered her telling me about the man she'd married who had turned her bastard theory on its head. That man was Peter. My son. He was a good man. She knew it. She had always known it. And together they had a son.

Despite the warmth of the room, I pulled my cardigan tight around me. Peter was right. I had never let Bibby go. I thought of how he'd likened it to a cancerous growth. If only he knew. Maybe he was right about that too. Perhaps there was a link between what festered in my mind and what manifested in my body. Dear God, it was at times such as this I realised that despite having lived 80 years, there was still so much to which I didn't have the answers.

On his return, Peter packed my things into my car.

'I'll be sorry to see you leave,' Matthew said as he handed me the bill.

'You've been very helpful, truly,' I told him as I withdrew the sum in cash from my handbag.

Peter's eyes widened. 'Where on earth did you…?'

'I could hardly pay by card,' I whispered as Matthew counted the notes. 'Mrs Jean Francis doesn't have a card, does she?'

Peter shook his head in disbelief, or maybe it was dismay, and said he'd see me outside. When Matthew finally handed me my receipt, I pushed another note across the counter. Waving my hand at his protests, I closed my handbag clasp and left the hotel for what I knew would be the final time. In one sense, I was sorry to leave. That beautiful room overlooking the sea had become my sanctuary, the place where I'd rested and contemplated my next moves. And this afternoon had been no different. Peter would follow me to Charmouth. This was where I'd decided it would be best for us to stay. It was only three miles east of Lyme, but not a place Charles frequented. Now all I had to do was find somewhere with vacancies, which I realised could be difficult at this time of year.

Looking in my rear view mirror, I checked Peter's silver BMW was behind me as I took the fourth exit off the roundabout. A large blue sign welcomed us to Charmouth, a National Heritage Site, it said, part of the Jurassic Coast. I drove slowly past the cars parked on the short steep hill that led down to the village centre, keeping my foot on the brake. I noticed several houses offering bed and breakfast and what looked to be a couple of hotels, but all had signs: 'No Vacancies'.

As the road levelled out by the Post Office, I slowed and on a whim turned right into Lower Sea Lane. A sign on the side of the local stores indicated it was the way to the beach and car parking. Perhaps it would be better if we parked and walked around the village in our search for accommodation. Some way along the road narrowed and a sign indicated that oncoming traffic had the right of way. About to bring my car to a standstill, I noticed a hotel on the left hand side set back from the road. The Hensleigh Hotel. More importantly, beneath the sign, which showed it was AA recommended, there was another which read: 'Vacancies'.

The woman on reception was charming and apologetic. 'I'm sorry. I was about to change the sign. We haven't even got one room, let alone two. We let our last room less than five minutes ago.'

I flopped down onto a comfy sofa. The day had caught up with me.

'Are you alright, Mum?'

I wasn't, but heard myself say, 'Just a bit tired, that's all. It's been a long day.'

Peter looked around as if searching for something. Someone. And I realised I must look as awful as I felt. 'I'll be alright in a minute.'

But he wasn't listening. He turned to the receptionist. 'My mother's really not well, would you mind her sitting here while I try and sort out some accommodation for us?'

She gave a genuine smile of concern. 'Of course not, would a cup of tea help?'

I intervened. 'I couldn't possibly trouble you.'

'Believe me, it's no trouble,' she said. 'But as for finding somewhere to stay in the village – now that could be a problem.'

She was right. Peter returned a while later, not having had any success. I felt drained as we left the hotel, and slightly dizzy, and Peter must have recognised this. 'We'll park your car up for a while and use mine,' he said. 'It's senseless using both cars.'

'Wait! Wait!'

I looked back and saw the hotel receptionist racing over to us, waving a bit of paper.

'Look, I'm not sure I should be doing this, but…' she looked around as if she didn't want to be overheard. 'There's a lady on the edge of the village who occasionally, very occasionally mind, lets out a couple of her bedrooms. It's not official or anything. And if you weren't too fussed about having en suite or anything like that…'

At that moment, I couldn't have cared if the toilet was at the end of her garden. All I wanted was a place to lie down. 'That sounds ideal,' I said. 'How do we find her?'

She handed Peter a slip of paper with a number on it. 'Try this. Mrs Kitchener her name is, and tell her Sonia gave you her number.'

As I thanked Sonia, Peter rang Mrs Kitchener on his mobile. She did have two rooms and we could go there immediately.

'It's not far,' Peter said, having got directions. 'I'll drive you there in your car and walk back for mine.'

Tempted though I was, I wouldn't hear of it. 'If it's such a short distance I'll drive. Go on, get in your own car and I'll follow you.'

Mrs Kitchener's cottage stood at the end of a short narrow no through road that we would easily have missed without directions. The lane, not much wider than a footpath, had grass growing in the centre and the hedge almost touched the sides of the car in places. Parking on a patch of broken concrete in the lane opposite the gate, we were immediately greeted by a smiling woman with rebellious red hair.

'I forgot to ask if you like dogs.'

'We love them,' I said, sensing by the look on Peter's face that he was about to make our excuses and suggest we leave.

'That's good. Now, how many nights was it for?'

'One,' Peter said.

'To begin with…if that's alright,' I added. I'd talk with Peter later, no point arguing about it now.

Mrs Kitchener led us up a chipped concrete path to a side door that led directly into a long low dark room with an inglenook fireplace at the far end. A shabby sofa and two winged chairs surrounded the fireplace, and the rest of the room was stuffed with furniture, making it almost impossible for us to enter. I rested my hand on a tall oak dresser that stood against the wall beside the door. After the bright sunlight outside, I needed to let my eyes adjust to the dark interior.

'Now, I'll just show you to your–' But Mrs Kitchener was interrupted by the sound of dogs barking outside. 'That'll be the boys, they'll have heard you and want to say hello. I won't be a mo.'

'You're not serious about staying here?' Peter said as soon as she left the room. 'No wonder she's not official and it's hardly surprising she's got rooms to spare, is it?'

The room was cold, despite the temperature outside, and I thought I caught a whiff of damp.

'I don't know,' I said, more in an attempt to convince myself, 'there's a certain charm about the place.'

'Charm! Now I know you're not well. Look around you, Mother.'

I did. Copper jugs, candle boxes and hunting prints lined the uneven walls and several wooden chests and chairs littered the rest of the space. Books tottered in piles on the flagstone floor which, from the little I could see of it, remained uncovered except for the occasional threadbare rug. And from what I could see through the two small windows opposite, the garden seemed in similar disarray.

'The place isn't clean for a start, it's full of…'

I held up my hand and sat on the corner of a large oak coffer. All I wanted to do was to take two painkillers and lie down.

'Peter, it need only be for one night.'

'OK,' he said, after a long pause. 'One night and one night only.'

At which point Mrs Kitchener came back into the room, accompanied by two ageing lurchers. 'There we are,' she addressed the dogs, 'We have nice visitors, don't we?'

The dogs, uninterested in the nice visitors, sniffed our legs briefly before curling up on the sofa together, at which point Mrs Kitchener turned her attention to me.

'They like to see who's around. Now, if you don't mind me saying, my dear, you look like you could do with a nice hot cup of tea and a lay down.'

I nodded. Her house might be unkempt, but she was perceptive and seemingly thoughtful. That would do me over star ratings anytime.

Surprisingly, the rest of the house was uncluttered and our rooms almost bare in comparison. They were neat and clean, each with tea-making facilities and a shared bathroom across the landing. I took the room with the single beds and made a cup of tea for Peter and myself whilst he collected my luggage from the car. He seemed more relaxed on his return, grateful, I think, that the rest of the house didn't live up to our initial findings.

'I'll take this to my room,' he said, lifting his cup of tea. 'I've got some phone calls to make. You might as well rest for an hour or so.'

I set my cup down on the teak beside cabinet and sat on the bed, but as he left the room, I called after him, 'Peter?'

He turned, his tall frame filling the doorway.

'Peter, it'll be alright. Everything will be alright.' I said, half-question, half-statement.

He stared at me blankly then shrugged his shoulders. 'Will it?' he said and closed the door behind him.

Chapter Thirty-Two

Charmouth, Dorset, Monday Evening, July 2006

It was almost dark when I woke and there were three missed calls on my mobile. One from Debs, one from Marilyn, the other from a private number. It irritated me when callers withheld their number.

A packet of egg mayonnaise sandwiches lay on the bedside cabinet, presumably put there by Peter. I crossed to the window which looked over the front garden and saw that his car was gone. He should have woken me, I hadn't wanted to sleep that long. Now where was he? I looked around the room for a note, but found nothing.

I opened the sandwiches and ate faster than was good for my digestion; I hadn't eaten anything apart from a croissant that morning. I needed to use the bathroom, but the flashing light on my mobile turned my attention back to my missed calls. I would ring Marilyn first.

It was comforting to hear her voice. The voice of a good friend.

'When are you coming home, Jetta?' she asked after I'd listened to her news and she'd confirmed the cats were well and so was she.

'Certainly by the weekend.'

'That long? And where are you now?'

'Charmouth,' I said, relieved I no longer needed to lie.

'Where on earth is that?'

'It's east of Lyme Regis. A coastal village, part of the Jurassic Coast, apparently.'

'Do you know, I think I might have been there years ago. I have a vague recollection of going there with my parents. Are you actually staying there?'

'Yes. And…and Peter's here too. He's staying with me.'

'Jetta, are you OK?' Marilyn asked after a short silence.'You're not…?'

'No, I'm not unwell…but I discovered something while I've been away, something to do with Peter. And me. Well, all of us, I suppose.'

'What's that? You're not making sense.'

'It's Peter. He's a father.' I was relieved to voice the words. 'He has a son in his 20s. I've got a grandson.'

'Grandson!' Marilyn couldn't hide the shock from her voice. 'You mean…did you know? Is that why you went away like that?'

'No, not at all. It's most strange.'

'Did Peter know? Oh, I'm sorry, what a bloody silly question!'

'No. It's not a silly question. He didn't know. He's never known…he hasn't even met him…yet…'

'Then how…?'

'I met him, Marilyn. I met him by chance, and there's no mistake. He's the image of Peter.'

For a moment or two neither of us spoke. 'You're absolutely certain, Jetta, you're not basing this on the fact that you've met someone who simply looks like…?'

'Of course not. There's more to it than that.'

'I'm sorry. I didn't mean to sound…well, you know what I mean. It just sounds incredible. You go off on a short break to a

random destination only to discover you've got a grandson you didn't know you had. You've got to admit it's pretty amazing.'

'It is. But my choice of destination wasn't as random as I let you believe. There was a purpose to it. But I can't go into it all now. It'll have to wait until I come back.'

After our goodbyes, I pressed the red button to finish the call. I didn't need to ask Marilyn to be discreet. I knew she wouldn't tell a soul, not even Tony.

I padded across the landing to the bathroom in my stocking feet, stopping outside the door. From one of the bedrooms I thought I heard a television. I wondered if Mrs Kitchener had one in her bedroom. It seemed unlikely, I hadn't noticed one in the sitting room and couldn't imagine her having one in her bedroom as neither my nor Peter's room had a television or radio.

Back in my room I was about to switch on the bedside light when I heard a car approach, its headlights lighting up the room. I crossed to the window and saw Peter draw his car to a halt beside mine. He didn't get out. He sat in the driver's seat, staring ahead. I watched him for a while wondering what was going through his mind. But eventually I switched on the lamp and drew the curtains. I wouldn't ring David and Deborah tonight, that could wait until tomorrow. I needed to see Peter first.

Some time later I answered a gentle tap on the door. It was Peter.

'You're awake then. Feeling better?'

'Yes. I've been awake for ages. Why didn't you wake me before going out? I had no idea where you'd gone. You could have left a note.' I heard the accusation in my voice.

'I popped out and brought you back some sandwiches, but you were dead to the world so I let you sleep. I went to a pub in Lyme, The Red Lion or some such place, had a bite to eat and rang you, but you didn't answer. And then I met that guy you–'

'It was you who called.'

'Meaning?'

'It said "private number". I didn't know it was you. I wish you wouldn't do that. Anyway, now you're here we need to talk about tomorrow and our plan of action.'

'Our plan of action? There is no our plan of action. I've got a lot to think about, but you might as well go home in the morning. I've got to get back some time tomorrow too.'

'You're going home tomorrow?'

'Yes, I've got a business to run.'

'But what about your son?'

'What about him? For Christ's sake, Mother, you can't just throw this at me and expect–'

'But don't you want to see him? Aren't you in the least bit curious?'

'Of course I'm curious. Why do think I went to Lyme? I found Bibby's shop but…but I'm not ready for this.'

Aware that our voices were raised, I leaned forward and whispered, 'No one could be ready for this. But it's happened. He's happened and he's your son.'

'Two days ago I thought my life was perfect. My business is doing better than ever. I've met a woman I want to spend the rest of my life with…'

'Life doesn't always time events neatly. What's more important, your son or your business?'

Peter retreated to the door. 'It's not that simple. You have no idea what I'm feeling or what's important to me. But rest assured, tomorrow I leave.'

'You can't.'

He closed his eyes momentarily. 'Why couldn't you have left things alone? What gave you the right to start playing Miss bloody Marple investigates and throw so many lives in the air?'

'I'll tell you what gives me the right.' This was the time to tell him. Tell him I was dying. Tell him that's what gave me the right.

I wanted to tie up loose ends before I cast off, before I signed out. 'It's because I'm…I'm…'

I faltered. He was about to make a fresh start with a new woman and all that involved, and now he'd learned he was a father. That he had been a father for 28 years. The impact of such news was enormous. Could I add to the weight of his problems by telling him I had only months to live? He might be 50 years old but I was still his mother. And he was right. I didn't know what he felt. But I did know I had to make him stay. I stood up from the bed. 'Please, Peter…please reconsider.'

'There's nothing to consider. I've made up my mind.' And, before I could say another word, he left, slamming the door behind him.

An hour or so later I went to bed, but couldn't sleep. I lay awake, worrying. Had Mrs Kitchener heard us shouting? Most of all, I worried about Peter and his future. I worried about my future too, all our futures.

And there was something else. Something Peter had said when he first got back about meeting some guy. And it niggled me.

Chapter Thirty-Three

Charmouth, Dorset, Tuesday Morning, July 2006

Before I checked the time, I knew I had overslept. My intention had been to get up early and waylay Peter. I wanted to stop him leaving. I couldn't let him go home, not now. Didn't he realise how much he risked losing? Untangling myself from beneath the bed covers, I crossed to the window and drew back the curtains. The ground appeared damp as if there had already been a shower, but I wasn't concerned. The recent heat wave was too much. I stood for a moment and watched pewter clouds drift across a darker sky. We would have more rain, I was certain of that – or maybe it was wishful thinking. Although overcast, the air remained warm and sticky and I rummaged through my luggage for a thin cotton blouse to go with my pale green skirt. Finding one, which ideally could have done with an iron, I hung it over the back of the chair. Hopefully whilst I used the bathroom the creases would drop, if only slightly.

Washing my face, hands and armpits made me feel more human and taking a pale blue towel from the edge of the bath I patted myself dry. Gathering up my toiletries, I poked my head outside the bathroom door and listened for signs of life. Except for the cry of a gull, I heard nothing as I crossed the landing. The blouse, though still not crease-free, would do and I applied a dab of make-up before trying to do something with my hair. I was in need of a hairdresser. Mrs Kitchener would be sure to know if there was one in the village.

I was about to give Peter a knock for breakfast when I heard a car. From the window I saw a dry patch of concrete where Peter's car had stood less than 15 minutes earlier. I rushed to his room, praying he hadn't gone for good and realised I seemed to have done a lot of praying lately for someone who hadn't yet made her mind up about such things.

I pushed open his door. There was no evidence he'd ever been in the room. No holdall. No jacket. No mobile. He'd left for good.

Mrs Kitchener handed me a plate of bacon and scrambled eggs. 'If you don't mind my saying, your son seemed preoccupied at breakfast. I couldn't tempt him with anything. Said he wasn't hungry, but I know that look.'

I nodded and bit into my buttered toast.

'Seems a shame to come to a beautiful place like this and bring your troubles with you,' she added.

For some reason, I couldn't take offence at Mrs Kitchener's words. There was something about her that suggested genuine concern. Intuitively I knew she wasn't interested in tittle-tattle. I looked across to where she stood against the ageing green Aga, her back to me as she lifted the kettle from the hotplate and topped up the teapot before bringing it back to the table. I cut into the thick bacon slice and, spearing the rasher on my fork, pushed it into my mouth. If I ate, I didn't have to talk.

'I always take myself down to the beach whenever I've got too much on my mind. The sea air does wonders.' She pushed a slip of paper across the table. 'I've put the hairdresser's name and number on here for you, but you could always call in on your way past if you're going down to the seafront. They're right in the centre of the village by the pedestrian crossing, you can't miss them. Sometimes they can do you straight away.'

I looked at the number and nodded. Unlike her, the writing was neat and uniform.

Mrs Kitchener poured herself another cup of tea, adding a heaped teaspoon of honey. I watched as she stirred the honey into her tea in a slow rhythmic fashion, her gaze following the swirling tea. 'Trouble is, people often think running away from things helps. Others believe that problems can only be resolved by confronting them. Yet in my experience it often pays to let problems go…but letting go isn't the same as ignoring things or running away. No, it's not the same thing at all.' She spoke in a quiet voice, almost as if speaking to herself. 'But sometimes we need to acknowledge when something, some problem or challenge, is bigger than us, greater than us. And when we do that the only sensible action is to let it go.'

'But how can you let go of things that mean so much to you and…things that have such enormous consequences not just for you but for everyone you love and care about?'

She didn't answer. She sipped her tea at intervals and I forced down the last of my breakfast, leaving only a crumble of scrambled egg and an inch of bacon rind.

Eventually, after she drained her cup of tea, Mrs Kitchener broke the silence. 'My dear.' She leaned over and patted the back of my hand. 'It's precisely because they mean so much that you have to let them go.'

Back in my room I contemplated my next course of action. Peter's leaving had left me in a ghastly quandary. I'd tried his mobile at least half a dozen times but all I got was a voice telling me that his phone was switched off. Blast him! He had no right to do this to me. I could pack, check out and go home, but what would that do? I couldn't just leave knowing I had a grandson who I might never see again. But if I stayed, what could I do? What should I do? What was the best course of action? Try to get to know my grandson, knowing in six months' time I could be dead? Was that fair on him?

I sank onto the bed and tried to switch my thoughts off, but couldn't. This was my comeuppance, surely. I'd come here with the intention of taking a life, why shouldn't I suffer? I'd intended to murder. What sort of person was I? What had I become? No, this was justice, alright. To end what was left of my days in emotional suffering was no more than I deserved. The random thoughts came thicker and faster than ever – Peter, my son; Peter, my grandson; Lawrence, Charles.

The thought of Charles filled me with sorrow. We could never be together, not even as friends and, worse still, I could never let him know why. My thoughts spiralled. Bibby, Murder, David, Debs, Andrea, Becky, Marilyn, cancer, pain-relief, doctors, hospitals, wills, loose ends…

And that's when I heard the sobs. Loud sobs. Sobs that reverberated throughout my body. And it took me a while to realise they were coming from me.

Pull yourself together, Jetta, I told myself, taking a crumpled tissue from my cardigan pocket and holding it against my eyes. For goodness sake pull yourself together. But I couldn't. I was overwhelmed. Overloaded. I had too many decisions to make. Looking at the crumpled tissue in my hand, I remembered the capsules. The orange capsules I'd once wrapped in tissue.

I removed the Secobarbital from my bag and lay them in a row on the blue bedcover. They looked pretty, the orange complemented the blue. This was justice, surely. I'd come to Lyme with the intention of killing, of murder. And here I was staring at the weapon I had chosen to take someone else's life. Only now I would use it to take mine.

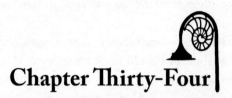

Chapter Thirty-Four

Charmouth, Dorset, Tuesday, Mid-Morning, July 2006

I don't know why I felt it necessary to kneel beside the bed. The hard wooden floor should have been agony against my bony knees, but it wasn't. Physically, I was numb. All I wanted was to stop the thoughts. I lay my cheek on the bedcover. A row of dazzling orange bullets stared back at me. A tumbler of water stood on the bedside cabinet. Waiting. There was no need for the capsules to disgorge their powder this time. There was no secret. I could simply pop one into my diseased body, followed by another. Then another. And another. Until I no longer thought about anything or anyone.

I picked up one of the capsules between my thumb and forefinger. The heat of my hands caused it to stick to my fingers. For a long time I stared at the capsule, twisting it between thumb and forefinger. Then a voice in my head asked: if it's that easy, Jetta Fellowes, why aren't you doing it? What's stopping you?

What was stopping me? Nothing, I decided. Absolutely nothing. But before I could act the voice was immediately followed by another. I could hear my mother telling me to pull myself together. The constant bombardment was torture and I sat back on my legs and looked up at the peeling ceiling.

'Please,' I begged aloud to some great unknown entity. 'Please help. Please, please help.'

Did I believe in God after all? Is this what happens when all else fails, when every other resource you've tried doesn't work? When desperation strikes? The thoughts served only to join the plethora of others and I dropped my head forward onto the edge of the bed.

I don't know how long I stayed there; minutes, maybe an hour. But after a while all I could think about were Mrs Kitchener's words at breakfast. No matter how hard I tried to dismiss them, I couldn't. *When your problems become too big, too great, the only sensible thing to do is to let them go.* Well, I was sensible, wasn't I? Hadn't I always prided myself on being sensible?

I stood up shakily and straightened my skirt. 'Let go,' I repeated over and over. Inside of me a spark reignited and whatever I did I knew I must never allow it to die. I couldn't allow it to be snuffed out.

I picked up the capsules and rewrapped them in the tissue. About to return them to my handbag, a thought struck me. I took them to the bathroom where, with the help of toilet paper and a toilet brush, they eventually disappeared around the u-bend and out of sight.

From my bedroom window I watched Mrs Kitchener stroll around the wilderness that was her garden. Occasionally she stooped to smell a rose or pull at a weed or two. Watching her re-tie a purple delphinium to its stake, I felt a stab of envy. Would I ever take pleasure in such small things again? I closed my eyes as the recently reignited spark dimmed. The thoughts and doubts and feelings began to escalate once again. I fought them, but it was hard, bloody hard.

I opened my eyes at the sound of a dog barking to see one of Mrs Kitchener's lurchers turning circles chasing his tail. I smiled despite myself. For once I knew my mother was right, I did have to pull myself together. It was the only way. And if that meant I had to go through life a day at a time, so be it. Or a minute at a time on the days I couldn't manage that.

The lurcher flopped down in a clump of rosebay willow herb, his antics over, and Mrs Kitchener wound her way through her maze of a garden towards an algae-covered greenhouse. There was a peacefulness here and I rather imagined that in another situation, Mrs Kitchener and I would have become friends.

Placing my suitcase on the bed, I began putting away the few bits I'd unpacked. There was no point in my staying. Not now. I would go home and resume my life. Pretend the last two weeks had never happened. What was it Debs always said? Fake it until you make it. Oh my goodness, the thought of Debs reminded me I hadn't returned her call. Leaving the case open on the bed, I picked up my mobile and dialled.

'Yes, I'm fine,' I reassured her again and again throughout the call.

'It's just we've never known you go off for this long before on a whim.'

'Well, if you can't act on a whim when you're my age, when can you?' I laughed.

'True. Will you be home by the weekend? We were hoping to come over on Sunday and the girls want to come too.'

'That'll be lovely,' I reassured her. 'I'll be home long before that.'

And deliberately keeping the call short, I muttered something about my battery being low. I wasn't in the humour for small talk.

On Sunday I would see my granddaughters, but I could never tell them they had a cousin. It wasn't my place to say anything. David and Debs would never know they had a nephew either, unless Peter decided to tell them, and I couldn't see him doing that somehow.

A knock at the door interrupted my thoughts. I opened it to see Mrs Kitchener holding a vase of flowers – crocosmia, honeysuckle, baby's breath, damask roses – all my favourites did she but know.

'I picked these from the garden. I thought they might cheer your room up.'

'Thank you.' I stood back to let her pass, careful not to brush the overhanging foliage and blooms. 'They're beautiful.' I added, immediately feeling guilty, knowing I wouldn't be around to enjoy them.

Mrs Kitchener placed the vase on the deep windowsill and spent a minute or two arranging the blooms. 'Did you ring the hairdresser?'

I hesitated. 'I didn't…actually, I'm thinking of going home today. And my son…'

'Dear me, I forgot to say, your son paid me this morning. He paid me for both rooms.'

'That's good.'

'Yes, for last night and up to and including Friday night. Although he did add that he might not be able to stay himself but he insisted on paying me anyway.'

Why had he done that? I didn't know what to say. 'I think he and I have got out wires crossed… As I say, I was packing and he…'

'There's no need to make up your mind now. Why not think about it after you've been into the village and had a walk down to the sea?'

'Don't worry about the money,' I said. 'Peter won't expect it back even if we don't stay, I'm sure.'

'Please, Mrs Fellowes, it's not the money.'

I wanted to shrivel away, ashamed I'd been so insensitive. Mrs Kitchener obviously wasn't the sort of woman to put money first. How could I have said such a thing?

'No, I know that, truly, I didn't mean to imply–'

'You didn't,' she interrupted. 'It's just that it's such a pretty village. It would be a shame to have come all this way and leave without seeing it. And I was serious about the sea. It often helps give things a fresh perspective.'

Sitting on the edge of the bed, I looked at her. I guessed she was in her 50s, certainly young enough to be my daughter. She looked odd, with her bright over-dyed hair, yet she exuded a calmness that was rare these days and I found myself drawn to her. Maybe she was right. There was no rush. Even if I didn't leave until four o'clock I would be home by seven at the latest, and that was allowing for a coffee and toilet stop.

I emerged from the hairdressing salon happier with my appearance. Seeing the Post Office open, I slipped in to buy some stamps and postcards. I could at least pretend I was on a proper holiday. I sent a view of Dorset Cottages to Marilyn and, knowing how much Debs enjoyed baking, I sent her and David one giving a recipe for Chideock Chocolate Cake.

Back outside the Post Office I admired the hollyhocks around the iron railings of the house next door. 'Charmouth Lodge' the sign said on the gate of the large white period house. Across the road, I recognised the lane as the one Peter and I had driven down yesterday in our search for accommodation. Was that really less than 24 hours ago? My goodness, how things could change in a day.

The main street through the village was busy and I thought it wise to cross the road at the crossing. People buzzed in and out of the shops and the cars parked either side of the road, uphill and down, caused traffic to move slowly. A young boy, carrying a bucket and spade, stood with his mother at the pedestrian crossing chatting excitedly and I joined them, unsure of where I was actually headed. I smiled at the young boy; surely it was only yesterday that David and Peter were that age. But the boy moved close to his mother and squeezed her hand tightly, unsure of the old lady smiling at him.

A number 31 bus approached from the direction of Lyme Regis and drew to a halt as the lights changed green, beckoning us to cross the road. Glancing at the stationary bus as I walked, I noticed a man near the front stand up from his seat. I couldn't believe it at first, but a second look convinced me it was Charles. Terrified he would look in my direction, I hurried and, once across, mingled with other shoppers. Without looking back I rounded the corner by Ida's Stores and only once I was sure I was out of sight of the bus did I begin to slow down.

Was it Charles? The man certainly looked like him, but why would he be here? He had no idea I was here. Besides, what were the chances of his coming to Charmouth today of all days? Nil, I told myself. I was being fanciful, and for the umpteenth time that day I told myself to pull myself together.

I knew if I kept on this lane I would eventually come to the sea and hoped there would be somewhere I could buy a drink. I needed a couple of painkillers. A stone wall around the Old School House looked an inviting place to take the weight off my feet for a few moments and I hoped its owners wouldn't mind. Despite the day still being overcast, I was perspiring. I slipped my handbag from my shoulder and half-leaned, half-sat on the wall next to a purple flowering buddleia. Taking a tissue from my bag I dabbed at my forehead and wondered how far it was to the sea. Perhaps I should have brought my car after all, although Mrs Kitchener had insisted it was within easy walking distance. But distance was relative, especially in this heat.

On the opposite side of the road a peeling green sign read 'Charmouth Tennis Club' and it was obvious from the sounds coming over the wall that a game was in progress. With the sound of balls hitting racquets in the background, I people-watched. Couples with children, some obviously on holiday, made their way up and down the lane. Cars too, many of which were left-hand drives with foreign number plates. Surely the world had got smaller. An elderly couple holding hands stopped as he helped her remove her cardigan and placed it over his arm. They looked comfortable together and briefly, I thought about Charles. Was he the sort of man who would hold hands in public? Would he be embarrassed by public displays of affection? Sadly, I would never know.

As I crossed to the other side of the lane, my mobile rang but the caller rang off before I could fish it out of my bag. Blast! The screen revealed one missed call but said it was a private number. Perhaps it was Peter. I'd call him when I reached the seafront though I had no idea what I would say. What was he thinking of, simply going off like that this morning? Had he no thought for me? The trouble was I'd always been too independent for my own good. I'd never deliberately put any pressure on either him or David to fill my life, even after Lawrence died. Especially after Lawrence died. I abhorred the prospect of becoming one of those mothers who kept their children on elastic. I had never knowingly placed the burden of my happiness on their shoulders. I had my own friends, my own interests…

Oh, what was the point of raking over things? I should still my mind instead of having futile conversations with myself over things that might never happen.

Chapter Thirty-Five

Charmouth, Dorset, Tuesday, Late Morning, July 2006

The rains came before I reached the sea and where the lane narrowed I stopped to shelter beneath an overhanging tree. Upon hearing a roar of thunder I moved as quickly as I could towards the stone buildings at the water's edge. Even I knew sheltering under a tree during a thunderstorm wasn't a good idea. By the time I entered the Beach Café, my freshly styled hair and clothes were soaked and I left a trail of water from the door to the counter. And for the second time that morning I wished I'd brought my car. I had to get back to Mrs Kitchener's yet.

I ordered a mug of coffee made with hot milk and paid the dark-haired woman on the till, who smiled sympathetically at my damp, dishevelled appearance. The café was busy and all but one table was occupied. I made a beeline for the vacant corner table and settled myself onto one of the chairs. Sipping at the hot coffee, I took my mobile from my bag and retrieved Peter's number. I hated using my phone in public. Aware I was within earshot of other customers, I spoke quietly when Peter answered.

'I have a missed call. Was it from you?'

'Yes…look, Mum, about this morning. I'm…I'm sorry I went off like that without so much as a word. It wasn't fair on you, but…'

Aware I was in receipt of a disapproving look from an elderly woman at a nearby table, I refrained from shouting; instead I said in a loud whisper, 'No, you're damn right it isn't fair, but as you rightly pointed out, it's not my business.' Then, remembering Mrs Kitchener's words, I added, 'Oh, look, Peter, I promised myself I wouldn't be like this. Only you can decide.'

'Anyway, I'm here now,' he interrupted.

'Where's here?'

'Lyme. I'm sat in Bibby's café right now.'

I took another sip of coffee to quiet the jolt in my stomach. A jolt that signalled shock and joy, possibly fear. I didn't speak.

'And when she has a moment she's going to join me.'

'You've…you've spoken to her?'

'Yes, a little, but not about my…not about Peter, not about my son.'

His son. He'd mouthed the words. His son.

'And I'm not sure I can talk about him, because I have no idea what I'm going to say yet. She was as shocked to see me as I was to learn about…about Peter. So I'm not making any promises, Mum. I can't. I won't. I have no idea where to start, let alone where any of this is going. All I rang for is to let you know I'm here.'

I stared at the rack of postcards near the icecream cabinet; revolving views of the Dorset coast and cliffs, cottages and harbours, sandcastles and beach huts, and I heard myself say: 'Thank you.'

Long after Peter hung up, the storm continued. Lightning gashed the dark sky and the noise of the sea and thunder combined meant I almost missed him. But a particularly loud thunderclap caused me to look up from my coffee. He stood in the doorway, rain dripping from his hair onto his shirt collar. As he scanned the café it was obvious he was looking for someone. And I knew that someone was me. I sank lower into my seat, hoping the large disgruntled woman at the next table would block me from view. I should never have come here. I should have trusted my instincts earlier. It was Charles I'd seen on the bus.

He turned from view and as he made to leave the café, I thanked God. Another couple of hours and I would be on my way home, never to see him again. But my thanks were premature. The rain kept him inside and it was only a matter of time before he saw me.

'Would you like another?' He nodded towards my coffee as he approached.

'No, I'm about to leave.' I added a thank you as an afterthought.

'For goodness' sake, Jean, we need to talk.'

I looked around the café in the hope nobody had heard him. He ordered himself a mug of tea, which he brought and placed on the table before sitting alongside me. I kept my gaze fixed ahead. Through the rain-spattered glass of the door I watched white seahorses ride the green sea. Eventually the rain stopped and the overweight lady and her friend on the next table left, leaving a pretty blonde waitress to clear the table ready for its next customers.

'You promised to come and see me yesterday,' he said. 'What happened?'

Aware he was watching me intently, I lifted the coffee mug to my mouth and drank, slowly. The best course of action was to put him out of his misery. To let him know it wasn't anything he'd said or done that had caused me to avoid him. But how could I tell him anything without revealing the whole truth? There was no future for us. There couldn't be. The best I could hope for now was to part amicably. There would be plenty of time for regret on my part later. For now I would be honest, or as honest as I dared.

Charles sat back in his chair. 'What did your son mean when he asked why was I calling you Jean?'

I swallowed hard. This was it. This was the moment I'd dreaded. 'Because my name isn't Jean. It's Jetta.'

'Jetta? Why did you tell me it was Jean?'

'And whilst we're on the subject, it isn't Francis either.'

'What do you mean?'

'Francis. My name isn't Jean Francis. It's Fellowes. Jetta Fellowes.'

There, I'd said it. I'd opened the hornets' nest. And I couldn't escape without getting stung.

'Fellowes?' He looked bewildered. 'What a coincidence. That's my daughter's name.'

'Yes,' I said. 'I know. It was her married name and she obviously kept using it after she left my son.'

'Your son? Jean…I mean Jetta, I don't understand. What's going on?' But before I had a chance to answer, he deduced it for himself. 'That man…that man you were with outside the hotel. That was your son. It's him she was married to, wasn't it? He was married to Bibby.'

'Yes.'

He frowned and his voice got louder. 'But what's all this about? What has any of this to do with you being here under a false name?'

'Initially I came here because I was curious. I'm not proud of it. I wanted to see your daughter, where she was living and how.'

'But why?'

'Because a couple of weeks ago I came across her by accident. She was in Bath and so was I. We were both attending a hospital appointment. She didn't see me, but I saw her and was surprised to hear her still using my son's name. I felt there was a significance to my seeing her, or rather I didn't want to believe it was just a coincidence. So I decided to investigate and discovered she was living in Lyme Regis. I drove down a few days later and booked into The Admiral's House Hotel. I didn't know how well known your daughter was in the town, if at all, and felt it was better to use another name so I could blend in as yet another grey-haired holidaymaker.'

'But what did you hope to achieve?' His voice was quieter again.

The thought of what I'd hoped to achieve shamed me now. From this vantage point, I couldn't believe I was ever that woman. That woman who in a moment of madness felt she had the right to play God. Yet I had achieved something. Something far more valuable. I'd discovered I had a grandson, and whilst I might never see him again, I believed Peter would. And I remembered the man in Lyme, Nomad, saying my search would bear fruit. And it had. Just not in the way I expected.

'Nothing. I hoped to achieve nothing. It was simply morbid curiosity on my part.' I heard myself repeat the excuse I'd given Peter.

'But that doesn't explain why you are avoiding me.'

'I'm not avoiding you. I…'

'You promised to come and see me yesterday.'

'Events overtook me,' I said.

'If I hadn't bumped into your son yesterday evening I wouldn't even have known you'd left the hotel.'

I recalled Peter's comments about the man he'd met and it all made sense. But it was no good. 'It really doesn't matter Charles, because I am going home in an hour and I won't be returning.'

'Why are you being like this? You know there is something between us. A spark. A meeting of minds. Call it what you will, you can't deny it. You feel it, the same as I do, I know.'

'I'm sorry if I gave you that impression. I've enjoyed your company whilst here Charles, but if I led you to believe there was more to it than that, then I…I apologise.'

The sting of my words was apparent. I saw it in his eyes.

'I don't believe you…'

'I'm sorry Charles,' I repeated. And despite his protests, I continued. A broken record punctuated with apologies. It took me a while to convince Charles I had no feelings for him. But eventually, in a voice that was brittle, barely audible, I succeeded. And he left. But I couldn't watch him leave. It's difficult to watch someone you love walk out of your life.

By the time I left the café the ground was almost dry and I was grateful for the gentle breeze that drifted inland off the now calm sea. I don't know how long I stayed at the table after Charles left, but was sure that more than an hour had passed. That would be enough time for him to be well away from here and to resume his life as it was before I came along. Life sans Jetta. I didn't allow myself to replay his pleas in my head. Or remember the look of hurt that betrayed his composure shortly before he left. No, I had done the right thing. I knew that. Yet I couldn't help my thoughts. The thoughts that inevitably began *if only*. But I stopped myself. There was no point.

Beyond the ice cream van in the car park I came across a narrow wooden footbridge that led over the mouth of the river. Halfway across I stopped to watch the Mallards and their young in the water below and the east cliff fell into shadow as drifting clouds once again obscured the early afternoon sun. I remembered the moment, just a couple of weeks ago, when I first learned of my diagnosis. How I'd wished and hoped it was all a mistake. *Why me?* I wanted to ask. But why not me? Why should I get a special dispensation?

Beyond the river I walked over the still damp grass to a pair of wooden benches that faced out to sea. I had my pick, both were empty. Sitting on the right hand bench the view almost took my breath. The wide open space, filled with sea, sky and shore was infinite; the light mesmerising.

I felt my shoulders relax as all tension seeped from my body into the earth. Earth trodden by those before me and those yet to come. From here I could see around the bay to Lyme Regis, its historic Cobb stretching out into the ocean. And not far from that place, in that small town, sat my son. I imagined him sat in the café, *her* café, with its beechwood tables and fresh flowers. Waiting. About to have a conversation that could change his life. Bibby's life too, I reminded myself. And I remembered the Bibby that was. Except this time my thoughts were of compassion, not murder. And I had Charles to thank for that. Dear Charles, who would never know how he had saved me from myself.

Peter's life was Peter's life, I could see that now. Mrs Kitchener was right, letting go was the answer. Really letting go I mean, as opposed to it simply being words that people say. Whatever decision he and Bibby came to, it would be the right one for them. I trusted that.

I held my breath as the salt air filled my nostrils. Surely this was one of the most beautiful places on God's earth. I smiled as I heard myself mention God yet again. Maybe that's what happens when you're presented with your final call-up papers. Except I was no longer concerned about those papers. I carried hope in my heart, and life, however long I had left, was for living. And with my family and friends, I would savour the joy of every moment.

I didn't hear him approach; I was too busy listening to the message on my mobile: *I'll see you back at Mrs Kitchener's. Perhaps I will stay another night, or two.* That was all Peter said. But it was enough.

Sensing someone there, I looked up. About to protest, to send him away again, I paused as momentarily the clouds parted and sunlight danced on the water before us. And as Charles sat beside me and placed his hand on mine I remembered that the sun is always there, shining, even on the days I can't see it for the clouds.

When I Die
Cry for me a little
Think of me sometimes
But not too much.
Think of me now and again
As I was in life
At some moments it's pleasant to recall
But not for long.
Leave me in peace
And I shall leave you in peace
And while you live
Let your thoughts be with the living.

Indian Prayer (Anon)

Sallyann Sheridan's previous books include *Using Relaxation for Health and Success, Getting More Business, Writing Great Copy,* and *The Magic of Writing Things Down.* Born in Wiltshire, England, Sallyann has a son Christopher, and she now lives on the Dorset coast. Please visit her website on www.sallyannsheridan.com

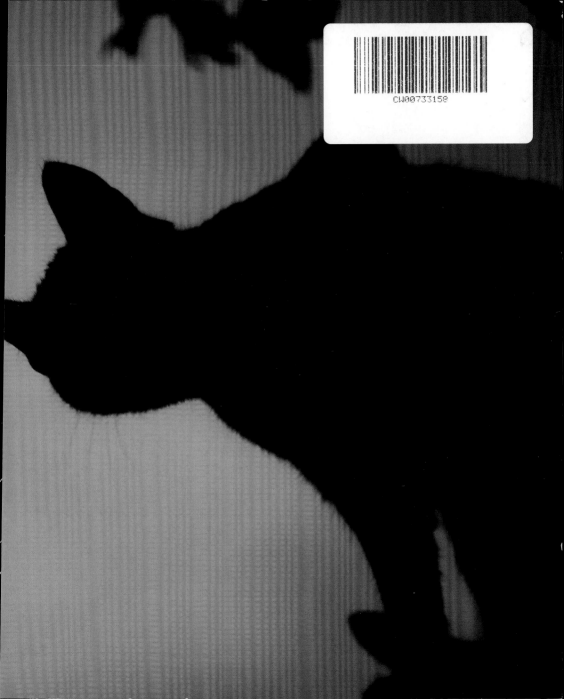

THIS BOOK IS LITERALLY JUST PICTURES OF CUTE CATS WHO ARE PLOTTING TO KILL YOU

Smith Street Books

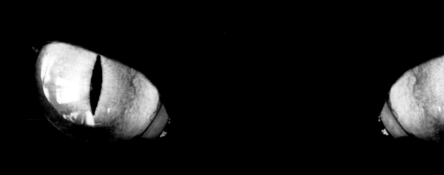

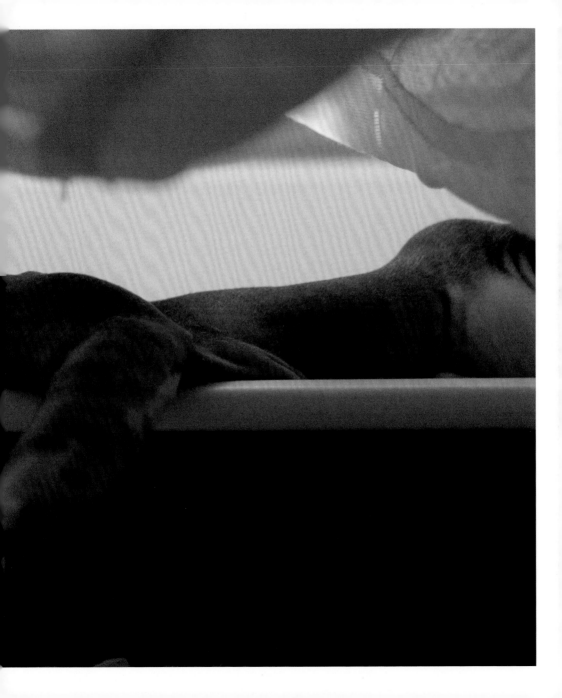

Smith Street Books

Published in 2024 by Smith Street Books
Naarm (Melbourne) | Australia
smithstreetbooks.com

ISBN: 978-1-9230-4932-1

Smith Street Books respectfully acknowledges the Wurundjeri People
of the Kulin Nation, who are the Traditional Owners of
the land on which we work, and we pay our respects to their
Elders past and present.

Publisher: Paul McNally
Design and layout: Hannah Koelmeyer
Cover photo: sdominick/iStock

iStock credits: gtly p2; Sdominick p8; Kech p11; Lightspruch p12;
helenaak p27; 101cats p44; Seregraff p45; fotoedu p50;
DebbiSmirnoff p59; Anton Ostapenko p63; Angela Kotsell p87

Printed & bound in China by C&C Offset Printing Co., Ltd.

Book 339
10 9 8 7 6 5 4 3 2 1